HEIR OF STARLIGHT AND TRUTH

CLAIMING ELFHAME
BOOK THREE

J.M. WALLACE

HEIR OF STARLIGHT AND TRUTH

CLAIMING ELFHAME
BOOK THREE

J.M. WALLACE

Contents

MARENTH
N
W
E
S
NEVENE
Rose Manor
Western Sea
Blackthorn Vei

AMARAN
Eastern Sea
Royal Palace
Mortal Realm

Blackth
Autumn Court
Western Sea
unseelie Palace
Winter Court
Elfhame

orn Veil
Seelie Palace
SPRING COURT
SUMMER COURT
Eastern Sea
N
W
E
S

Chapter One

The Queen was dead. The news rocked Kelera to her core. Even the brightly beaming sun did nothing to soothe the sweat on her brow. She couldn't believe that the fabled Queen of Seelie had at long last fallen to Samael's poison. Nor could she believe the overwhelming power that was surging through her veins now, crackling like lightning in a storm. It had flowed into her body like an arrow hitting its mark. But she didn't speak of it. Not out loud—not with her and Adrastus surrounded by so many strangers.

She held his hand as tight as she could while they walked up to the Seelie Palace gates. The frosted ground crunched beneath her boots. A frost that had no business spreading through a land of eternal spring. The chill that ran down her spine wasn't from the cold, though. Each step she took was heavy with guilt. Samael's magic was still seeping into the soil, which meant setting fire to the manor in the Autumn Court hadn't stopped him. If anything, it likely fueled his anger more. She shivered at the memory of screeches coming from the blazing home.

Trumpets sounded at their arrival, drawing her back to the present moment. The pooka, still glamoured in his pony form, pranced behind her, clearly uncomfortable being so close to civilization. From what she understood, pookas were solitary Fae. More comfortable roaming the land without restraint.

The pooka snorted and stamped his hooves on the ground. Kelera glanced between him and the tall gates. He didn't want to enter, that much was clear. Reluctantly, she turned to him, petting his soft, elongated ears—ears far longer than any real pony she had ever seen. He had the oddest way of showing up in her time of need. He'd taken her to the Unseelie Palace when she'd come to rescue Cierine from Samael and again when she was taking Adrastus to the lake to stop the Night Rider curse from destroying his soul. The emotions flooding in were a tumultuous storm, threatening to beat her down.

She summoned a slight smile in the pooka's direction. As much as she valued his presence, he didn't belong there. He should be in the Wildwood with the others. Softly, she asked, "You want to go back, don't you?" If she was being honest, she wanted to go back, too. They had gone through a lot to reach the Seelie Palace, but now that she was here, she feared what they might face inside those gates.

The pooka's ears flopped as he nodded eagerly and danced around in response.

It wouldn't be fair to try to get him to stay, so she held her smile carefully in place. The corner of her mouth twitched, threatening to fall into a frown as she said, "Then farewell for now, friend. I hope to see you again."

He nuzzled his head into her shoulder, and she smiled sadly at him. She had to trust he would keep himself safe during what was to come.

She spun away from him as the tall wrought-iron gates opened up to reveal a procession of palace guards led by the Seelie warrior, Oliver. Disappointment swept through her when she noticed Gadreel, Adrastus' brother, wasn't with him.

Adrastus cleared his throat, seemingly as disappointed as she was, and asked, "Where is Gadreel?"

Oliver beamed at the mention of his lover. "He'll join us later."

Adrastus gave her hand a reassuring squeeze. It was a relief to know that he had made it back to the palace after parting ways with her by the lake. As Oliver turned to lead her and Adrastus to the palace doors, Kelera glanced back the way they had come. The pooka was already gone. His stout figure was a small blur in the field.

Beyond him, she spotted the forest giants who had bowed to her near the hawthorn trees. Perhaps the pooka would join them. They had stayed behind with Ragnor and the other Guardians of the Wildwood. In the distance, their massive bark covered bodies roamed slowly as they surveyed the area for any sign of threat. Ragnor was somewhere in their midst, though she couldn't see him from this far away. He had insisted he and his men belonged out there, where they could keep an eye out for Samael and his Night Riders. It was their duty, after all, to be the first line of defense in the Spring Court.

Oliver cut through her thoughts. "Many of the villagers have gathered to see you into the palace. I fear we weren't able to dissuade them."

Kelera nodded in understanding. She couldn't blame them for wanting to sneak a peek at the infamous couple. The halfling and the Bastard Prince. Wanted for crimes they did and did not commit. She swallowed her embarrassment and followed quietly with Adrastus at her side. With him there, she knew she wasn't alone. It made the pain of parting with her friends a little more bearable.

They didn't make it more than a few steps when a sharp surge of magic flooded her chest. It knocked the wind from her like someone had punched her, forcing her to lean on Adrastus. The pain was not dissimilar to the moment near the hawthorns. She sucked in a deep breath and straightened. Now was not the time to show weakness.

Adrastus' brow furrowed with concern as he asked, "Are you sure you're alright?"

Afraid of drawing attention to the magical battle raging inside of her in front of these strangers, she answered quickly, "I'm fine."

"I can sense it through the bond. You're far from fine." His beautiful green eyes darkened.

She couldn't blame him for being worried. Between the bombardment of power and the debt she'd promised to the Elders in order to save him from the Night Rider curse, she had possibly piled on more than they could handle. Guilt racked her, and she averted her eyes from him. She didn't want to be the one to cause that concerned frown on his handsome face.

She gave his hand a small shake. "Let's just get through these next few hours." Not knowing exactly what to expect had her on the verge of madness.

She peaked up at him through her lashes. He pressed his lips together and nodded. She was grateful that he didn't push the matter. Soon, the sting of magic subsided, and Kelera was able to walk on without trouble. The sun beat down on them, but did nothing to melt away the frost. She pinched the bridge of her nose with her free hand, trying to stop the headache that threatened to present itself. She didn't know what any of it meant—the immense power and the forest giants rising. But from Adrastus' set jaw and the way his lips hardened into a thin line, it meant something to him.

And to the rest of them. The minute they stepped through the palace gates, they were surrounded by Spring Court villagers, all craning their necks to get a look at the halfling girl who had brought war to their doors. Not that it was truly Kelera who had been the cause of the looming battle. King Samael had made it clear that he was going to go through with his conquest, with or without her and her magic.

But it was her and her friends who had been the ones to bring the news to the Seelie Fae. They were the ones who had crossed Elfhame to ask them to take up arms against Samael and his Unseelie army. The villagers whispered in her wake as she passed by with the Guard.

"That's her. The halfling that killed Prince Ammon."

"They say she's bound to the Bastard Prince."

"Demon."

"She woke the Wild Hunt."

"She can't be."

"Looks just like her. The nose. Those eyes."

"But that scar..."

"Lost heir."

That last whisper disturbed her, leaving an empty pit deep in her stomach. The Elder Prophecy of the lost heir was one that had been passed around for so long that not even Adrastus had believed it. She'd hoped it was him. That he would be the answer to all of their troubles—the one to unite the courts in Elfhame and bring peace to the borders, even the mortal one. But instead, the forest giants had bowed to *her*.

Every instinct told her to deny it. It was impossible that she could be the heir to the crown. But the Seelie power flowing in her veins now was no longer just her own. She'd grown accustomed to her magic in the last weeks and the familiarity of Adrastus' Seelie and Unseelie magic dancing with it in harmony since the binding ceremony. The power that had driven into her as the horns blared—announcing the Queen's death—was not the same. It was something different entirely.

Whatever it was, and wherever it had come from, was a mystery to her still. One she hoped Adrastus could help her understand once they were alone again. She honed in on Oliver's dark head bobbing ahead of them from horse-back. Focusing on him did nothing to distract her roaming thoughts, though.

A woman bowed at the waist to Kelera as she passed. Her heart fluttered as a few others in the crowd did the same. She had spent her life bowing to her betters. Never in her wildest dreams did she imagine she would be on the receiving end. Her legs were suddenly very weak, and each step she took was shaky.

The palace grounds were larger than she'd expected, and she looked around to find carts and stands set up throughout as a market of sorts. As Kelera scanned the area, a dark form caught her eye. It was built like a man, standing behind the Fae who were bowing to her. It made no move to join them and although Kelera couldn't see a face, she could feel its eyes on her. Watching her every move in a calculating stare.

Her breath hitched in her throat and she grabbed hold of Adrastus' sleeve. "Do you see that?"

Adrastus surveyed the crowd. "See what?"

When she looked back, the shadowy figure was gone. She craned her neck, trying to find it again, but there was no trace of it. Only more villagers, leaning on one another and shoving in to get a better look at the procession.

She shook her head and said, "Never mind." It was her nerves. At least, she hoped it was. After all that had happened, she was bound to be on edge. Still, she eyed the crowd, searching for suspicious movement. With Samael's shadow shifting abilities, he would be more than capable of slipping in and out undetected. What sort of defenses did the Seelie have that the mortal court didn't? Would it be powerful enough to keep him out?

Her eyes widened as she looked up at the Queen's Palace looming over them. It was beautifully crafted with white stone that shimmered in the early morning sunlight. Kelera reached out to touch its marble-like walls. Magic emanated from them, extending out to her like a warm shield. It was so subtle compared to the power surging inside of her, she couldn't imagine how it would keep someone like Samael out. She inched closer, to get a better feel of the magic she assumed was there to protect the palace, but the thudding of a drum made her jump.

Three drumbeats sounded as the palace doors opened up to reveal several Fae dressed in flowery garments. Even the men wore floral jackets and vine ringlets on their heads. They were the very epitome of spring.

Their eyes bore into her, each varying from shades of green like Adrastus' to blue like hers. The rings in their irises were vibrant and alight with curiosity. A familiar, elegant tanned face caught her eye. He stepped forward and bowed at the waist to her. "Lady Kelera, it is so good to see you again."

"Lord Bothwell, I'm glad to see that you are well." Kelera curtseyed at him and smiled, genuinely happy to see a friendly face. The high master of the Queen's council had risked a lot in meeting them at the Beltane revel, and more so when he agreed to get her and Adrastus an audience with the Queen's council. If things went awry in the next few hours, then he might find himself ruined amongst his peers. A lifetime at court had taught her that one wrong move would tarnish a good name.

And judging by the narrowed eyes and scowls being directed by the courtiers in Adrastus' direction told her that right now, Bothwell's name was in a rather precarious position. Adrastus was the bastard son of the Unseelie King, after all. These Fae didn't care that Adrastus' mother had been one of them. His father had raised him in the darkness. Trained him to be ruthless. And that gave them more than enough reason to be frightened.

Adrastus' face was an unreadable mask of indifference. His magic was taught around hers as if it were reflecting the unease he was feeling. Part of her wanted to say something to comfort him, but until a moment ago, they had barely uttered a word to each other since leaving the hawthorns. Her lips hardened into a thin line, unable to hide the apprehension it gave her.

Bothwell's eyes darted between the courtiers. Then he smoothed his light brown hair back, maintaining his composure. "If you will follow me." He turned on his heel and strode through the palace doors. Kelera took a deep, steadying breath.

The courtiers gave them a wide berth, never taking their eyes off Adrastus. His magic hummed in her veins with a nervous vibration. She was getting better at reading him through their bound magic, but it wasn't helping to calm her own anxieties.

Adrastus couldn't hide the discontent in his voice as he said, "Here goes nothing."

The palace was breathtaking. Beautiful, polished marble shined beneath the sunlight that filtered in through the open ceiling. Kelera couldn't help but wonder what happened when it rained. Would the palace floors be drenched from a downpour? Or did the Seelie have a way of blocking it out? She stored all of her questions away for later, hoping she would have time alone with Adrastus soon so she could ask.

It was her hope that they would have a moment away from everyone soon. She'd just gotten him back and there was still so much to say... so much to apologize for. Even though they'd had an intimate moment by the hawthorns where she declared her love for him, she worried they wouldn't be able to move past the pain of her betrayal. She had left him behind, had unknowingly led Samael's men to him, and had barely gotten to him in time before the Night Rider curse destroyed his soul. And then there was the matter of the Lady of the Lake's debt she agreed to... It was no wonder his magic was having trouble settling down.

It hadn't been easy breaking down the walls he held around himself when she'd first come to the Unseelie Palace, and now she worried that he was going to start building them up again brick by brick. The only comfort came from his hand still in hers, granting her a small glimmer of hope.

Bothwell led them into a grand hall with a towering throne against the wall. Enormous windows were on either side of it, giving a generous view of the lush landscape of the Spring Court territory. The throne was expertly crafted with intricate carvings of flowers and wildlife. Small curious foxes made of stone bowed at the foot of it, while hand crafted statues of birds in mid-flight rose from its arms.

A heightened rush of power rolled through her body, nearly knocking her forward. The magic that had come to her in the woods was urging her toward the throne. Kelera resisted, clinging to Adrastus' hand. He looked down at her with worry clouding his vivid green eyes, but she said nothing, too afraid of one of the strangers overhearing her.

The room was crowded with council members, the Queen's Guard, and a few villagers that had been lucky enough to squeeze in. Curiosity was a powerful thing, and there was no doubt that they were eager to hear firsthand why the Bastard Prince of Unseelie had come to their court hand in hand with a halfling.

The courtiers and villagers that had crammed into the room began to talk amongst themselves. Their expressions were a mixture of disbelief and fear, as well as a few hopeful looks sent in Kelera's direction. All the attention had her stomach in knots.

It wasn't until Gadreel and Oliver strolled in side by side that she finally breathed a sigh of relief. They were dazzling in Spring Court attire. With dashing dark brown coats as rich as the soil and green sashes around their waists. It was a stark contrast to Gadreel's frost-colored hair and pale skin, but he looked incredibly handsome all the same. He embraced her in a tight hug, cutting off her air.

She squeaked, "Gadreel... can't... breathe."

He released her quickly and looked her over from head to toe. "I'm sorry, I just, I was so worried." Adrastus was silent, looking at his feet uncomfortably. The last time Gadreel had seen him was when the Night Rider curse was raging through his body. Was he ashamed that Samael had bested him? She knew those scars ran deeper than the marks on his skin.

Gadreel pulled him into a hug, whispering to him so that Kelera and the others couldn't hear. Allowing them a moment together, she stepped closer to Oliver. He shifted awkwardly, avoiding her eye. He'd never acted shy around her before. Maybe it was the stress of today's events. Between the news of the Queen and the uncertainty of Samael's plans, they were all on edge.

Kelera searched for something to say to comfort him, but they were joined by a petite mortal girl. Heat rose in Kelera's belly as recognition hit her. A small, mousey girl with rosy cheeks and light brown hair. The mortal servant girl, Mira, who had promised to help Kelera and Cierine escape the Unseelie Palace. Kelera's eyes fell to the sword strapped to the girl's side. *Her* sword. The one that her father had gifted her on her birthday. The one that Mira had stolen from her when she'd betrayed Kelera and the others at the blackthorns.

She hadn't thought much of the girl, expecting to never see her again. But the grief and frustration from the last few weeks slammed into her all at once. Fury overtook Kelera's senses, blinding her of everything and everyone around them. Power burned in her hands, begging for retribution. Hatred for Samael and the pain of Mira's betrayal was the spark to light the powder keg. So she did the only thing she could think of. She lunged.

Her fist connected with Mira's cheek, sending the girl flying to the polished floor. The throbbing in her knuckles left her with unexpected relief from the tension she'd been holding. Mira looked up at Kelera, eyes wide, and hands up to protect herself from another assault. But Kelera didn't feel the need to do more. Oliver put himself between her and the mortal girl, but Kelera stood as still as a statue.

Her throat tightened as Mira rubbed her cheek. Oliver helped Mira up, and she stood with tears threatening to fall from her eyes. Kelera didn't want to feel pity for her. Her actions had gotten several mortal women killed. Because of her, Kelera had been sentenced to stay in the Unseelie Court, forced to remain in Samael's presence. She was the reason Kelera hadn't gone home sooner.

She took a step toward Mira. Oliver held his hands out to stop her, but didn't dare to touch her. She balled her fists, trying to quell the memories, and looked around. Everyone was watching them. Some were whispering. No doubt gossiping about the out-of-control halfling.

Kelera kept her voice low as she said to Oliver, "You do not know the pain she has caused."

Mira peered around him. Her voice quaked as she said, "Please, understand. I-I..."

"Mira?" A frazzled girl came running to her side. She stared at Mira's cheek in bewilderment. "What happened?"

"It's fine, Diana." She reached up to caress the girl's flawless ebony face. Then she turned back to Kelera. "Please, let me explain. I couldn't stay there any longer. For years, I waited. Waited for my chance to escape." She looked lovingly at Diana. "Waited for the moment when I could reunite with my love."

Kelera's resolve softened, but the bitter memories of the women who were cut down like dogs at the blackthorn border still lingered. "So you sacrificed the lives of others."

Mira shook her head wildly. "No. I didn't think any of that would happen. Prince Adrastus swore he would protect you.

He said that no harm would come to you and that he had a plan to set everything right."

Kelera fought back angry tears. She'd felt so utterly betrayed that day as Mira ran off with her sword, leaving her to the mercy of Adrastus, who had been a stranger to her then. It was as much his fault as it was Mira's that the mortal women had not survived that day.

She glanced back at him. His mouth was drawn downward, and shadows danced in his eyes. "She's right, little thief."

"But the women..." Kelera could hear their screams in the back of her mind as clearly as if she was back at that border.

Adrastus held her gaze firmly. "What's done, is done. We have all made mistakes."

Kelera thought of his eldest brother, Ammon. The prince she had accidentally killed when she unleashed her power to save Adrastus. How many casualties had there been in their attempts to stop Samael? It didn't make any of it okay, but Adrastus was right. There was no changing any of it. All they could do was try to stop anyone else from being hurt. Now that her mind was cleared of blind rage, she could feel his magic spinning inside with her own. Like a reflection of the guilt and shame he was trying to cage.

Mira cleared her throat. When Kelera turned back, she found the girl holding her sword out to her. "I kept this for you. I prayed to the stars that I would one day have the chance to return it to you and tell you how very sorry I am."

Kelera took the sword from Mira's trembling hands and ran her fingers over the cold steel. It felt right, having it back in her possession. But it also made her miss her father terribly. Her heart ached in his absence. If only he were there to guide her. She hoped he and Cierine were faring well back in the mortal court. There was no telling what awful lies Samael had spun to King Tristan's council or if they had believed the horrible revelation that it was Alexander that had been working with the Fae.

She swallowed back her worries and met Mira's eye. Could she forgive her? Kelera had forgiven Adrastus for his transgressions. She had abandoned everything to save him, leaving her father and the mortals behind. She'd even killed when trying to protect him. All in the name of love. It seemed she and Mira weren't all that different...

Softly, she said, "We all have regrets that we must live with." She gripped the hilt of the sword, and Diana took a step in front of Mira to protect her. Kelera lowered the blade, pointing it at the ground, and continued, "But you have nothing more to fear from me. You have my forgiveness."

Mira's sigh of relief echoed in the hall. The crowd seemed to relax all at once too, finally whispering to one another again. Adrastus placed his hand on the small of Kelera's back and rubbed it softly.

During all the commotion, a small group of Fae had assembled near the throne. Oliver gestured to them and Kelera stepped forward with Adrastus at her side. Oliver hesitated, watching her closely, and said, "May I present the Queen's council?"

Six Fae, made up of both men and women, stood straight-backed at the foot of the empty throne. Their faces were a picture of pure disdain as they took in Adrastus' presence. Kelera was surprised, after her little display, that it was not her they were looking at. Their discomfort with him must have run deep. Was it really simply because he was an Unseelie Prince? Or was it something more? Adrastus was the first to admit that he'd done things he wasn't proud of. His magic, too, had been of a volatile nature; shadows and ice clashing with the Seelie power he held.

Kelera leaned in to whisper, "Do they know you?"

Adrastus gave a lighthearted shrug, but Kelera spotted the visible tension in his neck as his veins stuck out under the few scars he didn't bother to hide. He forced a smile as he said, "Not personally."

The council's silence was stifling. She gulped. "Then why are they looking at you like that?"

Adrastus gave a heavy sigh of frustration. "There are things they will not forgive." His words were clipped, and she could tell he didn't want to discuss it further. At least not here, with so many within earshot.

Regardless of what he had done to them or what they thought of him, now was not the time for grudges. Her mouth went as dry as the Summer Court sands. Someone needed to step up, but it was clear Adrastus wouldn't be the first to do so. If no one wanted to be the first to speak, then she would do it herself. She wasn't sure if they would listen to her after her outburst, but it was worth trying. She stepped forward with mock confidence. Magic rushed to her fingertips, eager as she inched closer to the throne. She clenched her hands into fists, wishing she still had Adrastus' hand to ground her. At least the cool caress of his magic around hers reassured her that his power was still there to balance hers out.

Kelera bit her lip, then dared to speak. "Gentlemen, and ladies." She bowed her head to the council members standing between her and the throne. "We are very grateful for this opportunity." She paused, her eyes lingering on the empty throne. The pit in her stomach grew as she thought of the poisoned Queen who should have been sitting there. Ignoring it, she added, "We know that this comes at a very difficult time for you."

A woman with hair pulled tightly back and a pointed face stopped her. "My name is Anaya. Your Grace, if I may?"

Kelera turned to Adrastus, waiting for him to tell Anaya to go ahead and speak, but he said nothing. Rather, all eyes were on her. If only she could make herself as small as the pixies so she could escape the eager stares she was getting from the crowd, who seemed just as confused as she was.

Anaya clasped her hands in front of her, making the colorful feathers on her gown rustle along the floor. She looked like a bird about to take flight. Her voice was gentle—like she was trying not to spook a creature in the forest—as she said to Kelera, "Prince Adrastus is not the one we address. He is not the one we have been waiting for." Her eyes flitted to Kelera's locket before she gestured to the council behind her. "A few of the others and myself have felt it. Since the moment you were first rumored to have stepped through the veil."

Anaya addressed the crowd. To Kelera's horror, she said, "The heir apparent has returned home at last." Loud gasps rang out through the room. "Flowers have blossomed in celebration. And the sunbeams rejoice its master at long last home again."

Kelera's mind was spinning. This was her life they were talking about and Anaya was announcing it for the world to hear. What if they were wrong? This woman should know better than to get the people's hopes up. She raised her chin as she tried to stop Anaya from going any further. "You can't possibly know for sure—"

Anaya gave her a stone-like look. "You disagree? Whispers say that King Cyrus sensed your power, too, though he was likely too blinded by his hubris to see the truth that lingered beneath his nose."

Kelera stubbornly argued, "King Cyrus wanted my power for the mere fact that he saw a use for it."

Anaya raised a slender eyebrow. "And Prince Samael?"

Kelera stood firmly. "Wanted Seelie power to solidify his chances of taking your land."

"And Prince Adrastus?" She put a hand on her hip. "You are bound to one another, are you not? Did you not find it interesting that an entire royal line coveted your birth-given magic?"

"Our reasons for binding ourselves to one another are nobody's business." Kelera wouldn't stand here and allow this stranger to insinuate that Adrastus was after her power for his own gain. They had saved one another time after time and she wouldn't let that be minimized or twisted into something ugly.

Heat tingled along her arms as her anger stirred her power to the surface. Adrastus grabbed hold of her hand. An ice cold sensation snuffed out the Seelie magic and Kelera shivered. Anaya studied the two of them, but said nothing. The room had taken on an anxious air, as no one seemed to know what to expect next.

Bothwell opened his mouth to speak but was interrupted by a door at the side of the room slamming open. It echoed through the hall and the room fell into an uncomfortable silence. The man who strode in wore the Queen's crest on the left breast of his jacket—directly over his heart. The delicate embroidered crown surrounded by beautiful hawthorn flowers clashed with his brutish demeanor. Kelera would have thought him very handsome with his golden blonde hair and piercing green eyes, had it not been for the sneer splayed across his face. His teeth showed like a wildcat in a cage and he walked to the throne with purpose.

He sat on the edge of it, drawing vexed looks from the council and deep bows from a few Fae in the crowd. The man ignored them, tilting his head to the side to study Kelera. "She has her eyes."

Bothwell's nose flared. "Of course she does."

Were they going to clue her in on the conversation or would they happily continue on as if she were not there? What mattered was the trouble at hand. She cleared her throat. "As I was saying—"

The man interrupted her, directing his ire at Bothwell, "Who is to say she is not a distant relative? Don't you think *I* would have known if my wife had born a *bastard halfling?*"

Kelera flinched at the insinuation. Having the eyes of the Fae in the room resting on her gave her a feeling that resembled spiders crawling on her. She didn't want to talk about prophecies and heirs. The man, who must have been the late Queen's husband, clearly had strong opinions on the subject. Regardless, who exactly did he think he was to speak of her in that sort of manner? Her days of standing by as people talked down at her were over.

Through clenched teeth, she said, "Enough of this. We are here to discuss King Samael, *not* me."

The man looked down with that same smug arrogance he'd walked into the room with. "You may have charmed them," he gestured to Adrastus, Bothwell, and Oliver, then continued, "but do not think for a second that you will have any effect on me. I don't care if you *are* Queen Mabine's daughter. You do not wear her crown yet." His eyes narrowed and Kelera had to take a deep breath to steady herself.

There it was. Someone had finally been bold enough to say the words out loud. The thing Kelera had been fearing since the moment the bells rang and the new magic drove into her body... Queen Mabine, of the Seelie Court, had been her mother. Her mother was dead.

Chapter Two

S houts rang loudly in the hall, echoing words of both outrage and hope. The enormous throne room was beginning to feel incredibly small. Between the bodies that had crammed into the space and the rising voices, Kelera was barely able to catch her breath.

She couldn't be the Seelie Queen's daughter, could she? Deep down, a voice inside whispered, *you knew it the moment that power touched your soul.* She pinched the bridge of her nose and shut her eyes. Her throat tightened as tears threatened to fall. She would not cry. Not here in front of that horrible man.

Adrastus put a hand on her shoulder and rubbed it gently. "Kelera, if you need to take a minute..."

She shook her head vehemently. "No. Not until we accomplish what we came here to do."

With a firm nod of his head, Adrastus turned toward the council. Raising his voice over the noise of the crowd, he said, "The matter we bring to your doorstep is of the utmost urgency. If you would clear the hall out, then perhaps we could speak to the council."

A few arguments were shouted from the wings of the chamber. Bothwell clasped his hands in front of him as he explained, "We are an open court here. Our people have the right to be present for this. Please, go ahead."

Adrastus began, "My brother holds the power of the crown, and we have reason to believe that the mortals will stand with him against the Seelie Court. It is important that we work together to stop him before he does any more damage."

The man on the throne held up an arrogant, silencing fist and stood. "We are well aware of the threat *your* brother poses. Our army is already preparing themselves."

Adrastus sneered at him. "And who will be leading this army now that Queen Mabine is gone?"

Kelera shivered. Gone. Queen Mabine was dead. Her mother was dead...

The man near the throne lifted his chin. "I will, of course."

Bothwell interjected, "King Herald, if this girl is who we believe her to be, then that will not be your place."

"This girl is not the crowned leader of the Seelie. As King Consort, it is my right—"

"If she is Mabine's daughter, then you no longer *have* the right," Bothwell hissed. It shocked Kelera to hear him speak with such venom.

Herald snarled back, "That is for the blood rites to decide."

A few in the crowd applauded and cheered in agreement. Kelera had read about the blood rites in Samael's room. If the ruler of Seelie died without a direct blood heir, then eligible Fae could vie for the crown in a battle to the death. Her stomach twisted into knots. Would he challenge her? Even as a direct heir to the throne? She hadn't come here to prove her strength. They had come for an army to stand against Samael. It was all she wanted from them.

Bothwell pointed at Kelera. "This is Mabine's daughter."

Herald bounded away from the throne and stood nose to nose with Bothwell. His words were low and determined as he asserted, "She had no daughter. And even *if* this halfling is what you say, there is nothing to stop me from challenging her and the legitimacy of her claim."

Bothwell didn't flinch. "I was there. On Beltane twenty years ago, I held the babe in my arms. I took her to her father's doorstep, and I left her there. With nothing but a few provisions, a note and a locket. The locket that rests around that girl's neck."

That shut Herald up. Kelera's hand flew to the necklace she'd clung to so many times before. The only piece of her mother she had carried with her throughout the years. What significance could a piece of jewelry hold that would have these men speechless? Both men stood face to face in a standoff of wills until another member of the council stepped forward. He was aged, with gray peppered hair that rested on his shoulders. His back was slightly bent, but he moved like a young man.

Kelera stepped away as he approached her. His gaze lingered on her locket, and she placed both hands over it protectively. A hush fell over the crowd as he asked, "Is it true? Did your mother give that locket to you?"

"Yes. It is all I have of her."

The old man whispered in awe, "*Under the hill, beneath the ash trees, the Elders await you with the keys.*" Hearing the phrase that Adrastus had spoken in the Summer Court sent a jolt of adrenaline through her.

Louder, the old man declared, "She holds the key of the Elders."

"Key?" Kelera narrowed her eyes. They were all acting absurd. "A key to what?"

Herald interrupted, sounding like a spoiled child. "Terrance, you can't know that it isn't a trick. A replica of some sort!"

"It is no trick," Bothwell interjected. "Queen Mabine placed it in the basket herself." His hands shook with so much outrage that even the courtiers around them seemed to shrink against the walls.

Terrance urged Kelera, "Open it."

She looked around at the curious faces. "I can't. It doesn't open." She'd tried many times as a child, hoping to find a picture of her mother inside. Desperately longing for just one look at the woman who had given her life. She had dug at it with her nails until her fingers ached. But each time she attempted to pry it open, she had failed.

Terrance reached his hand into his jacket, and a flash of cold steel caught her eye. Adrastus was between them before the old man had a chance to fully draw the dagger. Guards pushed in on them to separate the men, but Terrance raised his hands, pulsing them back with his magic.

Then he flipped the knife so the hilt was facing Kelera and explained, "It requires royal blood." His hard eyes met Herald's. "If she is indeed who they believe her to be, then it will open."

Kelera stared down at the hilt, unsure of what to do. She didn't come here for this. If the locket opened, then it would mean that the mother she had once longed for was dead. There would be no reunion. All she would be left with was a crown she wasn't sure she wanted and questions that would be forever left unanswered. On the other hand, would not knowing be any better?

Adrastus placed his palm on her cheek. "You don't have to do this..."

"I think I do." Kelera unlatched the delicate chain and held the locket in one hand. With the other, she took the knife from Terrance. Without flinching, she ran the blade along her palm, drawing blood.

The world stilled as she placed the locket in her bleeding hand. She held her breath as she closed her fingers around it and waited. Magic shimmered around her closed fist and up her wrist. Then something clicked. When she opened her hand, the locket was open and a delicate, ash-colored key sat tucked inside.

Bothwell held his hands out to Kelera. "She is what the prophecies have foretold! She is the one to unite us all!"

Kelera couldn't take her eyes from the key in her hand. Before now, she could deny the truth. Could turn a blind eye to it all and shove it away to deal with later. But now that it was staring her in the face, she was no longer able to hide from it. She was the heir to the Seelie crown.

Adrastus murmured to her, "Kelera, are you okay?"

All she could do was shake her head. She was too stunned to utter a word. There weren't even any emotions to grapple with. If anything, she felt numb. Not even her magic stirred. The room, however, turned into a spectacle. Men were shouting for the blood rites, claiming she wasn't raised in Elfhame and would not know how to rule their people.

Others were kneeling to her with tear-filled eyes. They were looking at her as if she were the answer to their prayers. But she wasn't. Couldn't they see that? She wasn't prepared for any of this.

The Fae who had bowed to Herald when he'd entered looked down at her with disdain. It was something she'd grown accustomed to in the mortal court. But those days had passed. Acceptance couldn't be forced. If the Seelie Fae had made up their minds about her, then she wouldn't be able to change them.

And after their reaction to Adrastus, did she want to? If they grew to accept her, but not the man she loved, then that would be just as painful. Her magic pulsed toward the throne as if trying to throw its own opinion into the mix, but she shoved it back down with determination. Bothwell tried to quiet the discontent, but the crowd was out of control.

One of Herald's supporters spat. "The Elders never would have prophesized an heir of mortal blood!" He lifted a fist in the air as he continued, "Do you honor our lands? Have you ever shed a tear for the Fae? *You are not one of us.*"

Adrastus' magic flared in her veins and for a moment, she thought it would unleash its icy wrath on them all. She wrapped her Seelie power around it, grounding it back down to a chilly ebb of power, but it nearly knocked the wind out of her to do so. The binding strained itself as it held together, and it left her with an uneasy feeling in her gut.

His voice was thunderous as he argued with the man, "You are wrong. She has spilled both tears and blood for the innocent, both mortal and Fae alike."

Kelera didn't notice the reactions of the crowd because she couldn't bring herself to look away from him. This was the Adrastus that had frightened and intrigued her when she'd first come to Elfhame. The strong, confident Prince of Unseelie who had battled his brother to claim her in the pits. His fierce presence swallowed everything whole. Kelera's love for him stirred and her heart warmed. In times of uncertainty, there was one thing she could always count on. Him.

Herald scoffed, but before he could voice his opinion on the matter, the door opened. The crowd parted to reveal Ragnor and the Guardians. And behind them were Gilby and Tobias—Adrastus' friends from the Winter Court—and Ferden, the boy Kelera had shared a lashing with, and his mother, Grace.

Kelera sucked in a breath as they strolled past the Seelie Fae as if they owned the place. Grace raised her slender face and pushed her silver hair behind her shoulder. All eyes were on her and her enchanting beauty as she said, "Aye, we have witnessed her selflessness first-hand."

Herald didn't bother containing his outrage as he hissed, "How dare you bring Unseelie in here? You think we can trust the word of the very people who threaten to take our land?"

Grace narrowed her eyes. "You are a fool if you believe that all the Unseelie support Samael and his mad reign. He is tearing our villages apart to force us to join him in this fight. Are you so ambitious that you would ignore the warnings Lady Kelera and Prince Adrastus are giving you? That you would denounce her as the rightful heir?"

Oliver stepped in now. "What further proof do you want? I myself witnessed the lashings Kelera took to save that Fae boy at the King's revel." He pointed to Ferden.

Herald raised his voice to the crowd. "Bias at its finest!"

That was enough. Kelera had heard what she needed to. To Adrastus, she said, "I need to get out of here."

"Let's go." He took her hand, but she pulled away from him.

"No, stay. I just need a moment."

It wasn't that she didn't want to speak with him alone. But how could she get the words out if she hadn't been able to process it all in her mind first? She shoved the locket into her pocket and raced to the door, avoiding the confused faces in the crowd. As she slipped from the room, she heard voices rise again in dispute. She gritted her teeth. Let them argue themselves to death in there. She would have no more part in it. What she needed was a quiet moment.

She let the door slam shut behind her and ran.

Chapter Three

Kelera's footsteps echoed through the marble halls. She tugged her hair up with frustration and tied it with a leather strap she had tucked away in her pocket. Still, sweat beaded on her forehead and down her back. Servants hopped out of her way as she stormed down the corridors, but she barely noticed them. Her thoughts were racing too fast for her to focus on anything other than escaping the council and their bold opinions.

Maybe at one time it would have bothered her that people were voicing all of her insecurities out loud, but not today. She knew as well as any that she wasn't prepared to rule a kingdom. What would she want with a crown? It was bad enough having to keep herself and Adrastus out of harm's way. Adding an entire realm to that responsibility was unimaginable.

She rounded a corner with a huff. So what if she was the Queen's daughter? Herald could have that throne he fancied so much. She'd done what she came here to do. The council had officially been warned. And he'd said it himself. The army was readying themselves. Mission accomplished.

But then why did it feel like there was a forest giant sitting on her chest? It shouldn't matter to her whether they accepted her or not. If they triumphed over Samael, she could happily spend her days in the Winter Court with Adrastus and their friends. Right? It was hard to decide what she honestly wanted when their very lives were still at stake.

From the corner of her eye, she saw a shadow shift against the wall. She stifled a startled gasp and squinted in its direction. With the open ceilings, sunlight was plentiful, but that didn't stop shadows from being cast into the corners. Thanks to Samael, she feared she would never look at a shadow the same again. Cursing under her breath at the paranoia, she continued to walk.

Power surged through her limbs, tugging her forward. Confused, Kelera scanned the hall for anyone who might be trying to use magic on her. But she was alone. She quickened her pace through the spacious corridor, not willing to go back into the throne room where everyone was arguing about *her* fate. How could she make the decision that was best for her if she was surrounded by people pressuring her into choosing one way or the other? If only her father were here to confide in. There were so many things she wanted to ask him. Would he finally open up about her mother now that the truth had been spoken out loud?

The pulse of magic grew as she neared tall columns and open walls that surrounded a small garden. Lush green bushes were perfectly manicured and planted alongside stunningly bright flowers. Drawn by their beauty and the magical pull, she stepped from the marble and into the little grove. The new power that had settled into her bubbled up to the surface the moment her feet touched the grass.

The hidden oasis was so quiet and still that she almost wondered if anyone was allowed to be in there. Maybe it was for observing from the outside only. She glanced around, suddenly feeling like a child that would be scolded for wandering into some place she shouldn't be. But there was no one there. She was all alone.

Without anyone present to tell her otherwise, she walked deeper into the garden until she came to the center. Delicate blue flowers, the color of Kelera's irises, surrounded a bench of some sort. It was long and rectangular with a statue laid on the top.

The white stone was expertly carved into a woman's likeness. Kelera reached out to run her hand over the smooth stone, but stopped short and gasped. The statue's face staring up at her might have easily been mistaken for her own. Carved with waist-length wavy hair and full lips, the only difference was the striking angular shapes of her cheekbones. The effigy's arms were sculpted in a way that allowed her hands to rest on the center of her chest. Above them was a carved locket. It matched the one in Kelera's pocket perfectly.

Shivers slinked down her spine. This wasn't just any statue. It was her mother's casket. The blue petals were crushed under her feet as she turned to leave, but she couldn't bring herself to take a step. Her heart felt heavy, and she clutched at her chest. After all this time, she couldn't just walk away.

As she turned back to the casket, she caught sight of a portrait propped against one of the shrubs. Vibrant blue eyes, like Kelera's, stared back at her from the painting. It was the first time she had ever seen a likeness of Queen Mabine. Beautiful wasn't a worthy enough word to describe her. With flowing, wavy golden hair and a welcoming smile, she reminded Kelera of sunshine.

Careful not to touch the stone coffin, she walked over to the painting and studied it. Mabine's smile didn't quite reach her eyes. Instead, there was something both sad and powerful in them. It brought tears to Kelera's own eyes.

As much as she had tried to ignore it, grief was catching up to her. Her heart longing to mourn for what had been taken from her—a mother to guide her. Kelera's voice was no more than a pained whisper as she said, "I should have come sooner. If I hadn't taken that horrendous detour to the mortal court, then maybe we would have had a chance to meet."

"She would have loved that." Bothwell's voice jolted Kelera out of her confession.

She wiped the tears from her cheeks before facing him. "She could have come for me. All these years, she stayed away. If she wanted to meet me, she knew where to find me." Grief and anger were vying for a place in her mind and heart.

Bothwell stood by her side and made no move to break the silence. His mouth was turned downward in a frown and his strong shoulders were slumped. It made Kelera regret speaking so harshly. Mabine had been his Queen and his friend. And it was painfully clear that he was grieving for her.

Kelera tried to make up for it as she added, "The depth and determination on her face is striking. It is as if she had something to prove."

"She did." He sighed as he continued, "She had much to live up to. And she did. But it was at the cost of what she truly wanted."

If Kelera's father wasn't there to give her answers, then maybe Bothwell could. "And what was it that she truly wanted?"

He gave her a knowing look.

Kelera's throat was dry as she croaked, "Me?"

"Mm," was his only response.

After a moment, Kelera asked, "Did she ever speak of him? My father, I mean."

"Only to me. We grew up together here in the palace. She spoke to me in confidence, as only old friends can do."

Kelera thought of her own friend and confidant, Cierine. She hoped she was safe in Nevene. That she hadn't been punished for helping Kelera escape her trial and execution.

Bothwell went on, "Mabine often whispered of the mortal man who was different from the rest. She dreamed of the life the three of you might have had if she had been able to go with you."

"Then why abandon me? As Queen, she would have had the power to keep us safe here."

Bothwell grimaced. "Anyone who lives in the shadows of the throne is never truly safe. Even the Queen herself." He gestured to the stone casket. His eyes were pleading when he turned back to Kelera and said, "You must understand. It wasn't safe for you. The Wild Hunt rode on the night you were born. The entire birthing room was set ablaze, and it was all I could do to put it out in time. You were so powerful... and yet so defenseless. When she met your father, she was betrothed to Herald. She had gone to Nevene for one last night of freedom. Who could have realized what would come of it?"

Kelera's heart hammered in her chest. The Elders knew. They had prophesized it. Which meant her mother had known what she was all along. Had she believed Kelera would prevail? Or did she send her away because she knew it was a lost cause? Kelera couldn't help but wonder what her mother would think of her confliction to take the throne. Bitterness reared its ugly head, and she balled her hands into fists. Those were questions she would never get answers to.

Bothwell took hold of Kelera's hands and gave them a slight shake as he continued, "The only way to protect you from King Cyrus, from Herald, and from every other person who longed for the crown of Elfhame was to hide you away. Where better to stow away the most powerful Fae to ever be born than in a realm where magic is forbidden?"

Kelera's heart broke in two. She had imagined a million scenarios over the years—reasons why a mother would abandon her child—but she never imagined this. She bit her lip and tried to will away the tears threatening to fall.

Clearing her throat, she said, "She should have come with me."

Bothwell shook his head sadly. "She was afraid of what would happen to her people if she left them. Your grandparents raised her to believe that the crown comes before all. She trusted that your father would raise you with all the love you would need."

"I was angry at her for so long. When I was young, I dreamed of the things I would say to her... now I'll never get the chance. I can't help but wish things would have turned out different."

Bothwell released her hands and turned to the stone coffin. "She never did realize that she could have the life she wanted. She was too afraid. Too worried about living up to other's expectations. Those are mistakes I hope you will not make as Queen."

Kelera dug her nails into her palms to distract herself from the weight of his words. She had just escaped a life of trying to be perfect. All she craved now was freedom. Why would she want to be Queen? Especially after hearing about what her mother had given up for the crown.

With a firm shake of her head, she confessed, "I don't know how to be their Queen." Visions of a throne room engulfed in flames and ashes drifting from the ceiling clouded her memory. In her nightmare, she had been wearing a crown and everything she touched had been destroyed.

Bothwell watched her carefully, his eyes dark with concern.

She changed the subject. "What will they do with her?" She nodded to the stone coffin.

"They will take her body to the ash trees and light a pyre. They will return both her physical form and her soul to the earth."

"And her magic?"

"It will stay with you. Magic of royals does not return to the land, but rather passes to the heir. You feel it, don't you?"

Kelera bit the inside of her cheek and nodded. The power swirling within her had been a part of her mother. Whether or not Kelera was willing to accept it, she did have to respect and honor it.

Bothwell sighed. "In the meantime, there will be a feast." He patted her on the shoulder. "Shall I show you to your chambers?"

She turned to follow him, then thinking of the shadows she'd seen earlier, she asked, "Is the palace secure? I mean, will the magic hold against Samael if he tries to come here?"

Bothwell stiffened, but answered calmly, "I admit, the council is worried it may not. Between the transfer of the crown's power and the frost inching closer to the gates, it is taking a lot more effort to keep it intact."

It was far from the answer Kelera had hoped to hear. Would it strengthen again if she accepted the crown? Would she be strong enough to keep them all safe? As they reached the palace hall, she gave her mother's statue one long look. It wasn't the meeting she had always dreamed of, but there was something comforting in knowing the truth after all these years. All that was left to do now was to move forward. At least her mother had left her in capable hands as far as the council went. If they had the good sense to fear Samael, then they wouldn't hesitate to help her and Adrastus take him down. Samael's threat was imminent and she wouldn't be free until he was gone.

She owed it to her friends to set aside her feelings about the mother she had never known. To lock away any grief for Mabine's death. It could wait. The living needed her now.

Adrastus was waiting at her door in a dashing forest green jacket and black pants. It brought out the varying hues of springtime green in the rings around his pupils and reminded her of the Wildwood. His gaze narrowed when he caught sight of Bothwell by her side.

He sounded defensive as he asked, "Is everything alright?"

Kelera kissed him gently on the cheek. "Bothwell was just giving me some insight on my mother." The word felt foreign to her, and she had to swallow the lump in her throat that followed it.

Bothwell bowed deeply to her. "Now I must be off to oversee tonight's event. I can send someone up to show you to the ballroom—"

Adrastus stopped him. "We can find our own way."

Kelera added, "Though it is kind of you to offer." She nudged Adrastus in the side for being rude.

Once Bothwell was gone, Kelera opened the door to her rooms. It was elegant with small golden accents and soft earth tones. And it was gigantic. When Bothwell had mentioned chambers, she had imagined a room with a private bath, not several rooms bigger than her father's home back in Nevene.

Adrastus lingered in the doorway. "Should I come back for you when you're ready?"

Puzzled by his sudden distance, she insisted, "No, stay." She tried to lighten the air as she added, "Who knows when we'll get the chance to be alone again?"

Shadows passed through Adrastus' eyes as he stepped into the room. His sour mood gave her an uneasy feeling in the pit of her stomach. Was he still upset with her about Samael and the curse? She wouldn't have been quick to forgive herself for it, either. There was a fracture between them. One that she had caused. It would be up to her to mend it.

He closed the door gently behind him, and she stepped closer to say, "Dras, about what happened with Samael—"

"It's fine," his words were clipped.

"It is not. I don't want to pretend that my decision to storm off on my own didn't have consequences for you."

His jaw twitched as he warned, "Let it go, little thief."

He had to know her better than that. "Samael almost destroyed you because I left you."

Adrastus tugged at his jacket collar and his face reddened. "Yes, Kelera. You walked away from me, and it was the worst moment of my life." His voice trembled with rage. "Is that what you want to hear? That you nearly broke my heart when you left?"

"Dras..." her voice faltered.

He ran a hand through his raven hair and sighed. "I have no intentions of holding your mistakes against you. I have already forgiven you, little thief. I forgave you the moment I opened my eyes to find you beside me at the lake."

Kelera's heart pounded in her ears, accompanying his words in a loud symphony, as she listened to him continue, "Samael almost destroyed me because I wasn't careful enough. I was reckless and underestimated his reach in the Seelie Court. I'm not angry with *you*. I'm angry at myself!" he raised his voice and the glamor that hid the scars on his face—the ones given to him by his brothers when he was a young boy—showed through. They were jagged and severe, even after all these years.

Her heart ached, and she fought the urge to reach for him as she responded, "There's no way you could have known."

Closing the space between them, he grabbed hold of her arms. His tone was a low rumble as he said, "Because of *me*, you now owe a debt to the Elders. Because of me, you are here in this precarious position. For star's sake, Kelera, they're down there talking about *blood rites*."

She tore away from his hold. "Then it seems we are both to blame for how things have gone. But, Dras, you have to be able to talk to me about these things. Be angry with me. Even be angry with yourself. But don't shut me out. I *promise* you, I will not leave you like that again. Not ever."

Adrastus grunted in response and loosened his grip on her arms. They ached with the need to have him touch her again. It hurt to know that he blamed himself for the debt she had promised in return for his life. More than anything right now, she wanted to make him forget about it.

Reaching for his jacket, she took it in her fingers, caressing the fine fabric. Her face burned with a blush as she tugged it from his shoulders. A growl of longing came from deep in his throat and shadows danced in his eyes. Shadows that had once frightened her. But now, they were as much a part of her as they were him.

The jacket fell to the floor in a crumpled heap, setting their passion into motion. They tore at each other's clothes, ripping them off and leaving them in a trail to the enormous bed. Adrastus' hands were rough as they pulled at her hair, tilting her head back for easy access to her neck. He nipped and licked lower and lower until he reached her chest.

Kelera's breathing came fast, and she struggled to contain the little moans that escaped her. Adrastus drew back with hunger in his eyes. Her own gaze drifted down, drawn to his lips. The need to have those lips on her body was almost too much to bear. Heat spread between her thighs, and she gripped his shoulders possessively.

No matter what came next, they belonged to each other. They had both saved and risked each other's lives enough times that she'd lost count. Debt to the Elders be damned. The debt she and Adrastus owed to one another was the only one that mattered. And that one would be paid in love.

A shudder of pleasure coursed deep below her belly as he took her. It was as if all his anger and guilt were channeled into each thrust, and Kelera welcomed it. She called out his name, encouraging him... begging him to bare his soul to her.

When they reached the height of euphoria, Kelera sighed softly. Adrastus stilled and buried his face in her hair. They stayed that way for a moment, content to remain as one. The tension left his shoulders, and he whispered her name.

When he shifted on the mattress, she followed, snuggling into his arms. Neither of them spoke, but it felt as if something had been rekindled between them.

Adrastus pulled the blankets over them and she trailed her fingers along his chest, tracing his battle scars. Her voice was hoarse as she said, "We've walked into quite the mess, haven't we?"

He shut his eyes tight and rubbed his temples. "We sure have. It's... a lot to process."

Kelera snorted. "Tell me about it. Up until a few hours ago, I thought our greatest challenge would be to convince the council we could be trusted. Now an entire realm is arguing over my fate like I have no say in it what so ever."

The night stars twinkled in the window, reminding her of the time. She squirmed from the bed and grabbed the chemise that had been left for her. Then she walked over to a grand writing desk made of the same smooth marble as the floors, but with specks of purple and pink throughout it. Bending to grab her pants, which had somehow ended up across the room, she reached into the pocket for the locket. Quickly, she withdrew it and shoved it into the drawer. She didn't want to put it back on. Not yet.

Adrastus leaned on his forearm and his face softened. "I didn't mean to place more pressure on you. I can't imagine what you must be feeling."

Kelera strolled through the room, running her hand over the velvet sage green couch. "Anger, grief, confusion, shock. You name it. I'm feeling it."

"Right." Adrastus rose, pulling his pants back on, and took a seat on the sofa. "But it's not just the matter of you being heir to the Seelie throne. Samael is out there somewhere. He is coming for all of us, and once he learns of who you really are, he will stop at nothing to destroy you."

Kelera joined him on the couch. With so much happening so quickly, guilt for what she'd done at the manor hadn't had the chance to gnaw at her. But now that the intimate time they had shared moments ago wore off, she was feeling it full force. She needed to tell him what she did.

With a deep breath, she started. "When we left your family's manor in the Autumn Court, I did something."

Adrastus furrowed his brow. "Whatever you did, I'm sure it was justified."

She hoped he would see it that way. Before she could lose her nerve, she blurted out, "I set the house on fire with Samael, Kane, and Beatrice inside."

His jaw dropped. The wait for him to respond was agonizing. She tapped her foot on the floor until she couldn't take the silence any longer, then said, "They weren't going to stop. You were slipping away to the curse, and I just wanted Samael to feel even an ounce of our pain—"

"Why didn't you say anything sooner?" There was no regret or sadness in his voice as he asked, only confusion.

"Because I know Samael. A house fire would never be enough to stop him. And on the way here, when I saw that the frost was getting worse, I knew that he was still alive. We couldn't go into the council meeting letting them believe that there was a chance he hadn't survived. They wouldn't have felt the sense of urgency we needed them to. And there were too many people around for me to risk telling you and having them overhear."

She bounced her leg anxiously, waiting for him to respond. His family had abused and tormented him, but would it still strike a nerve deep down? Families were complicated, even one as malicious as his.

To her relief, he said, "You made the right choice." Kelera jumped as he barked with laughter. "You set my childhood home on *fire*? Perhaps you need a new nickname. *Little arsonist* has a ring to it, doesn't it?"

Kelera swatted at him, but she laughed too. It was good to see a smile on his face again. When their laughter died down, she leaned back on the couch. His fingers trailed along her collarbone, sending delicious shivers down her spine. She moaned as he pressed his warm lips against her neck. She gripped the cushions as he kissed and nipped. If only they could stay in this room and lock the rest of the world out forever.

She tensed as she stated, "What if I don't want the crown?"

Adrastus looked up in surprise. To her relief, there was no judgment in the way he looked at her. Instead, he leaned in, pressing his forehead against hers, and said, "I didn't realize when I brought you here that I was leading you into a game of chess. One in which you were the Queen. I am afraid for you."

The brutal honesty in his words was jolting. She confessed, "I wish it had been you. That you were the lost heir. I had been so sure of it."

He brushed her hair back behind her ear and his hand rested on her cheek, over her scar. "I know. I wish it too now. Simply so I could protect you from what's to come."

"I could give it to Herald. The power, the crown..."

"Is that really what you want?"

Kelera's eyes fluttered shut. "I don't know."

His lips pressed against hers, and she leaned into the kiss. When he pulled away, he said, "What you need to know is that I believe in you. I always have. And know that I will stand by any decision you make."

She did know. It was the only solace in an otherwise dire situation. She settled into his side and closed her eyes. This was one of those small moments of happiness that she would cherish and hold on to in the days to come.

Chapter Four

It took Kelera longer than she'd expected to prepare for the feast. Bothwell had been kind enough to send a few lady's maids up to help her get into her gown. Adrastus, try as he might, had been no help at all with the intricate lacing in the back.

To her delight, it hadn't stopped him from attempting it. The focused women raised their eyebrows as Kelera laughed out loud, recalling the way his fingers had fumbled with the ties. She hadn't been able to resist peeking back at him to find pure concentration on his face. He'd been biting his lip, taking the task as serious as if he were strategizing battle plans. By the time he finished, the entire thing was knotted up worse than a briar patch. The lady's maids hadn't seemed as intimidated by him as the courtiers and didn't bother holding back with the scolding they gave him for making their job harder than it had to be.

After that, he had graciously excused himself as the women fluttered around like tiny hummingbirds poking and prodding at her. She envied Adrastus' ability to throw on a jacket and appear immaculately put together. Whereas she—as she'd become accustomed to, growing up as a lady of the mortal court—was expected to fasten herself into a maze of stockings, lace, and ribbons.

When the ladies finished, Kelera barely recognized herself. In true Spring Court fashion, the dress was adorned with elaborate florals. They were blue to bring out her eyes. Something she suspected Bothwell had done on purpose to solidify the resemblance between her and Mabine.

Surprisingly, though, the gown wasn't layered with fabric like many of her dresses in Nevene had been. Rather, it was a light silk that flowed down to the ground with a cinch at the waist, accenting her wide hips in the most flattering way. She adored it.

Her long, dark, wavy hair was tamed and braided down her back with flowers and vines tucked in. She wasn't sure how the ladies had accomplished it, but she truly looked like Seelie royalty. The only thing she had fought them on was the tiara they had tried to mount on her head. There was no use in giving the courtiers false hope when she still hadn't decided on what to do.

The lady's maids fluttered out of the room like a flock of tiny birds, leaving her to find her own way to the ballroom where the feast would be held. As she stepped into the hallway, voices drifted up from a grand staircase. Follow the noise. Should be simple enough.

The halls were lit by golden candlelight, casting dancing shadows along the vine painted walls. Kelera took her time as she walked, not in a rush to go to a feast honoring the mother she never had the chance to know. It only served as a reminder of what she had missed out on. Her spirits were low, but she knew Adrastus' company would cheer her up. It was a specialty of his, after all.

A clatter at the other end of the hallway stopped her in her tracks. Her breath hitched in her throat, half expecting to find the shadow from earlier if she turned her head in the direction of the noise. She groaned with a sigh of relief as she spun around to identify the culprit... an open window someone forgot to latch. It was swinging in and out with the night breeze.

The hall was eerily quiet, and the air was surprisingly stifling. Her nerves were as jumbled as the ties on her dress had been, and with good reason. The threat of Samael haunted her. The sooner she got through tonight, the sooner they could move on to more pressing matters.

Shaking her head at her silly paranoia, she straightened out her dress. The lady's maids had promised there would be dancing as it was less of a wake and more of a celebration of the life Queen Mabine had lived. No doubt if there was, then Adrastus would ask her to dance. Her stomach filled with butterflies as she daydreamed about how divine it would feel to have his powerful hands on the small of her back. The prince couldn't lace a dress to save his life, but his hands certainly weren't lacking in other expertise. With her cheeks burning from a blush, she turned back to the staircase, but slammed into something solid.

Hands gripped her shoulders, digging in with ferocity, and suddenly her back was against the wall. She opened her mouth to call out, but shadows wormed their way down her throat, threatening to cut off her air.

Panic swelled in her chest at the sight of Samael's face only inches from hers. Inflamed red burns streaked his once flawless skin. Burns caused by her fire. Even though her heart had leapt into her throat at the initial shock of seeing him, it was nothing compared to the disappointment that he'd escaped the fire with no more than some ugly scars.

He remained far too close, with his lean body pressed against hers. The faintest smell of smoke drifted into her nose as she stood frozen in place. Her eyes darted around the hall, desperate for the Seelie guards' presence. Bile rose in her throat as she spotted blood seeping onto the floor near an open door. It seems Samael had found the guard first. Her own heartbeat thundered in her ears.

Samael whispered, "Surprised to see me?"

Truthfully, she wasn't. Samael had proven himself capable of slipping into the unlikeliest of places when he'd started infiltrating King Tristan's palace in the mortal realm. It was unnerving to find that the Seelie magic that protected the stronghold here wasn't as strong as she'd hoped. It was something that would need to be rectified.

His shadows slipped slowly from her mouth and he put a finger up to his lips in warning. Her thoughts warred and anger rose like a bonfire, replacing her fear. She could call out for help, but she would risk him slipping away or hurting someone else. Deciding to wait and play his game, she locked eyes with him and spat, "Surprised? No. Terribly displeased to see that you're alive? Incredibly."

Amusement flickered in his eyes. "That's an awful lot of confidence coming from a woman at my mercy."

She flinched as he leaned in and caressed her neck. Her skin crawled as his icy fingers trailed up to the puckered skin of her scar. A deep moan of pleasure came from Samael as he pressed his lips to her jaw. His tongue was warm—a stark difference in his bitter touch—as he licked the scar that he'd given her from her jawline up to her eyebrow. Her stomach contracted and heaved at the violation, but it didn't seem to faze Samael as he pulled back with hunger in his eyes.

Power rumbled in Kelera's chest. Not just her own now. Not only did she have the power of an Unseelie Prince attached to her own, but she now had the power of the crown to back her up. Imagining a million fiery arrows, she channeled them down her body to where he was touching her. Samael hissed as it burrowed into him, and he leapt away from her. She backed slowly toward the staircase, ready for his assault. He wasn't going to get the jump on her again.

"You *bitch*." He shook out his arms as if trying to rid himself of the pain of her magic.

She tilted her head to the side with mock concern. "What? Don't like the feel of fire on your skin?"

His nostrils flared in response. But his usual arrogant confidence returned as he retorted, "I just wanted to see you one last time before I destroy any hopes you have for saving this wretched realm."

He wasn't there to kill her? As the Seelie heir... the lost heir, she would have expected him to be there to assassinate her. Did he not know yet? It was somewhat comforting to learn that he might not have any spies inside of the Seelie Court. But if not to murder the heir of the throne he so desperately wanted for himself, what could he possibly be doing there?

"Perhaps it would be a more productive visit if you just turned yourself in." Kelera inched back, hoping to reach the staircase where she could call for the guards. Trapping him in the hall and having herself positioned by the open stairs would give them the upper hand. If she tried to take Samael on her own, then she could do damage to the palace and the incredibly large amount of Fae who had gathered for the funeral feast.

Samael cooed, "Admit it, you've grown fond of these little interactions of ours. Especially now that your confidence in your magic has increased." He stalked toward her like the predator he was.

But she'd survived Samael this long. She wasn't about to falter in front of him now. "I admit that I am stronger than when you ambushed me in the Nevene palace." She thought of the night that he'd come into her room. The same night he'd taken Cierine and put all of these events into motion.

His eyes roved over her and the possessiveness in them sent a chill up her spine. He licked his lips and nausea rolled in her stomach as the dead skin around his burns cracked. This was another one of his games. He couldn't help himself. Making her feel small and helpless had become his new favorite pastime. Especially when she decided to fight back—it only presented him with more of a challenge.

He taunted her. "Fate seems to want our paths to cross time and time again. Perhaps it was just my luck that those incompetent mortals didn't have the chance to execute you."

Kelera stumbled another step back, but her satin shoes slipped on the marble floor. She regained her footing, but he had already taken the opportunity to nearly close the gap between them. Fire burned in her veins, begging for her to consume him with it. But she couldn't. Not here. Not with the new power that she held. There was no telling how much control she would have over it when unleashed.

Samael's eyes lingered over her breasts as he continued, "I have big plans for you. Of course, I cannot allow you to sit beside my throne after how disobedient you've been. But I'm sure I can think of something more creative and... entertaining."

Kelera's skin crawled with disgust. She dug her nails into her palms, trying to distract herself from her rage. The power was getting harder to control with every step closer to her that he took.

Taking a risk of looking back to the stairs, she saw that she was only feet away from them. This was her chance. Still, she knew better than to allow relief to creep in too soon. She shouted, "Guards! Samael is here! He has breached—"

Something slapped her hard across the mouth, stunning her into silence. When she looked back at Samael, shadows were dancing around his hands. Footsteps came stampeding up the stairs. They were coming for him. She just had to make sure he didn't escape before they arrived.

Kelera touched her lip where he had split it open and glanced down to see the blood on her fingers. It seemed she wasn't the only one struggling with control. It didn't matter what he wanted with her. What mattered was that he couldn't resist confronting her. If this were a game of chess, she would be saying "check mate" right about now.

She stuck her lip out in a pout as she said, "Face it, you are *alone*. You think you have the upper hand? Adrastus and I have each other. Who do you have? A brother who lusts only after blood and his own mother?" She scrunched her nose in disgust as she mentioned Prince Kane and Queen Beatrice of Unseelie, then continued, "And an army who have been coerced and cursed by you? No one loves you, Samael. And because of that, you will never be the High King of Elfhame."

His eyes widened, but he didn't say a word. She'd struck a nerve somewhere in that dark heart of his. Ragnor's voice bellowed through the hall as he and the other Guardians of the Wildwood reached the top of the stairs. From the corner of her eye, she welcomed the sight of Jinx and Tepin, the friends she and Adrastus had made when they passed through the Summer Court. Her confidence grew in their presence.

Ragnor called from behind her, "Has he hurt you?"

Kelera sneered at Samael as she answered, "No." She ignored the sting of her mouth where he'd struck her. Admitting that he had hurt her would give him too much satisfaction.

Samael bared his teeth at her, but before he could make his move, Kelera imagined a tiny spark of light overtop his heart. And with a grin, she snapped her fingers. The spark caught on his jacket over his breast pocket. It took only a miniscule amount of her magic and she hoped it would remain contained long enough for the Guardians to subdue him.

But as the men advanced on him, Samael raised his hands. Shadows swarmed from them, wrapping around him and clouding her eyesight. The palace guards bounded up the stairs, shouting as they caught sight of the altercation. The men bumped into her, trying to navigate their way through the pitch black shadows. After a moment, it disappeared. And with it, so did Samael.

"Damn it!" Kelera cursed. Ragnor, Jinx, and Tepin shared the sentiment, yelling profanities that would have made the most seasoned guard blush.

The guards, however, didn't notice. They were in a disarray. None seemed to know exactly what should be done. Kelera watched as they looked around the hallway in bewilderment. Someone had to do something. So she commanded, "Go. Send search parties throughout the palace and the grounds. He can't have gotten far."

A few nodded their heads to her, but some lingered as if they were unsure if they should heed her command. After all, she wasn't yet the crowned queen. Bothwell, with his impeccable timing, shouted to them from the staircase, "You heard her! Go! I want every single guard hunting that animal down."

That got them moving. They saluted him and bounded away in various directions. Kelera gave Bothwell a grateful smile as he approached her. Adrastus wasn't far behind. He catapulted from the stairs, straight into Kelera's arms. Both men scanned her for any sign of injury.

She assured them, "I'm okay, I promise."

Bothwell pulled a kerchief from his pocket and handed it to Adrastus. He patted it against her lip with a gentle hand. It glowed under his hold, and she felt immediate relief as he healed the cut. When he finished, there wasn't even the faintest throb of a bruise that would have been forming without his magic.

She kissed him on the cheek. But his eyes were hard and angry, with shadows dancing in them. They were darker than she'd seen in a long time, and it was as if he were looking right through her. Cautiously, she asked, "Dras?"

He blinked rapidly, and the shadows cleared to reveal springtime green. "I'm fine."

Kelera eyed him carefully. Was he fine, though? She had only seen shadows in his eyes like this when his magic was at its most erratic. But that had always been in times of battle. With the rogue Fae in the Winter Court or the bounty hunter in the Summer Court. But now they seemed to be coming more frequently and with frightening ease. Even Ragnor shuffled a few feet back, giving Adrastus a wider berth.

Bothwell's voice shook as he claimed, "The guards will find him."

Adrastus growled. "Not likely. He knew what he was doing coming in here. There is no way he didn't have an escape planned." He nodded to Kelera, seeming distant as he urged, "Tell us everything."

She described quickly, but in detail what had happened. When she finished, Bothwell mused, "Why risk it? All so he could get under your skin?"

She shrugged. "If so, it didn't work. I mean, it's unsettling that he was bold enough to find me here," she paused and lowered her voice to a whisper, "but at least now we know that he hasn't learned the truth of who my mother is."

All the men nodded in agreement.

Bothwell straightened and said, "Well then, we'd best get back to the feast. If we do not present a confident, united front, then they will worry. Let us allow them this one last night before we thrust them into battle."

Kelera squeezed her lips into a firm line. How could she drink and eat when Samael was lurking in the shadows? Worse, how was she supposed to mourn for a mother she never knew?

Jinx scratched beneath his eye patch as he chimed in, "We'll join the search, just in case."

Ragnor agreed, "Aye. Maybe it would be best to cancel the feast."

Bothwell's mouth popped open in shock. "That would be a grievous error. The best thing we can do for the court is to go down there and appear calm and collected. As I said, there is no need to cause a stir."

Kelera hugged herself, unsure of whose advice to take. She turned to Adrastus. "What do you think?"

He was thoughtful before responding, "Bothwell might be right. I would wager that Samael is long gone and if he isn't, he may decide to try something at the feast with so many high standing courtiers gathered in one place. Better for you and me to be there if he does."

It was a good point. But still, something nagged at her. Samael was an expert at infiltrating heavily guarded places, but the Seelie magic should have been strong enough to ward him off. Shouldn't it? She pointed the question at Bothwell. "How did he get past the defenses?" She raised her chin to look him in the eye, hoping he wouldn't try to sugar coat his answer.

He gulped, then said, "I fear the frost may be weakening our land magic. The magic responsible for protecting the palace walls."

The admission made her so dizzy she could do nothing but grab onto Adrastus' arm. As the Guardians rushed off to join the Queen's Guard in their search, Bothwell and Adrastus looked at her as if waiting for a sign to proceed. If she agreed to the crown, it was something she would have to get used to. The amount of pressure it placed on her was surprising. It would take time to adjust after years of taking someone else's lead.

Each step she took felt heavy as she followed Bothwell with her arm looped around Adrastus'. He patted her hand, but the reassurance fell flat. She glanced back, half expecting to catch a glimpse of Samael's slippery shadow. Relief failed to come when she didn't find it. Wouldn't it be better to know where he was?

She descended the stairs on unsteady footing. The staircase was far larger than she'd anticipated. They looped around the large curve of it, passing intricate carvings of solitary Fae like bogies and pookas. For a moment, she wondered what would happen to them if Samael stole the crown. She hadn't read anything about their stance on Elfhame politics. Would the witches and the other Fae like them who wandered the realm with no attachments choose a side? Had they already done so without her knowledge? She suppressed another shiver.

When they reached the bottom of the stairs, she wasn't prepared for what she saw. An all white stone ballroom gleamed under massive candlelit chandeliers. It brightened everything and everyone beneath it. Pink flower petals were scattered along the floor and fully naked Fae posed on pedestals. Their skin was painted with a shimmering gold, and they had thin vines wrapped around their arms and legs. They smiled and danced to the soft music drifting through the room. Kelera's jaw dropped at the indecency.

Adrastus joked, "Yeah, that's how my face looked too when I first came in here. I thought my father's revels were extravagant, but this..."

He trailed off as two Summer Court Fae danced in front of them. They were wearing nothing but seashells, which clattered as they moved their bodies in rhythm. Their hands roved along one another with smooth expertise. They winked at Kelera, and Adrastus chuckled. But she was too overwhelmed to see the humor.

She took a deep breath before she said, "I need a drink."

Adrastus furrowed his brow. "Are you sure you're alright?"

"Yes." It came out as a snap and she regretted it immediately. "I didn't mean to sound cross. It's just a lot to take in. And I guess I might still be a little shaken up."

"Understandable. If Samael is still on the grounds, they will find him. I have faith in Ragnor and the others."

Kelera gave him a skeptical look with her eyebrow raised. "Do you have the same faith in the guards?"

Adrastus draped his arm over her shoulder. "How about I show you how to spot Elfwine so you can avoid it?" His evasiveness of her question spoke louder than his words could have.

A hesitant laugh bubbled up from her throat at the mention of Elfwine. The Beltane festival in the Spring Courts Wildwood had been the first time she'd gotten truly drunk and although she didn't want to relive it, she found that she could joke about it now.

Rich spices wafted through the air from the long tables set up with food. Between the scent of the grand feast and the uplifting beat of the music, Kelera felt a pang in her heart. What would her father think of it all? They mourned differently in Nevene. With sorrowful ceremonies as quiet as death itself. But here in Elfhame, they embraced the passing of their loved ones. Celebrating the life they lived and the glory that awaited them in the afterlife.

It was too bad her father wasn't there to celebrate with them. Though he hadn't talked about her mother, Kelera knew he cared for her. His silence was far more telling than any stories he could have shared with her. She glanced at Adrastus. She couldn't imagine a life without him and the love they shared. If she had lost him to the curse, she imagined it would have been difficult for her to relive the memories with him as well.

Adrastus handed her a glass of deep purple liquid. The scent of lavender drifted up from it and Adrastus took a moment to point out the difference between it and the Elfwine that sat filled to the brim on the table.

The room never seemed to end as they navigated their way through clusters of Fae—courtiers, villagers, entertainers, and anyone else they could fit into the great hall were there. There was a small pond encased between the marble floors and she stepped over glittering stones to cross with Adrastus in tow.

When they came to the other side, she spotted a long table placed at the head of rows of other tables. It was the first similarity she'd found between the Seelie Court and Nevene—the spot where royalty and their guests and advisors sat to overlook all others.

As Kelera began to set her drink down on one of the tables below, Bothwell sidled up to her. He wrinkled his nose as he said, "Oh no, not here." He took her by the elbow and turned her toward the table of honor. "Your place is there."

The pleading look she shot Adrastus with did nothing to save her from Bothwell's firm grip. Adrastus followed quietly behind them as they ascended the steps to the table. Bothwell ushered her to the center and gestured for both her and Adrastus to sit. Her nerves were jumbled as she took her seat. She didn't belong up here. Adrastus maybe, but certainly not her.

Adrastus seized hold of her hand under the table and leaned in to say, "Give me the cue and I will whisk us out of here. You don't have to do anything you don't want to do, little thief."

"I don't know what I want to do. That's the problem." Part of her yearned to stay and see the send off they were going to give her mother. But another part of her was terrified. Would they expect her to cry? Or did they expect her to hold her composure as a queen would?

Fae filtered in from the other half of the ballroom and took their seats. Their faces glistened with sweat and golden paint as they smiled up at her. She shifted uncomfortably under their gaze. It was hard to know how long this would take or what they would expect of her, and it took everything within her not to default to her old ways of trying to act how she thought they would want her to.

The hall quieted as heavy footsteps echoed behind the table. A few—although surprisingly enough, not many—Fae stood and bowed as Herald approached her. Kelera braved a look in his direction to find him staring down at her with open disdain. That's when she realized she and Adrastus were sitting at the center of the table in the spot where the King and Queen would sit. Her heart dropped. This was a public affront to him. One that Bothwell had planned without her knowledge.

He'd dressed her up like royalty and placed her in a position of honor for all to see. Like a prized pony. How could he do this to her without speaking with her first? Her cheeks warmed as she shot a glare in his direction a few chairs down. Herald grumbled as he sat to the right of her and she tensed.

Adrastus gave her hand a squeeze in his usual reassuring manner. Grateful for his presence, she leaned into him, resting her shoulder on his arm. Herald ignored her completely, downing an entire glass of wine and filling it up immediately.

Meanwhile, Bothwell stood and announced over the crowd, "Friends, we gather here to bid farewell to our beloved Queen Mabine." Tears filled his eyes and he choked them back as he continued, "At dawn, her body will return to the land from where it came. But tonight, we honor her spirit!" He gestured to Kelera, "And her daughter."

Murmurs spread through the room, and Kelera wanted nothing more than to crawl under the table. Herald gripped his wine glass so tightly that his knuckles turned white. Gadreel and Oliver stood at the back of the room, looking around nervously. She wished she was down there with them, hiding in the darker corners, away from prying eyes.

Gadreel leaned in and whispered something into Oliver's ear and when he finished, they both let out loud whoops and started clapping wildly. Applause rippled through the crowd until nearly every Fae was standing and cheering for her. Would they be so jovial if they knew their enemy had slipped through her clutches only moments ago? Perhaps it was a mistake to have come to the feast.

Kelera's breathing was coming in sporadic spurts and there was a tightness in her chest that was becoming hard to ignore. She turned to whisper to Adrastus, "Is it too late for whisking?"

Adrastus smiled and clapped. Through his teeth, he responded, "I think so."

Chapter Five

Oh, how right Adrastus was about that. Once they finished dinner, Fae after Fae approached the table to offer their blessings. It was an endless procession of well wishes, long-stemmed roses, and trinkets. None of which Kelera desired to receive. After each one, her eyes darted around the room, searching for any shadows that didn't belong. Still, through it all, she plastered a gracious smile on her face and held it there until the muscles in her cheeks ached.

When the Fae were finished, they set about dancing or chatting amongst each other. Bothwell crept up behind her and bent down to her level. His face was glowing with pride as he said, "You've done well tonight."

She turned to confront him with an incredulous look on her face. "How dare you," it came out as an exasperated whisper.

"What's wrong?"

Her magic flared like lightning, but Adrastus' firm grip on her thigh calmed her back down. Steady, she responded, "You're parading me around as a Princess of Seelie without asking me first if I am comfortable with it. Perhaps I didn't make myself clear enough this morning in the garden. I have not made my decision."

Bothwell's face fell in genuine remorse. "I didn't mean to upset you or try to force your hand." He glanced around and his eyes rested on Herald, who had made his way across the hall and was huddled close with some courtiers—the very ones that had knelt to him and snubbed Kelera. Bothwell's voice was grave as he continued, "It is important that we establish your place here. If we do not solidify your claim to the crown now, then it won't matter what you decide later. Should these Fae see you as anything other than the rightful blood heir of the Seelie throne—as Mabine's daughter—then you won't have the option of claiming it if that is what you choose in the end.

Kelera groaned. He was right. If she chose to give up the crown and Mabine's power, then none of this would matter. But if she changed her mind and wanted to rule, without first presenting herself as the rightful heir to the throne, then no one would follow her. The decision would be made for her.

She relented, "Fine. But promise me that you will discuss these things with me first from here on out. Do not manipulate me. I've had enough of that to last a lifetime."

"Understood." He gave her a curt nod and excused himself to join the other council members below the dais.

Adrastus scanned the room like a hawk, but when he spoke, it was low so no one would overhear. "You handled that well."

Kelera raised her chin. "I did, didn't I?"

His gaze snapped to hers and laughter twinkled in his eyes. "You would make a good Queen, you know. Even if you choose not to take the Seelie crown..."

"Go on," she said cautiously. Where was he going with this?

He shrugged as he took a sip of his drink. "When this is over, someone will have to rule Unseelie in Samael's place."

"Would that someone be you?" She was surprised at the turn in conversation. He'd been adamant that he didn't see himself fit to rule over his father's territories. Was this a change of heart?

He shook his head. "I don't know. Gadreel would be capable." He chuckled. "He'd likely paint the palace purple. But I think he'd do well as king."

Kelera spotted Gadreel in the crowd with Oliver's hand secure in his own. A few courtiers shot disapproving looks in their direction, and she remembered that a relationship between Seelie and Unseelie was frowned upon by some. It had to be hard on their love life, though you'd never know it by the way the two of them were looking into each other's eyes right then.

Kelera bit her lip, thinking of hers and Adrastus' own relationship. "If I claimed the crown of Seelie... or Elfhame, would people accept the two of us together?"

Adrastus clucked at his teeth and exhaled loudly. "Some would. Some wouldn't."

She turned to face him, bracing both of her hands on his legs. "I won't do any of this without you. Whatever my decision, I want you to be by my side."

"I don't want to make things harder for you."

"It would be a million times harder *without* you."

Adrastus turned his head to glance back at the party and didn't press the subject any further. After a few silent beats, he excused himself to go speak with Gadreel. It was important to let Gadreel know about their older brother's break in, even if Bothwell wanted to keep the courtiers in the dark. Kelera remained in her seat, more comfortable there than having to walk around the crowd reminiscing about the Queen she hadn't had the opportunity to meet.

She was just beginning to relax with the music drowning out her warring thoughts, when Herald sat down beside her. He scooted his chair close to hers so that their legs were touching. Kelera's mouth twitched in disgust. She made a point to ignore him as she took a small sip of her lavender wine.

He drawled, "Enjoying yourself, *Princess?*"

She gave him an annoyed look. He was incredibly handsome, like a storybook prince. But that's where his charms ended, in her opinion. She wasn't sure how her mother could have stood to be with someone like him or why he inspired such loyalty from some of the courtiers. He came off as arrogant and entitled in the way he had taken his seat on the throne and in the manner in which he spoke to Kelera.

She wanted to offer a snarky retort, but bit her tongue and said instead, "It is a very lovely feast. I'm sure Queen Mabine would have been pleased." In truth, she wasn't sure. It was becoming increasingly more difficult to figure out the complicated woman that her mother had been.

He snorted. "She would have thought it was too much."

Kelera perked up at that. "Really?"

Herald tipped his head back as he drank from a smooth horn, then said, "Yes. If I'm being frank, I can see similarities between the two of you."

She couldn't contain her interest. "How so?"

He studied her for a moment. "For one, you're both stunningly beautiful. But you also have that same irritating determination." He leaned his elbow on the table. "You want to set things right. I can see that. The whole damn court can see that. But do you really think you could rule these people successfully? From what I've heard, you have been raised to be a lady of the court. To *serve* royalty. Not to *be* royalty."

Kelera scoffed. "And *you* are better suited, I suppose?"

He puffed out his chest. "I am. I was *born* for this. I know how to control all that power you now hold. Can you really say the same? From the moment I opened my eyes to view the world for the first time, I have been in training to rule at the Queen of Seelie's side. It is my Elder-given right to take her place now."

"According to Bothwell, it is actually *my* Elder-given right." She wasn't sure why she was wasting her energy arguing with him about this. Especially when ruling over an entire land was beginning to seem less and less appealing. But something about him irritated her and she couldn't help herself.

He grimaced as he responded, "Except that you have idiotically bound yourself to a monster. More than that, you love him. Anyone looking at the pair of you can see that you will not give one another up. But that is precisely what you will have to do if you take the Seelie crown."

"Dras is no monster. And he also has Seelie blood."

"Perhaps. But they will never trust him. Not after all that he has done."

"He is trying to make up for his mistakes."

"I knew you would say as much." Herald leaned back in his seat, raised a hand in the air, and snapped his fingers. "That's why I have arranged for a little demonstration."

Doors opened at the side of the room and courtiers in emerald green cloaks ushered a man in. They sat him down on a chair at the center of the room and stepped away. The man was ragged and filthy, wearing tattered robes. His head rolled from side to side, and he was muttering to himself.

Kelera's eyes met Adrastus' from across the room and his face went wraith-white. He looked as if he was going to be sick. Gadreel whispered something to him, but he shoved him away and approached the man, stopping short of reaching him.

Herald plastered on a poor excuse for a solemn look as he stood to address the crowd, leaving Kelera incredibly confused. He raised his voice and said, "You have all come here tonight to not only bid my dearly departed farewell, but to also embrace the daughter who has, at long last, returned home. But do not make the mistake of welcoming all who step through these palace doors today."

Kelera stood now too, unsure of where he was going with this, but ready to defend herself, nonetheless. With a sweeping motion, Herald gestured to the man in the center of the extravagant room. Courtiers gasped and covered their mouths with their hands and villagers watched with horrified faces. A wretched cackle bubbled up from the man's throat. His voice cracked from lack of use as he shouted incoherent words to no one in particular.

Herald continued. "This man's mind was shattered not so long ago by someone in our midst. A Dark Prince of the Unseelie Court. A Prince of the Night. The honorary guest of Princess Kelera."

The title he bestowed upon her would have caught her off guard coming from his lips if she hadn't been so consumed with worry for Adrastus. He was visibly trembling, but she wasn't sure if it was from embarrassment or anger. His face was a mixture of emotions as he glanced between the man and Herald.

Herald turned to Kelera, closer than she was comfortable with. She tried to take a step back, but bumped into one of the chairs. There was venom in his words as he said loud enough for everyone to hear, "Do you see the sort of man you are bound to for eternity? The man you would subject your people to, ruling with him by your side?"

Adrastus shouted, "Enough!" He took a few long strides toward the dais. "Step away from her. Now." His threatening words were cold and deadly. Enough so, that they caused Herald to take a shaky step back.

Herald feigned innocence as he smiled and said, "I just thought the people had a right to know what sort of rulers they would be getting."

Adrastus bared his teeth. "I have no desire to lord over your people. Perhaps that is the sort of king consort *you* were. One always trying to control your *beloved* and sway the council to take your side. If Kelera chooses to accept the crown, then that is her choice. It belongs to her."

Her stomach did a small flip. If she had to choose between him and the crown, then there was really no choice to be made. It would always be him. Always. Her mouth felt dry and she couldn't think of anything to say. The people looked so uncertain she knew she had to do something, but what could she say to convince them that Adrastus was not like his father, King Cyrus?

Adrastus spoke before she had a chance. He turned to face the crowd, gazing upon each and every one of the Fae there. Pointing to the manic man, he explained, "Do you all forget who this criminal is?"

A few murmurs sounded through the crowd. Some of the onlookers appeared just as taken aback as she was. But many spat in the man's direction, glaring at him in recognition and hatred.

Adrastus continued to speak to them, "He put you all in danger when he broke the accords with the mortal realm. Stealing babies from their cribs and children from their gardens! Your *King* Herald here did nothing to stop it. Those young lives were lost, and for what? So this man could take their innocence for his own magical gain?"

A few of the Fae shouted in anger, recalling the horrible acts the man had committed out loud. Angry glares were shot at Herald, who had become very quiet by Kelera's side. She crossed her arms in satisfaction. His little stunt was backfiring.

Adrastus didn't stop there. "Perhaps it was not my place to interfere with Seelie justice, but I would not sit by as this man destroyed innocent lives. So, yes, I did what I do best. I *broke* him. I burrowed into his mind with the shadows passed down by my father *and* my *Seelie* dream magic, and I shattered it. And I would do it again."

The majority of the crowd shouted in agreement and support. Mira, clinging to Diana's arm, shot a seething glance in Herald's direction. It appeared that even with the support of some council members, he did not have the support of the courtiers. They, too, shared Mira's heated gaze.

Bothwell stared at Herald with a look of triumph, then called to the men who had brought him in, "Take this man back to the dungeons!"

They obeyed, dragging the man away as he laughed and cried hysterically. Kelera was flooded with relief once he was gone. She'd seen the effects Adrastus' magic could have on men when his Seelie and Unseelie power collided. But hearing the story behind this particular incident brought nothing but a sense of pride for the kind of man Adrastus was. One who would not stand idly by in the face of treachery.

Courtiers bowed their heads to Adrastus in a show of respect. Maybe she was wrong about the Seelie and they would find it in their hearts to accept him. This was just the glimmer of hope she needed.

She turned to Herald and spoke under her breath so no one else would hear her. "It seems I would not have to choose after all."

She sauntered away to leave Herald to think about how his actions had backfired on him. The Fae returned to good cheer, as if nothing had happened, but she could see the council members watching her carefully. As she approached Adrastus, Herald bounded down to them. When he reached them, he grabbed Kelera by the arm and pulled her into him roughly.

Adrastus shoved him back and placed himself between them. He warned Herald, "You do not touch her. Ever."

Courtiers and villagers shot wary glances in their direction, but the council circled around to block out their view. Anaya's feathered gown fluttered around her as she chided

Herald and Adrastus, "This is not the time, nor the place. Your little stunt has interrupted quite enough, King Herald."

Herald balked at her. "How can you support this?" He shot a dagger-like look at the council around them. "How can any of you possibly want a halfling with a bastard Unseelie Prince ruling the Seelie Court?"

A frail council member with long black hair streaked with silver spoke, "If the prophecy is true, then it will not be the Seelie Court, it will be all of Elfhame. This *halfling* could be our savior."

Herald hissed through his teeth as he said, "You would see the courts combined? You would have us give our power over to *them?*"

She raised her wrinkled chin. "If the Elders wish it. Yes."

Herald opened his mouth to say more, but the grand glass windows around them shattered, accompanied by blood-curdling screams. Kelera whipped around to see the large skeletal horses and the rotting men who haunted her dreams. The Night Riders were here.

The room broke out in chaos as Samael's cursed Riders trampled courtiers and villagers. Bones crunched beneath their savage steps. A swarm of tattered cloaks and skeletal armor blotted Kelera's view of the room. She searched the crowd, desperate to catch sight of Gadreel and Oliver. But as she scanned, her gaze landed on Adrastus. The shadows in his eyes were back, bobbing in and out rapidly.

"Dras," she called to him, but he didn't notice. His attention was locked on the Night Riders. The very monsters he had nearly joined. He stared at them, unblinking as sweat beaded on his temples.

Kelera tried again, more determined to break through to him, "Adrastus!"

He pinched the bridge of his nose and shook his head. Now that he had snapped out of whatever trance he'd been in, he pressed his back against Kelera's and shouted to Bothwell, "Where are the guards?"

Bothwell's face was a sickly shade of green as he said, "We sent them all out to find Samael."

Damn it. Kelera had been so distracted she hadn't considered how long the guards had been gone. She hadn't had much faith in them finding Samael. He was far too slippery for that. But she should have inquired sooner. She never should have listened to Bothwell. They should have been repairing the wards on the palace instead of infighting with Herald and his pride.

Adrastus cursed under his breath. "That's what he was doing here. That sneaky son of a bitch. He knew we'd send every guard out to search for him, leaving us completely exposed in here."

The council had spread out now and was using their combined powers to create a shield around them and Kelera. The older council woman shouted, "Protect the royal family!"

"No," Kelera argued. What they needed to do was protect the people. The Seelie were doing what they could to defend themselves, but it wasn't stopping the Night Riders from tearing weaker Fae down with blades made of sharp bone. It cut through magic and flesh like butter. Was the Seelie's magic faltering just as their palace wards were? Surely Samael would have felt their depleted power when he set foot on the palace grounds. If her instincts were right, and if they didn't act now, then this would be a massacre.

She grabbed hold of Adrastus' hand and tugged him through the council's protection spell. It resisted at first, but Kelera's fire-fueled magic melted it away. Once they were free of the council, they faced the Night Riders. Gaunt faces stared down at her. Though their eyes were shrouded in shadows, she could feel their gazes boring into her.

As she called on the bound magic that she and Adrastus shared, it defied her. Like fabric snagged on something, she feared if she pulled too hard, it would tear. Carefully, she tugged until it released enough to liberate shadows and ice alongside the heat of her Seelie magic.

Adrastus' face dripped with sweat, but he didn't back down. Together, they blocked the Riders from the party-goers. Crackling came from a Rider walking to the corner where Mira and Diana had been standing. He raised a finger and pointed it at Mira, whose face turned an unnatural white. Kelera's heart skipped a beat. Did he remember Mira from the woods in the Autumn Court? When she had fled from them in an effort to reach the blackthorns? The glove the Night Rider wore couldn't hide the smell of rotting flesh and it turned Kelera's stomach.

"Dras, over there!" she shouted and before the Night Rider could slash its blade into Mira, Adrastus slammed shadows into its wrist. The sword fell, leaving Diana the opening she needed. The decorative vines that were slinked around the columns responded to her, wrapping tightly around the Rider like a snake. It squeezed until Kelera heard the sound of old bones snapping.

Relieved to see that the courtiers could protect themselves to a certain extent, Kelera turned back to the fight at hand. Pain lanced through her shoulder as a Rider slashed his sword out at her. She reached around and pulled her hand away to find blood staining her fingers.

The Night Rider leveled his gaze at her. "The High King sends his regards."

Kelera pushed through the pain as she retorted. "Where has your fearless leader run off to? If he wanted a fight, I'd have given it to him."

Adrastus' magic wove itself around her wound, giving her just enough relief that she was able to raise her arms at the cursed Fae. An entanglement of ice, shadows, and light slammed into him, throwing him from his steed and into a crumpled heap on the floor.

The Seelie Fae charged at the other Riders with newfound confidence, using their magic to snuff out what was left of the Riders' lives. Pools of blood coated the pristine marble where both Seelie and Night Riders had been slain.

When she turned to where Adrastus was fending off one of the cursed Fae, she saw another creeping up behind him. He was twice the size of Adrastus, but eerily quiet. As he raised his sword, Kelera's power flared like never before. She was blinded by a fearsome white light as it overtook her. The blast of it knocked her back into a wall and her head slammed hard on the stone.

For a moment, it was so quiet that she thought she'd lost her hearing. She couldn't hear the clash of bone and magic anymore. There were no war cries. No creaking of ancient armor. Just silence. She reached for her head and felt something wet under her hair.

Her panic was suffocating. Images of Adrastus' eldest brother, Ammon, being slammed into a cavernous, frosted wall and his lifeless eyes staring up at her flooded her memory. The horrifying scene from her nightmare in which her fire consumed everything in its path took the breath from her. What had she done?

She could see nothing but the blinding white light. A fresh wave of panic hit her as she shut her eyes tight and willed her sight to return. When she opened them, she winced. Slowly, the silvery light faded, revealing a room littered with bodies. Night Rider bodies. She breathed a heavy sigh of relief as she noted the courtiers and villagers standing tall around the room. A sob escaped her as Adrastus ran to her and knelt down in front of her.

"It's alright. You're alright," he reassured her, but fear was laced in his words.

"Did I hurt anyone?" She didn't want to cry when so many were watching her, but between her panic and the magic she was having trouble reeling back in, it was hard to regain her composure.

"No one that mattered." He smoothed her hair away from her sweaty brow and ran his hands over the back of her head. She hissed in pain and he pulled his blood covered hand away in alarm. "You're hurt."

Holding in Queen Mabine's power was excruciating, like daggers trying to tear through her skin. "Dras," she squeaked, "I can't contain it much longer."

His eyes widened. "It's going to be okay." Icy magic ran along her body, trying to coax the Seelie crown's power back down, but it burned her like frostbite. Tears of pain streamed down her sweat and blood streaked cheeks.

She whimpered, "It's not working."

Bothwell joined them. A cut at the corner of his eye was bleeding profusely and the vessels inside had burst, filling it with red. He glanced between her and Adrastus. "What is it?"

Adrastus snarled, "The crown's magic. It's too much for her. You need to get everyone out of here."

Bothwell ignored him and placed his fingers on Kelera's temples. "Don't worry, Your Grace. We'll fix this." His words echoed from a distance as her vision went black and she drifted off into nothingness.

Chapter Six

K elera woke to angry, bitter voices. The men were arguing in hushed tones, but their words hammered into her throbbing head, nonetheless. The room was dimly lit, revealing a carved stone ceiling above her like the one in her own bedroom. Hesitant to leave the soft feather down pillows she had been placed on, she rose to rest on her elbows.

Adrastus and Bothwell stilled like children who had been caught staying up past their bedtime. Bothwell smoothed his hair back and straightened his jacket. But he wasn't fooling Kelera. His distress was obvious judging from his rosy cheeks and thin pressed mouth.

Adrastus was at her side in the blink of an eye. He studied her carefully, as he had done numerous times before when she'd lost control of her magic. Only this time it hadn't necessarily been *her* magic she had lost control of. It was Mabine's. Whatever power had been transferred to her by her mother was impossible to contain. Memories of bodies littered on the floor forced Kelera to shut her eyes tight in an attempt to block them out.

She pinched the bridge of her nose as she inquired, "How many?"

Bothwell's footsteps approached, and she peeked up at him through heavy eyelids. His face was twisted in confusion, and he asked, "Dear?"

Kelera fought the urge to speak out of frustration. Instead, she maintained her decorum and elaborated, "How many did I kill?"

Adrastus grabbed hold of her free hand. "No innocent lives were ended by you, little thief. Not one."

Bothwell agreed, "Only the Night Riders. It was as if the blast passed right through all of us and into them." He wrang his hands together in a jittery motion. "A few of our own were injured, though only with slight burns. Nothing the master healers can't handle."

The blood drained from her face. She had burned them. The nightmare that had come to her the night of the Beltane revel flooded back. Everything she touched had been swept away in a blaze of fire, leaving ash in its wake. What if the horrid dream had been warning her of something like this? The crown's influence was too much for her to handle.

Bothwell reassured her, "If not for you, Samael might have claimed victory tonight. None of our people were killed at your hand, Princess."

Kelera shot each of them a glare. "This time. But what happens the next time? What happens if I can't control it again?"

Adrastus rubbed his thumb along her knuckles, soothing her. "You won't. We'll ground it. Just like before."

This was different. Couldn't he see that? This power was like nothing even he had experienced before. She tried to make him understand as she said, "This magic is extraordinary and stronger than I could have predicted. It is dangerous in the wrong hands." She drew her hand away, wrapping her arms around her stomach to quell her nerves. "And it took me weeks to finally get control over my magic before. We don't have that kind of time now. Samael was clever enough to distract us before the feast. He made his move of attack tonight and failed. If he meant to chip away at our confidence, then his wounded ego won't allow him to wait long before he tries again."

Kelera looked at Bothwell, and he dropped his gaze to the floor. He had to know she was right. They both did. Men like Samael always had something to prove. Any slight—especially one in which his prized Night Riders were defeated—wouldn't go unpunished. It was only a matter of time before he retaliated.

Bothwell broke the silence. "The wounded Seelie have been taken to the healer's quarters. We lost lives tonight, but it would have been catastrophic had it not been for you, Princess Kelera." He sighed, "The council wants to see you in the morning to discuss... what is to be done."

"About Samael?"

He hesitated, twisting his hands together, before answering, "About your power."

She smiled bitterly. "So, they agree. It's too much for me."

Adrastus growled, "If someone would shut Herald up, then maybe they wouldn't be so quick to doubt her." He didn't look at anyone in particular as he spoke, but Kelera could practically feel the tension between him and Bothwell.

Nausea rolled in her stomach as she ventured, "They want me to transfer it to Herald?" She should have seen that coming. He was the next logical choice. It seemed her little display tonight had given him the perfect opportunity to challenge her. And maybe he was right. Perhaps he would be better suited for the job.

Bothwell shook his head vehemently. "No. They will still support your claim, should you wish it. But they believe you need a blessing." He was gripping his hands so tight they were turning white now. There had to be more to it than he was letting on.

Adrastus leaned his shoulder against hers and added, "From the Elders." His muscles were taut against her. The Lady of the Lake's warning of the debt echoed in her mind. If she went to the Elders, would they call in what she owed them? And what would that be, exactly?

Kelera held her composure as best she could. "How would that even be possible?"

Bothwell spoke next. "You hold the key."

Kelera's eyes drifted to the drawer where she'd tucked the locket away.

Adrastus chimed in again, "With it, you can enter the hollows beneath the ash trees."

"It's that simple?" Kelera's voice was filled with doubt. Things in Elfhame were *never* as simple as they seemed. Even dancing with Adrastus in the Summer Court had been an act of opening her heart to him. Going under a hill to meet with the world's most ancient Fae sounded terrifying.

Adrastus gave Bothwell a pointed look. His face was hard and his eyes were narrowed. Bothwell shifted uncomfortably under the gaze and cleared his throat before speaking. "No. You must go alone. Only a King or Queen can pass through their veil."

Adrastus spat, "You mean only a King or Queen can survive." This is what they must have been arguing about when she woke up. He was trying to protect her from Bothwell's plan.

She hugged herself tighter. "But I am not the Queen."

Adrastus directed his clipped response at Bothwell. "Exactly."

Bothwell held his hands out to them both. "But she is as good as Queen. You are the heir, Kelera. Mabine's blood and her magic runs in your veins. This would not be the first time a royal heir has had to go under the hills to solidify the grasp on their power. Your mother, herself, did it before she took the crown."

Kelera's heart skipped a beat. Mabine had struggled with her magic too? Thoughts and emotions warred in her mind again. If she did this, then she could take hold of the power they needed to defeat Samael. But wouldn't presenting herself to the Elders be the same as agreeing to become Queen?

She raised her chin to meet Bothwell's eyes. "What if I deny the crown? What if I want to give it to someone more worthy?"

Adrastus stared at her in wonder. "Is that what you think? That you aren't worthy of it?"

She ignored him, not wanting to get into it at the moment. She simply wanted to know if it would still be possible to give it up after she went to the Elders.

Bothwell's eyes filled with sorrow, and his face fell. It was the look of a broken heart. But he nodded and said, "Actually, it will be the only way to give up the power. You must have control of it in order to willingly channel it into another. Whomever that may be."

It could be him. The idea hadn't occurred to her before. But if she had the option of giving it to anyone she wanted, then she would much rather hand it over to him instead of the power hungry King Herald. But all of that would have to wait. As of now, she couldn't do anything with Mabine's magic. Decisions did not have to be made until she had the Elder's blessing.

She placed her hands neatly in her lap as she said, "I'll do it. I'll go to the Elders."

Bothwell didn't look at all relieved. He bowed and said, "I will alert the council. We will make preparations. When the sun rises, we will bid farewell to Mabine's body, and then you can take your leave."

He headed for the door, but she stopped him before he could reach for the handle. "Lord Bothwell... what will it be like? Down there?"

His lips parted, and he hesitated. With a deep sigh, he admitted, "I cannot speak from experience. Mabine was reluctant to talk about it when she returned. All she would say was that it was a world of immense power. One that confronted you with the truth, whether you were ready for it or not. She alluded to the restless souls there, wandering aimlessly with unfinished business. You must be steadfast in your endeavor, Princess."

Kelera's skin clammed up at the foreboding words. She allowed them to sink in as he exited without another word, leaving her and Adrastus in tense silence. Adrastus stood abruptly and paced beside the bed. His hands trembled as he rubbed at the stubble on his chin. She watched him move unceremoniously back and forth until she grew dizzy.

"Dras, sit back down, please."

He stopped pacing and growled, "I cannot let you go into the realm of the dead alone. Bothwell cares for nothing but his territory. He knows the risks, yet he wants to send you there, anyway."

"He's doing what he must, and so am I. You felt it, didn't you? The power and the turmoil that came with it?"

His face softened slightly. "I did. I tried to reach out through the bond to quell it, but it was as solid as a fortress. There was nothing I could do."

"What if it's affecting you, too?" She thought of the shadows clouding his eyes.

He stiffened. "What do you mean?"

With a steady voice, she said, "Don't pretend with me. Especially not now." She inhaled deeply through her nose, trying to remain level headed. Allowing her frustration to rise wouldn't do either of them any good. And would only push him away.

"Something's wrong," he admitted. "I don't know if it's Samael's frost that's dampening my Seelie power, or if it's the wild strength of your new magic..." he groaned and ran a hand through his hair. "Whatever it is, the bond isn't anchoring my Unseelie power like it should."

"All the more reason for me to go to the Elders."

It was clear he had felt as helpless as she did. She reached for him, pulling him back into the bed, and rose to her knees to embrace him in a hug. The tension in his shoulders soon melted away, and he wrapped his arms around her. It was good to have him holding onto her. To be holding onto each other again.

Kelera kissed him on the neck, letting her lips linger on his scarred skin. She trailed her kisses along his jaw until they reached his mouth. When he kissed her back, it was with fierce hunger. Heat flooded between her legs and before she knew it, she was lying on her back against the soft pillows. His powerful arms were on either side of her like a stronghold that would keep all threats away.

They kissed passionately, giving in to the desire that had been building beneath their worry for one another. She gave herself over to Adrastus' expert hands as they explored. When it was just the two of them, like this, her mind could not wander. They were all that existed.

She rolled on top of him, mounting him with ease. His moans of pleasure gave her a boost of confidence and she moved her hips in a steady rhythm, delighting in the way he felt inside of her. Time seemed to still as they explored one another, finding endless ways to bring about intense ecstasy. All thoughts of the Elders and the shadows slipped away with each touch and kiss.

After a while, they finally tired, finding themselves lying in each other's arms dreamily. Adrastus trailed his fingers along her back, sending shivers down her spine. After the excruciatingly long day and recent ballroom battle, the bliss she was lost in now was divine. If only they could remain like this forever...

With the husky voice of someone tirelessly satisfied, she said, "This is what I want."

Adrastus laughed huskily. "A big feather down bed?"

She swatted at his chest and nuzzled into him. "You. This. A life together without the pressures and responsibility. I mean, the fate of the world is quite literally resting on our shoulders right now. Wouldn't it be nice to spend a simple life together? I want us to be free..." She paused and chuckled, adding, "and yes, I also want a big feather down bed."

"Say the word and it's yours." His voice was soft, like he was fighting the urge to drift off to sleep.

"I know."

But there was still so much to be done. Between Mabine's magic, the unclaimed crown, and Samael, there was no way they could take control of their life together until the rest was resolved. And what would it mean for them if they did walk away from their duties?

He kissed the top of her head and she felt her hair catch on his stubble as he pulled away. She did her best to smooth it down, but supposed that, too, would have to wait. At least until the morning.

Sleep began to claim her and her eyelids grew heavy until Adrastus spoke again. "You are worthy of it, though. I just need you to know that. You are worthy of the crown and so much more, little thief."

She didn't answer. Instead, she closed her eyes tight and steadied her breathing so he would think she'd already fallen asleep. She knew deep down that he only wanted her to be happy. But she also knew he had reservations about ruling. He'd voiced his reluctance to her, himself. And when it came down to it, whether she wanted the crown or not, she would choose him.

Chapter Seven

The world was clouded by smoke. Thick, gray, and suffocating. Kelera choked on it as it filled her lungs. There was no escaping it. Frightful cries burst from all directions. It was the sort of wailing that came from deep within the soul. The sort that only appeared when grief was rearing its ugly head.

Her body trembled as she stumbled through the field. Burnt grass crunched beneath her boots with each step she took. But through it all, she could only think of finding Adrastus. The air was smoldering like there was still fire burning nearby. Was she surrounded by it? Was he?

Desperately, she tried to call out to him, but her voice wouldn't come. A tall, lean man caught her eye in the distance. His stark silvery hair was unmistakable. He did, after all, haunt her dreams often. Ammon walked ahead of her, unphased by the smoke and the raging fire nearby.

Kelera couldn't think of what she should do, so she followed him. Each step she took was painful. Her legs were heavy with exhaustion. Worse than the heat in the air, was the burning inside of her. Her skin screamed as it relentlessly coursed through her.

A bright light appeared before Ammon and he stepped through it effortlessly, disappearing on the other side. Kelera ran as fast as her legs would carry her, afraid to lose him. When she reached the light, she jumped through without a second thought.

The scene on the other side was worse than she ever would have imagined. The fires were gone, leaving only crackling embers behind in the field. Trees which once stood strong and proud in the Wildwood of the Spring Court were now barren and dead.

But that wasn't all. Kelera's breath hitched in her throat as her eyes met the fallen on the battlefield. The bodies on the ground were unrecognizable. Their skin was black and red. Their armor melted into their skin. The only thing to set them apart from one another were the crests they wore. Bits and pieces of a crown surrounded by thorns and others with pinkish white flowers.

Ammon was standing mere feet away from her. His icy blue eyes met hers and he smiled as a woman joined him. Kelera hadn't laid eyes on the witch since she was a child and had ventured too close to the blackthorns, but she would never forget her intense gaze or the spiderweb of wrinkles that lined her face.

The witch's words felt like spikes against her skin as she said, "The world will succumb to frost, and be reborn in fire. You did it, Your Majesty."

There it was. The same prophecy that continued to haunt her no matter where she ran to in Elfhame. Kelera croaked, "I didn't do this."

"Do not be ashamed. It was fate." Ammon looked at the sky above Kelera's head, where a tiny white piece of ash drifted down.

She watched it as it moved toward her, but the closer it came, the brighter it became. A slight glow emanated from it, like one of the stars in the Elfhame night sky. She was frozen in place by its illuminating beauty. It finally reached her, landing on her nose with a peculiar tingle.

Kelera raised her hand to touch it and the moment her skin met the strange ash, it burst with blinding white light.

She opened her eyes with a gasp. She sucked in fresh air, relieved to be free of the smoke that had burned her lungs. But the excruciating heat beneath her skin remained. She sat up, struggling to calm her racing heart.

Warm hands cupped her cheeks, and she looked up to find Gadreel staring back at her with the same icy blue irises as Ammon. She raised the back of her hand to her mouth and stifled the sob that threatened to escape.

Her breathing was ragged and coming in short bursts, and Gadreel was saying something she couldn't quite make out. Only when Adrastus joined her at her side did she find the steady strength to calm herself.

"Breathe, little thief. Breathe."

She obeyed, taking a deep breath in through her nose and out through her mouth. With each one she took, the burning fever on her skin began to melt away. Gadreel had a strong hold on one of her hands while Adrastus rubbed the other with her head resting on his chest. Oliver caught her eye at the edge of the room. He looked like a frightened deer, pressed against the wall.

With as much composure as she could muster, she said, "It was a dream. Like the one before. I destroyed everything."

This time Adrastus didn't dismiss it as nothing more than a nightmare the way he had done when she'd dreamed of the burning poppy field in the Summer Court or the burning throne room in the Spring Court. He caressed her hair and allowed her a moment of silent contemplation.

The prophecy's phrase was a vague one. It had never stated who would bring the frost, but they all knew now it was Samael. If they were to go beyond the palace grounds, they would see the evidence of the icy curse with their own eyes. But every Fae she had talked to since coming to Elfhame had been sure that the lost heir would be the one to rebirth the land. Even since it had been revealed that it may in fact be she who was that heir, she'd never stopped to consider what rebirth actually meant. What if it was a cleansing through destruction?

She sat up and looked at the three worried men, too distraught to wonder why they were all gathered in her room at such an early hour. "What if the Elders don't want my power to be controlled? What if they're counting on me losing a handle on it and unleashing it on the world?"

Gadreel shook his head. His usual lighthearted spirit had dimmed, and his face looked gray like he had fallen ill. "They wouldn't do that."

"Wouldn't they?" She knew none of them had met the Elders. The last Fae to go beneath the hollow hills were King Cyrus and Queen Mabine. But her own experiences in Elfhame had proved how foolish it was to underestimate any Fae, regardless of how powerful. They all excelled in trickery.

No one answered. It only solidified her fears, locking them deep inside her like the mortals had done to her in the dungeons. These men were as in over their heads as she was. To her surprise, that made her feel slightly better. She'd spent the last few weeks fumbling her way through Elfhame culture and politics. It had forced her to rely on Adrastus and Gadreel in ways she had never relied on anyone before.

This evened things between them. She knew it was a petty and selfish thing, but it gave her the confidence to say, "Then I suppose I should go find out."

The sun had barely risen when they reached the ash trees. Before meeting the large forest giants who had bowed to her, Kelera would have thought these trees to be massive. Now they looked mundane and average with their full green leaves and wide trunks. They also lacked the same magic she had felt at the hawthorn tree line—the shield that had tried to prevent her from reaching the lake in time to break Adrastus' curse.

The council had already arrived and were circled stoically around a pyre. Magnificent colored flowers and golden trinkets lined it. But her heart skipped a beat when she spotted the shrouded body lying at the top. Kelera was relieved that her mother's corpse wasn't visible from where she stood. To see her face to face for the first time this way would have been more heartbreaking than she believed she could handle at the moment.

While the Fae around her wore their finest clothing, she was well dressed for travel. But despite her long-sleeved shirt and leather vest, she shivered. The frost was particularly bad this far from the palace. Even the large group of guards that had accompanied them blew on their hands to keep warm.

The walk there through the village had been revealing. With Samael's icy curse spreading so fast, crops were dying in the fields and villagers were struggling to find game during their hunts. It was forcing them to tap into their food stores. Samael would bleed them and their land dry. Each face she passed engrained itself in her memory. These were the people relying on her the most.

She tried to focus on the ceremony now. Council members took turns speaking. Some reminisced about their time with Queen Mabine, while others spoke of strength in the face of great strife. Kelera's mind wandered. Soon she would be parting with them all to undergo possibly the greatest challenge of her life thus far. Though she couldn't imagine anything more frightening than being under Samael's control, Bothwell's warnings of the dangers under the hill were hammered into her head.

Gadreel and Oliver drew her attention with their whispers. They were huddled tightly together, their heads so close Kelera feared if one of them moved, the other might topple right over. Desperate for a distraction, she continued to watch them. Adrastus remained between her and her friends, so she wasn't able to overhear them, nor did she want to. Whatever intimate secrets the lovers were sharing belonged to them and them alone.

She smiled softly to herself as Gadreel handed Oliver a kerchief to wipe away his tears. Gadreel's hand drifted to Oliver's shoulder, then wrapped tightly around him. He trailed his fingers along Oliver's jacket, touching each thread tenderly. The gesture reminded her so much of Adrastus when he tried to comfort her, that her heart swelled. These were good men. Strong, loving, and unashamed to show it. Gadreel deserved his happily ever after as much as she and Adrastus did, and she prayed to the stars that he would receive it.

The ceremony dragged on, and she masked her wariness as best she could throughout it. As it came to a close, she could feel everyone's intense gaze on her. They watched solemnly as the council and Adrastus accompanied her far into the grove of ash trees. Shadows danced over the men and women's faces. It only made the whole situation more menacing than it should have been.

Bothwell stood in front of her with a look she had seen on her father's face many times growing up. Sir Aldric had given it to her the first time she'd fallen from her horse, the first time one of his knights bested her in a duel, and when she'd prepared to cross the blackthorn veil for the first time. It was a mixture of pride and fear.

Bothwell smiled softly. "May the fates be with you."

The Fae gathered around and all of them, except for King Herald, echoed the words. Herald was seething with a red face and arms crossed over his chest. But she ignored him. This wasn't about his ambitions or his pride. This was about Elfhame. About claiming the power that they would need to defeat Samael and his army. It was bigger than any of them.

Adrastus approached her next. His face was unreadable—the mask she'd seen him use many times before—but his embrace was warm and comforting. When he drew away, he pressed his lips to hers. The kiss deepened only for a moment, and before she was ready for it to end, he pulled away.

He leaned his forehead against hers as he said, "You are the strongest, most capable person I have ever known. You can do this. And when it's done, I will be right here waiting."

She closed her eyes and ran her hand over the side of his face in a gentle caress. There was no telling what she would encounter when she journeyed under the hollow hill, but she wanted to hold and cherish this moment for as long as she lived.

She whispered, "I love you."

"I love you too, little thief."

Afraid that she would lose her nerve if she lingered any longer, she pulled away and walked toward the hollow. Holding an arm out, she trailed her fingers along the diamond-shaped ridges on the ash tree's bark. Magic bloomed to life as she did, prickling her skin as it flowed into her.

With a deep breath, she stepped up to the low, round hill. Anywhere else, it would have looked like a random mound of dirt. But the harder she stared, the more the glamor dropped to reveal a hole just large enough for a person to pass through.

Pulling Mabine's necklace from her pocket, she knelt on the ground. There was a small stone embedded in the side of the mound. Drawing a dagger from her sheath, she slid the blade across the palm of her hand, mustering just enough blood to place on the small locket. With a simple click, her journey was set in motion. Inside, the key's magic beckoned to her like it had been waiting for this very moment. Just as Bothwell had coached her when they walked through the village, she placed the key inside the stone.

The ground inside the hollow rumbled so softly she had to strain her ears to hear it. She stood, and this time, clasped the locket around her neck. Its familiar weight on her chest comforted her, giving her the courage that she needed to move forward. With a gulp, she took a step inside.

Power surged around her, sucking her in like the black-thorn veil had. It was like being underwater and at one time it would have filled her with dread, but now, she was used to the strange pull. The sounds of birds chirping in the trees and the murmurs of the council were drowned out.

On the other side, purple crystals dangled from the ceiling of the cave like icicles. They shimmered bright, lighting her way as she ventured further into the cavern. It wasn't quite what she had expected, though she supposed she had no idea what she thought she would find once she passed through.

There were no sounds as she explored the cave deeper—not even the sound of her own footsteps could be heard. Her heart began to race the further into the glittering cave she went. What if it hadn't worked? What if they were wrong about her being able to access the Elder's realm before her crowning ceremony?

It felt as if every step she took got her nowhere. She clenched and unclenched her fists in an effort to relax. Panicking now wouldn't do her any good. But still, the cavern took her nowhere. The crystals all looked so similar that she couldn't decipher how far she'd gone or if she wasn't going anywhere at all.

For all she knew, she would be trapped there forever. She paused and looked around. She could turn back. But then what? Go home and tell the people that she had failed them? Or worse, what if she returned to Seelie and her power destroyed them all before Samael had the chance to do it himself?

Her voice echoed as she said, "I am here in the name of Elfhame. I come seeking the Elders."

To her dismay, nothing happened. There seemed to be no other choice but to turn back. They would figure it out. They always did, right? Hope began to flutter away like a bird taking to the sky, but a shimmering wall of magic caught her eye.

It hadn't been there before. Of that, she was certain. But now, it glimmered in the dimly lit cave as clear as day. There was no mistaking what it was... A veil. Kelera took a deep breath as she reluctantly approached it.

It reminded her of the first time she'd sliced her hands on the thorns of the blackthorns, uncertain of what would happen. She'd been a frightened girl, then. Afraid of how others perceived her. Terrified of being found unworthy.

She squared her shoulders, reminding herself that that girl was gone. Replaced with a woman who had stared death in the face numerous times and lived to fight again. She wasn't weak. She was a raging fire, ready to face anything that came her way. Failure was not an option. Adrastus was right. She could do this.

With newfound courage, she plunged herself into the veil.

Chapter Eight

Bothwell was wholly and utterly wrong about what Kelera would find beneath the hollow hill. This was no dangerous underworld. Lush, magnificent landscape stretched as far as the eye could see. She was standing in the center of a forest littered with flowers she'd never seen before. Each was so unique that she wasn't sure she would ever be able to describe them to anyone back home.

Some were tall with stems as wide as her arm, while others twisted like braided loaves of bread, reaching up to her knees. Birds fluttered around the treetops with feathers that left trails of glittering dust in their wake. Even the light breeze drifting between the towering trees shimmered. Back in Elfhame, one could physically feel the power emanating through the land, but here in the Elder's realm, it was visible to the naked eye. It was ethereal, and Kelera could do nothing but take it all in.

As she circled the clearing, doing her best not to crush any of the smaller flowers, she called out, "Hello? Is anyone there?"

Though she hadn't known what to expect, she had thought that someone would be there to greet her. If not an Elder, then at least one of their servants. If they had any, that is. The Fae believed that when they died, they would return to the land along with their magic. If that were so, then where was everyone? Where were the souls of the Fae? It was jarring to think that only moments ago she and the Seelie had been bidding her own mother's soul farewell, sending it down to this very place.

Kelera's throat scratched with sudden dryness at the prospect of crossing paths with Mabine... if such a thing was even possible. Doing her best to keep on task, she chanced a few steps further into the forest, not quite sure what she was looking for. Surely, the all-knowing ancient Fae would sense that she had entered their realm. If this was their idea of a game, she wasn't interested in playing.

They were wasting her time. And knowing Samael, he was already planning his next move. It sent shivers up her spine. But as she came to a dark path, she realized it wasn't the thoughts of Samael that were making her uncomfortable. The path was twisted and foreboding, with lifeless branches that looked eerily similar to the Night Riders' slender skeletal frames. She glanced back at the elegant flowers and lush trees and every instinct in her body screamed for her to turn back.

But she couldn't. Not when she'd made it this far. If the Elders weren't going to come to her, then there was only one choice, and that was to go forward. When her feet hit the rough ground of the path, the magic shifted. Its power crept into her bones—damp and heavy. She swallowed the lump in her throat and focused on putting one foot in front of the other.

Still, there was not a soul within sight, which suddenly made the lack of Adrastus' presence painful. If only he had been able to come with her. She missed the solid comfort of him and his sly smiles. Reaching deep into her magic, she felt his power caress her. It was a comfort to know that a part of him was with her wherever she went. Giving her the small spark of hope she needed to continue on.

It was dangerously dark now, and she stumbled over roots hidden beneath the shadows. One particularly large one tripped her, and she tumbled to the ground with a curse. Someone nearby let out a throaty laugh. Her stomach leapt to her throat as she found the source. A ghastly beast stood mere feet from her. How had it moved so quietly through the trees?

Scrambling back, she reached for her magic. It flared at her fingertips in warning, lighting the wooded area around them with a soft glow, but the creature didn't balk. He stared down at her with a tilt of his head. Though his face and body resembled Fae, the broad horns protruding above his ears were as sharp as daggers, and his massive claws were as long as her forearm. She'd never seen his likeness in any of the books she had read, so she couldn't put a name to what he was.

That, however, was the least of her troubles. The more pressing issue was that she didn't know if he was peaceful or dangerous. Wanting to avoid a fight, she rose slowly and drew her magic back slightly. It dimmed to a low flicker, but her heart continued to pound in her chest.

Her voice shook as she declared, "I'm not looking for trouble. I only seek the Elders."

The creature's bushy eyebrows pinched together as he frowned. He made no move to advance on her, so she took a cautious step away from him. She was careful not to turn her back on him, waiting to be sure if he was friend or foe.

As Kelera debated on whether she should try talking to him again, the creature opened his mouth. His jaw elongated to reveal three sharp rows of teeth reaching back into his throat. Terror flooded her as a vicious roar tore from him. Her magic flared in response, knocking them apart. The burst of light swept the creature away and out of sight.

Kelera shook in shock as she lay in the dirt. Her body ached from the impact and her skin burned with the strength of her power. She took several steadying breaths and tried to regain her composure. It would be a good time to run before the monster came back, but the use of so much of her magic left her drained and trembling.

The familiar masculine voice that often haunted her dreams drifted through the darkness. "Looks like you could use some assistance."

With a start, Kelera shoved her wild hair from her face and looked up. First the monstrous horned beast, and now this. Bothwell may have been right about the hollow after all. Dread overwhelmed her as she met Ammon's leveled gaze and stuttered, "I-is it really you?"

She'd dreamt of him so often that she was used to his haunting, dead eyes, but here they seemed to glow with life. They were remarkably bright, especially in the blackened forest. Her heart skipped a beat as she got back to her feet. She didn't dare move toward him. The memory of moths pouring from his mouth and pelting her in the face and arms was still too fresh. And accompanied by her most recent nightmare from the previous night, she feared she might cough up her breakfast.

He smiled sadly at her. "I don't believe I've ever met anyone who carries as much guilt as Adrastus... Until you."

Her eyes burned as she stated, "I never meant to hurt you."

"I know that." He tilted his head. "But it is not *my* forgiveness that you need."

Her attention snapped to the sound of bones crunching behind her. When she turned, she spotted a vision of Ammon's body lying in a crumpled heap on an ice cold floor. Her heart plummeted in her chest as she watched herself abandoning him so she could run to Adrastus. When she turned back to Ammon and the dark forest, there was no hatred in his eyes, only pity.

Before she could say anything, screams tore through the quiet air. When she looked to the right, she saw a servant woman being torn down with magic and steel at the edge of the blackthorn veil. The mortal women she had dared to try to save when she'd rescued Cierine. She watched as a vision of herself left the women to fend for themselves so she could push her best friend through the veil. She recoiled at the gruesome sight of the women lying on the ground with lifeless eyes.

Chanting to her left grabbed her attention next. The Guardians of the Wildwood were gathered around Chaz. Thin black lines coated his golden brown skin and putrid green pus oozed out. The pain and grief on their faces was so overwhelming that Kelera squeezed her eyes shut.

She snapped at Ammon, "Stop it!"

"It is not me, Kelera. This is all you." His voice was so soft that she opened her eyes to meet his gaze.

"I never wanted to hurt anyone. All I ever wanted was for everything to be..."

"Perfect? Life, as you now know, can never be so." There was no judgment in his words, only truth.

"I know," she whispered. "I just want to set things right. Tell me how I can do that."

"You need to let go of all of this guilt." He gestured around them at the horrible scenes of her past played out over and over again in a symphony of heartache. He continued, "It is the thing that drives you and your magic. Filling you with fear that someone else will succumb to these same fates. But that is not how things work. You are no more to blame for these tragedies than the stars in the sky. It is simply the way things were meant to be."

"You did not have to die. If I would have been able to control myself, you would still be alive."

He held a silencing hand in the air. "I made my choices. My fate was already on its course long before you came into our lives." His eyes were wide and pleading now as he said, "Let go of the guilt and embrace what is meant to be."

Kelera sucked in a deep breath between her teeth. It was easy for someone to tell you to let go when they themselves did not have to do it. He could show her the things that haunted her dreams, but he could never understand the weight of the guilt she felt. How was she supposed to move past it all?

"Tell me, then. What do I have to do? How can I get the Elders' blessing?"

Ammon stepped aside and swept his arm toward the path. It brightened slightly with moonlight, giving her just enough of its glow to allow her to see where she was going. His body faded as she came closer until she reached the edge of the moonlit path.

His voice sounded distant as he instructed, "Face the greatest of your fears. Only then will you be found worthy."

Then he was gone. Just as quickly as he had appeared. Had she simply imagined him? Was it a trick played by the Elders? Or had it truly been his spirit? He'd looked at peace and because of that, she hoped it was the latter. That he had discovered eternal life in the realm of the Elders. It was better to remember him this way than to think of the haunted version of him that visited her nightmares.

As she walked, the path glistened with magic again. It wove around her boots, lighting them up like warm sunlight. But just as she began to relax, the putrid smell of burning flesh filled her nose. She wiped at her brow, which was beading with sweat. The air became unbelievably hot and stifling, as if she were walking through fire. She sucked in a ragged breath as the trees around her crumbled into ash.

They fell to the ground in heaps of it, allowing her to see past them. Where the vast forest had stood only seconds ago, there were now houses crumpled to the earth. Creatures from the Wildwood, Lesser and High Fae alike, cried out in mind splitting screeches. They were in pain. Not just pain. They were dying.

Massive bodies plummeted down from the sky like flaming starlight. Kelera's hand flew to her mouth as they landed near her. Warriors with once beautiful steeds lay with twisted limbs. A sword, glistening and enchanting, flashed beside a corpse. She recognized the enchanting steel. Had seen it strapped to the side of the man who vowed to stand with her when the time came. It was Woden's sword. She pressed the back of her hand to her nose to block out both the smell and the horror. This was the Wild Hunt.

Her mind spun as she looked around for the one person she worried for the most. Dark raven hair caught her eye, and she ran to him. Adrastus was on the ground with a rusted blade sticking out of his side. His once mesmerizing green eyes were wide, with milky shadows clouding them. She collapsed beside him with a sob.

This was it. Her greatest fear. A world blazing with fire and the man she loved, dead. She let out a loud frustrated scream, "What do you want from me!" The Elders had had their fun. It was time for them to show themselves. "How am I to let go of my fear when you won't stop reminding me of it?"

She buried her face in Adrastus' shoulder and cried. People had been telling her all her life that she was unworthy. And now the Elders were showing her just how weak and helpless she truly was. If they wanted her to be the savior of the realms, then why were they torturing her with visions of her failure?

Suddenly, hot hatred filled her. This was their fault. If they were all knowing and powerful, then why hadn't they stopped Samael? Why were they dragging this out instead of giving her the blessing that she needed in order to defeat him? They had thrust Mabine's power into her and that meant any blood her failure wrought would be on their hands, too.

The hatred bloomed, spreading like a wildfire in a field of poppies. This was her mother's fault as much as theirs. Instead of training her to control her power, she'd abandoned her. She had left Kelera defenseless and clueless. She thought of the burning pyre and the Queen who had laid upon it in a shroud.

If her mother's spirit was here in the realm of the deceased, then she would take this chance to say what she needed to. Gripping Adrastus' body tighter, she cried out, "You left me unprepared for all of this!" The screeching and popping of fire ceased and her voice echoed as she said, "What am I supposed to do? Who am I supposed to be? These are questions I have had to live with my entire life. All because you abandoned me! All because you were too afraid to face what fate had in store!"

She was breathless by the time she was done. Her shoulders slumped as the anger dissolved—released with her heated words. Adrastus' body became light beneath her grasp and she gasped as she looked down to see the vision of him fading away. It was all disappearing. The fire, the homes torn to the ground, and the creatures who were suffering.

All of it vanished, replaced by the glowing forest. Kelera placed her hands on the ground to stabilize herself. Tension coiled inside of her stomach as she braced herself for the next nightmare to be shown.

Instead, she spotted a man and woman sitting together on a hill. At first glance, she thought it was her and Adrastus, but as she stood and walked closer, she saw that the woman had golden blond hair. But it was the man holding the woman in his arms that caught her attention. It was a face she knew better than any. She studied the mild differences. Her father's warm eyes were no longer lined with the signs of age. He was a young man, nearly hers and Adrastus' age. And he was smiling in a way she'd never seen before.

The woman sitting beside him whispered something and pointed in the distance. When Kelera turned, she saw nothing but darkness. Her father hesitated to look away from the woman as if nothing she could be pointing at could possibly be as fascinating as her. The adoration was undeniable, and Kelera felt as if her heart would break for him.

Throughout her life, her father had dodged marriage proposals, even ones that would have been to his benefit and aided in Kelera's standing. There had never been a woman who could hold his attention long enough for her to notice. She certainly had never seen him look at a woman this way. Like a man madly in love. It must have been incredibly lonely for him. She knew the ache that only loneliness could bring. And now, thanks to Adrastus, she knew the elation of finding love. She didn't want to imagine what it would be like to have it taken away immediately after finding it.

Tears welled in her eyes at the heartache she had for her father. She reached for him, but the couple faded as her fingers met his shoulder. The vision changed to the same woman, with kind eyes that matched Kelera's, pacing on a balcony in the Seelie Palace. A comforting floral aroma drifted through the open doors, making Kelera's ribs grow tight out of homesickness.

Bothwell joined the woman, resting his hand on her rounded stomach. He soothed the woman into stillness. "Please, Mabine, reconsider."

"I can't." Mabine's hair glowed in the sunlight as she shook her head. "Once the baby comes, I will have no choice but to fulfill my duties. I will no longer be able to hide away."

Kelera glanced down at Mabine's stomach, covered by a thin blue nightgown. She blinked rapidly at the sight of her pregnant mother, unable to believe what she was seeing. The vision continued, with Bothwell reddening in frustration.

His voice trembled as he warned, "Herald will make a grab for power the first chance he gets. You cannot trust him, let alone marry him."

Mabine placed an elegant hand on his cheek and closed the gap between them. The baby inside her belly was the only thing standing between them now. Her eyes sparkled with tears as she declared, "I will do what I must."

Kelera took a step closer and reached out for her mother, longing to touch her just once, even if it was all an illusion. Her breath hitched in her throat as Mabine and Bothwell faded away. But the room did not. Spotting Mabine out of the corner of her eye, Kelera turned to find her lying in a bed. She was holding a baby in her arms, looking lovingly into its soft pink face.

There were tears in her eyes as she said, "This is for the best. It is not safe for her here."

Kelera looked around frantically. Who was she talking to? But all she could make out was the dark shape of a man sitting at a writing desk. She didn't dare reach out this time, afraid that she would lose the vision again. And this was one she wanted to hold on to.

Mabine began to hum a soft tune. A lullaby. The same one the witch in the poppy fields had hummed and the same that Adrastus had used to calm her to sleep in the Summer Court. A Seelie lullaby. One filled with love and safety.

The humming grew distant and Kelera cried out as Mabine and the baby were quickly replaced with a man in a hood carrying a small basket. Yearning for the vision to come back, Kelera shouted, "No!" but it was no use. The man hurried to her father's door in Nevene and set the basket down gently on the steps.

Taking a step closer, she watched as he tucked blankets around the baby with care. The hood slipped from his head to reveal Bothwell. He hadn't changed much in Kelera's twenty years, but he looked pained here. It showed in the dark circles around his eyes and in the downward pull of his mouth.

He whispered to the baby, "I will keep her safe, just as your father will keep *you* safe." The baby—Kelera—began to fuss, and he hushed her with a kind tone. Tears streamed down his face as he said, "You will return home one day, and I will welcome you with open arms, Princess."

Kelera wiped away the tears on her cheeks. She'd heard what had happened and had imagined how things had gone, but seeing it with her own eyes was different. The love that her parents had shown each other, the pain in her mother's eyes as she made the decision to give her up, and the regret in Bothwell's voice as he saw her safely to the mortal realm... it was completely and utterly heartbreaking.

A soft voice came from behind her. "He tried his best. We all did."

When Kelera turned, shock and realization hit her like a tidal wave. It was accompanied with a pain like a thousand pins being pushed into her heart as she stood face to face with the woman she'd longed to know. The woman whose locket she had carried with her as long as she could remember, no matter how painful. Queen Mabine was only inches away from her, standing in a floor length white gown.

Her mother had come for her after all this time.

Chapter Nine

Mabine glowed with ethereal beauty. It clashed with the dark forest, and Kelera was afraid to even blink. Was this another vision? Or had her mother's spirit come to answer her heated call? The new power that passed to her at her mother's death pulsed stronger. It expanded as if to reach out to its previous master.

Kelera held her breath, praying her mother would be the first to speak again. She had no idea what she should say or how she should act. When she'd been very young, she had dreamed of the woman who might show up with arms opened wide. In her daydreams, she imagined jumping into the safety of that warm embrace and how the world would feel complete as she did.

When the rest of the little girls at the mortal court had walked hand in hand with their mother's, Kelera had always stood on the sidelines. Watching and praying that one day she would have that too. When her mother didn't come back for her, hope was replaced with bitterness. Any woman who would give up their child and never look back was heartless and cruel.

But now, after all she'd learned about hers and her mother's past, she couldn't find it in her heart to hate her. Even the anger that had overcome her moments ago no longer presented itself. She'd judged her mother harshly many times over the years, but when it came down to it, Bothwell was right. Fear ruled Mabine. Something Kelera must have inherited from her.

The silence was unbearable, so Kelera summoned the courage to speak. "I didn't expect you to answer me when I called."

Mabine's eyes flitted to the ground, and she clasped her hands tightly in front of her. The gesture was so similar to what Kelera often did when she was trying to contain her emotions, that it stunned her.

She jumped slightly as Mabine finally spoke. "I am sorry it took me so long. But it was necessary."

Kelera balked. "Necessary? To see the destruction I'm sure to cause? Trust me when I tell you that I am well aware of the danger I pose to our people."

Mabine smiled softly and repeated, "Our people. I never thought I would have the opportunity to hear you say those words."

Kelera shrugged awkwardly. Honestly, she'd never expected to say them. Before coming to Elfhame, she never imagined seeing the Fae as anything other than a threat. But it had all changed. It was why this was so important. Without the blessing, none of it would matter. Not the fact that she now called Elfhame home, nor the love she had for Adrastus and the Fae. It would all be worthless in the face of the destruction Samael and her own erratic magic posed.

Mabine studied her for a moment before saying, "I see so much of him in you."

She could only be referring to one man. Her father. It gave Kelera a start. "Funny, he used to say the same about you." Any time she'd been caught playing in the garden with the tiny Fae creatures, he'd reminisced about how alike she was to her mother. Though he hadn't told her much, she'd detected glimpses here and there in the small moments like that.

Mabine reached for the side of Kelera's face where the ugly scar Samael had given her resided, but she took a step back before Mabine could touch her. Sorrow flickered in her mother's eyes, but Kelera raised her chin. She didn't want her pity, not when she had lived through Samael's terror. If anything, the scar was a sign of her victory. Even if they lost this war—if Samael killed her—she would die knowing that she'd gone out fighting.

Mabine drew back and clutched her hands together tightly. She sounded wistful as she admitted, "I regret that things did not turn out differently for all of us. And I am sorry that you have had to face these trials." She bit her lip and tears swelled in her crystal blue eyes. "I only ever tried to do the right thing. I couldn't have known what fate had in store..."

Kelera took a tentative step toward her. "I am not here to dwell on regrets. I am here to fix it all. Please, tell me what I need to do to get an audience with the Elders. Time is not on our side."

As much as this reunion should have meant to her, it was overshadowed by the worry settled deep in her belly. Her mother was no longer a part of the living world, but Adrastus and Kelera's friends *were*. They were all relying on her.

Mabine reached out more boldly this time and took Kelera's hand. It sent goosebumps along her arms, but she wasn't sure if it was the fact that a spirit was touching her or if it was because this was the first and only physical contact that she would remember having with the woman who gave her life.

She resisted the urge to pull away, and Mabine smiled before saying, "There is still time, but it all depends upon you. Releasing guilt cannot be done with the snap of a finger. It will take time. Like a caterpillar who breaks free of its cocoon to be reborn as a butterfly. You simply have to open your mind to the possibility. Admit that every horrible thing that has transpired is not solely because of your choices. The threads of fate are many. No one decision, no single person can take credit. Just as your power is a collective of all those who have come before you and those that will come after... So is the pain of the past and the future."

Kelera's cheeks were wet with tears. She wasn't sure when they had started to fall, but she couldn't stop them. Mabine wiped them away with slender fingers. She rested her hand on Kelera's scarred cheek.

Her mother was right. Ammon had made his choice to follow them into Samael's room of shadows. He had decided to take Samael's side, knowing the danger. Chaz had always been a man driven to help those in need. It was why he had jumped in front of the sand wielder's stinger to save Kelera's life. The servant women had wanted so badly to be free from King Cyrus that they had risked everything.

Still, even though she was able to admit all of that to herself, their deaths still weighed heavily on her heart. Mabine shivered, drawing Kelera's concern. The hollowed hills were neither cold nor hot, in her opinion.

"What's wrong?" She studied Mabine's face. Could a soul catch a cold in the afterlife? The prospect didn't seem likely. But there was clearly something wrong.

Mabine was the epitome of composure as she said, "I'm afraid that the boy king's curse is seeping deeper into the land."

"The frost?" Kelera's words were as sharp as Samael's icicles.

"I fear it will continue to spread until both land and ancestral magic are depleted."

Kelera sounded small, like a child, as she pleaded, "Please, tell me how to get to the Elders. Explain to me how to do what needs to be done?" She'd never asked anything of her mother before—though she'd never really had the chance. But Mabine owed her this. After leaving Kelera, no matter the justifications in doing so, she owed her help.

Mabine's face beamed with pride. "Oh, my love, you have already begun." Her eyes drifted over Kelera's shoulder.

When she turned to see what Mabine was looking at, her magic prickled under her skin. The dark forest was gone. They were standing in a chamber of sorts. It was made of the same sleek stone of the Seelie Palace, with an open ceiling covered in lush grass and fully bloomed flowers dangling from above.

Jarred by the strangeness of it, she stumbled back a few steps. But when she looked down, the confusion grew. The floor allowed a full view of a beautiful night sky. Stars shined brightly, lighting the room clearly. It was as if the world had been turned upside down. It was so enchanting that Kelera could only imagine beings as powerful as the Elders residing there.

A shaky breath escaped her as she turned back to Mabine. Her voice cracked as she said, "Thank you."

Mabine pulled her into a hug. There was such strength and emotion in the gesture, as if she'd been waiting years for the chance to hold her daughter in her arms once more. Kelera breathed in the scent of her—like a field of flowers in the springtime.

After a moment, she released her. It was too soon. Kelera longed to reach for her again, but Mabine had already stepped back. She placed a hand over her heart as she said, "Goodbye, my love. Remember that you are worthy of the world and so much more. We are all born to play a role, each and every one of us. From the smallest pixie to the most powerful royal. I have done my part, and now it is your turn. I regret that I will not be there to guide you," she continued with tears gliding down her cheeks, "but you have so many around you to rely on."

Kelera opened her mouth to speak, but no words seemed sufficient enough to express the mixture of grief and gratitude in her heart. She held back her own tears, hoping she appeared stronger than she felt.

Mabine added, "Please tell your father that I never stopped thinking about him. And that I regret that we did not get the chance to meet again in his lifetime..." She began to fade away and Kelera's heart hammered in her chest. She was losing her all over again. Before Mabine drifted into the shimmering air, she said, "Perhaps we will meet in the next."

And then she was gone. Kelera took a deep, steadying breath. She would grieve later. There was no time to allow those feelings in, not when there was still a job to be done. When she turned back to the large chamber, she was startled to find six sleek black thrones.

In each one, sharp, angular faces stared down at her. They were striking in the way that the Fae were, but there was something frighteningly powerful about them. Their eyes were bright pools of starlight and if they stood, they would have been at least ten feet tall. They all wore the same deep purple-blue robes. The colors swirled slowly, as if the fabric itself was alive with magic.

This was it. The moment she had been waiting for. She straightened, mustering the dignity she imagined one needed when meeting powerful, mystical beings. Showing she was respectful but not intimidated seemed like the right course of action to take.

She raised her chin to meet their gazes and spoke first. "Your eminences." She winced as it occurred to her that she wasn't sure what titles she should use. Continuing, she declared, "I am here to ask for your blessing."

An Elder sitting on the end laughed. It sounded so human-like that it startled her. The Elder was a woman. When she leaned forward, the hood of her cloak fell from her head, revealing full, ringleted hair. It was bright red like a flame and between that and the fierce glint in her eye, she reminded Kelera of Cierine.

She was the first to speak. "We know why you're here, Kelera, daughter of realms. You need not explain it to us."

The man beside her had a more serious tone as he added, "We see all. Hear all. Know all."

Kelera didn't shrink under his scrutinizing gaze. "Then you know how imperative it is that you bless my power and allow me to return home with the full force of my magic."

The woman regarded the other Elders. "Yes, we all know how desperately you want to return just so that you may rid yourself of the benevolent gifts we have bestowed upon you."

Kelera's mouth gaped open. Did they think her ungrateful for her hesitation to ascend the throne? Judging by the disdainful looks the rest of the Elders were giving her, that was exactly what they thought. She chose her words carefully, worried about offending them further. "I simply want to do what's best for Elfhame and the mortal realm. I am not sure I'm equipped to rule. Wouldn't the Seelie Court fare much better under the rule of someone who knows the people and their ways?"

Another man spoke up. The robe didn't seem to fit his massive frame quite right. He looked like he belonged with the Wild Hunt rather than on an ancient throne. His voice was kind as he mused, "You are still frightened."

Kelera nodded. "Yes. I have seen the visions. I know how terribly things can go if I rule Elfhame." If they saw all as they claimed, then surely they had witnessed the throne room in her nightmares turned to ash, and the field ravaged into a sea of embers. If her nightmares were any indication of what was to come at her hand, then the best thing she could do for Elfhame was to walk away.

The woman chuckled. It grated on Kelera's nerves. There was nothing amusing about this situation. Though perhaps for beings who were so far removed from man-kind, it was quite entertaining.

The woman's eyes glinted as she explained, "You misunderstand. What we sent you was a warning of your fate should you choose *not* to embrace your power and your destiny."

Kelera furrowed her brow and looked at each of the Elders. They all nodded in agreement. A chill ran through her and she crossed her arms over her chest protectively. She *had* embraced her magic. Had grown to love Elfhame and was ready to stay to build a life amongst the Fae. Most of all, she had faced her fears and come all this way to find the means to save the people she loved.

Through a clenched jaw, she replied, "I am trying. I have given up everything for this. I left my home in the mortal court. Twice. I am here to stand with the Seelie. To fight for Elfhame. What more do you want from me?"

The warrior-like Elder rose, towering at least twelve feet high. He looked down at her and she imagined she appeared as nothing more than an ant to him. The room rumbled with the tenor of his voice as he said, "A debt cannot go unpaid."

A debt? Her stomach dropped as she recalled the Lady of the Lake. Kelera had made a deal to save Adrastus' life. She still owed that debt to the Elders. She took an uneasy step back. Whatever they asked, she would be forced to give them. This is what Adrastus had feared would happen if she came to the Elders. Even with the debt in the back of her mind, its danger hadn't fully hit her until now. She had walked into their realm to ask for their help when she already owed them payment for the aid they had given to her before. Of course, they wanted her to pay up before granting her anything more.

One of the other Elders drifted to her feet, too. The man sat down to let her take the floor. Her voice was high and light, like wind chimes. "Forgive my brother's brashness. You see, the world has always required balance."

As she spoke, a shimmering dust rose from the sky-floor like snowflakes. They drifted above and she waited for them to fall on her, but they stopped well above her head. They spun in a circle, forming a colorful picture of purple and blue like the night sky. It showed six Fae coming together out of the darkness. As they conjoined hands, life began to form between them. Trees sprouted, rivers flowed, and animals opened their eyes for the first time. It was beautiful, giving Kelera a sense of hope as she watched the beginning of creation.

The woman continued, "Seelie and Unseelie. Light and dark. Without one, the other simply cannot exist." The magic forming between the Elders in the vision split into two halves. One danced with shadows and ice and the other pulsed with light and fire. Kelera listened carefully as the woman went on, "But we did not account for love and free will. We didn't consider what would happen when the lines blurred." The split magic swirled together at the edges, forming a man and a woman embracing one another.

"Not all Unseelie are bad. And not all Seelie are good, as you yourself have witnessed."

Kelera thought of Gadreel and Adrastus. And of their friends from the Winter village. She also thought of the man who had been devouring children in the Seelie Court. She nodded in understanding, too entranced by the vision to speak.

The woman continued to weave her tale above Kelera and said, "Babies born of two courts..."

Kelera pictured Adrastus and the gleam in his eye when he smiled at her.

She sensed the woman's eyes bearing down on her as she added, "and babies born of two realms. And so, my brothers and sisters and I realized that was precisely what the world needed. No longer a great divide, but one ruler to bring the realms everlasting peace."

The magic above her blinked out, leaving only the starlight to illuminate the room. Kelera understood, she truly did. They needed someone who would unite Elfhame. But how could she do that? She was not Unseelie. There was no guarantee that she would be able to persuade the Autumn and Winter Courts to follow her.

She cleared her throat and said, "That is why you prophesized the lost heir. But how can you be certain that it is me? I am a halfling. It will already be a challenge to get the Seelie Court to accept me. How am I to get all of Elfhame to follow? If we could put the right ruler on the throne of Seelie and if we can overthrow Samael, placing someone better suited in his place then—"

The first woman interrupted, "You want to defeat Samael? To keep your nightmares of destruction from coming true? Then you must accept the truth of your fate. Lost heir or not, you belong in Elfhame. Whether you are ready to admit that, it does not matter. You have come a long way since first crossing the blackthorn veil. You have let go of many of the things that were holding you back. But until you can accept who you are meant to be, then you will never be able to take the power you need in order to win this war."

Kelera grabbed hold of her locket. "And the debt I owe you?"

"You are the debt."

Icy fear shook her. It wasn't the first time someone had spoken those words to her. Before, it had come from Adrastus' mouth. This was worse. The Elders were all powerful, ancient beings. They were capable of crushing her like a bug under their boot if they chose it.

She shrugged her tense shoulders. "What does that mean?"

The woman leaned forward and spoke as if she was talking to a child. "You belong to Elfhame. You can never return to the mortal realm." She sat back and mused at the others. "I do believe it is the most generous deal we've ever made." They all chuckled.

Kelera, on the other hand, still didn't see the amusement. But she couldn't talk, couldn't think straight. Elfhame had become her home. But in four little words, the Elders had made it her prison.

The woman elaborated, "You belong to Elfhame now. You and any that come after you. That is the debt."

Kelera desperately wanted something to hold on to. The starry sky under her feet spun. Or was it her head? She could never leave Elfhame. What about her father? Cierine? She clutched the locket around her neck tighter and ran her fingers over the thorny engravings. "What of my family and friends in the mortal realm?" Her heart skipped a beat. "What if Samael triumphs here?" If Samael succeeded in taking Elfhame, the mortal realm would have been the only place for her and Adrastus to flee to. She felt like the world was crumbling around her.

The massive man spoke this time. "Our word is final. We will not force you to wear a crown that you do not want. But for your debt to be repaid, you can never leave the realm of the Fae."

"And if I *don't* take the crown? If I stay in Elfhame and do not lead it, what then?"

He shrugged. "You can stay, accept the crown, and use your full power to fulfill your destiny."

The wind chime woman finished, "Or you can deny the crown and watch Elfhame succumb to the frost."

Kelera clutched the locket so tight it dug into her palm. The choice they were offering her was a facade. Life or death. Or worse than death if Samael had his way. And nowhere for her to run.

One of the Elders, she wasn't sure which one now because she couldn't bring herself to look them in the faces, said, "You must truly search within yourself. What is it that your heart sincerely desires?"

"Adrastus," his name escaped her before she could stop herself. She looked down to avoid their eyes. "I want to be with Adrastus. I will choose him above all else."

"We know," the wind-chime woman said softly. "But whether or not you get the life with him that you dream of, will be up to you. Should you choose the path of your destiny—"

"And if I deny it? If I leave here without your blessing... or if I give the crown to another. What will happen to us? Is there another way to stop Samael?"

The Elders shot nervous glances at one another. It was unnerving to see such powerful beings look so unsettled. She pleaded with them, "Please, I just want the truth."

The first woman spoke. "The truth? If you do not wield the power that has been gifted to you, then the prophecy will not be fulfilled. The world will succumb to frost and be *destroyed* by fire."

It was like a punch to the gut. The nightmares. All of them would come true. She would destroy everything and everyone she loved if she wielded her power without their blessing. The only way she and Adrastus would survive this war was if she took the crown and lived up to her destiny.

She could hardly catch her breath. Suddenly, the room seemed very small, and the starlight was more dizzying than before. She swayed slightly on her feet. Though she had considered honoring her duty as the daughter of Queen Mabine, it now felt like shackles on her wrists. The power inside her was meant for her and only her. And the Elders would not bless it as so unless she agreed to take the throne.

But none of it mattered as much as protecting Adrastus and their people. If the only way to keep him safe at her side was to rule, then he would understand that, wouldn't he? He promised to stand by her no matter what. In that regard, would it be so terrible to agree with the Elder's terms?

Adrastus had been working in the dark for years to help his people. He had risked his life to take care of them when his father would not. With her on the throne and him ruling beside her, then perhaps they could help to turn the Unseelie Court around. Rid it of the fighting pits and the fear the citizens held toward the royal family.

With Adrastus' help, she could learn how to lead. He'd taught her how to control her magic. And they had support. Gadreel, Oliver, Bothwell... They knew the ins and outs of Elfhame politics. If they stood with her, then there was no telling how much good they could accomplish. And more than that, they would have the best chance of repairing the broken trust with the mortal realm.

As she considered all of this in silence, she realized the truth *was* indeed there all along. She could have everything she ever wanted and so much more. She clenched her fists and stood tall as she looked back up at the Elders. They were on the edge of their seats, waiting for her response.

The magic in her veins pulsed, giving her the rush of adrenaline she needed to say the words. "I accept your terms. I will embrace my destiny. I will wear the crown."

The first woman smiled proudly at her. "Then you have our blessing."

Power surged from the Elders. It swirled around her like a storm of starlight engulfing her completely. It flowed from the tips of her toes and up her body until it reached the top of her head. Her hair whipped around her face until the magic settled on her like a crown. The moment it did, the immense power inside of her calmed.

It no longer burned and rose like a wildfire that she couldn't contain. Tension she hadn't even realized she'd been holding dissipated. She felt incredibly light. All this time, her body had been battling to hold the magic in, even when she wasn't trying. Like a reflex. One that was no longer needed. The power Mabine had passed to her was solidified. It was a part of her.

Her own power was grounded, like it had been when Adrastus soothed her with their bond. Quickly, she felt for it.

She hadn't considered that she might lose it if she received the Elder's blessing. Hadn't considered how it would make her feel to not be connected to him in that way anymore.

The warrior-like Elder smirked. "Do not fret. It is still there. What is bound may not be broken except in death."

Cold ice filled her veins, and she grasped onto it with her power, channeling it to her chest like a hug. Adrastus' magic was still a part of her. She shuddered, remembering the shadows in his eyes. "Can I ask one more thing?"

Amusement flickered in the Elder's eyes. "You are worried about the young Prince's magic."

Surprised, Kelera stammered, "Y-yes."

The warrior-like Elder pursed his lips before speaking. "It is not a simple matter. Nor is it one we typically meddle in."

Kelera's shoulders slumped. It wasn't what she hoped to hear. If they had the power to help, then why wouldn't they just do it? "I cannot... will not, do this without him. If there is something I can do to help him, then I need to hear it."

"Prince Adrastus must overcome the darkness from within. We have no doubt that you, Queen Kelera, have the ability to shine a light on that darkness. Rely on old friends and they will guide you."

She puzzled over his vague words, only to realize what he had called her. Queen Kelera. The weight of something still rested on her head and she reached up to find cool, smooth metal. Grasping onto it with trembling fingers, she withdrew it. The crown was made of a glittering steel she had never seen before. It was the most mesmerizing thing she'd ever seen, twisted around in the shape of thin branches or vines. She clutched it tightly as she looked up at the Elders.

The first woman bowed her head as she said, "Go with strength and courage, and hold on tight to it. For you will need it more than ever, Queen Kelera."

Magic buzzed around her, and the room began to fade away. The last thing Kelera saw before she was thrust into the darkness was the Elders standing and bowing to her.

Chapter Ten

The darkness didn't last long. It faded just as quickly as it had come, revealing ash trees and an ice-covered ground. Kelera tightened her grip around the crown in her hand and shivered as she peered around in confusion. Samael's magic had done a number on the land. The once lush, green grass was completely coated. Not one blade had survived the cold. Everything looked drab and gray, and she felt as if she might be sick at the sight of it. How long had she been gone? Was she too late?

Someone grabbed her from behind, and she swung out a fist to ward off the attacker. It connected with a sturdy frame and she yelped to see Adrastus rubbing his shoulder. His eyes were darker than usual and his skin had paled significantly.

He did his best to give her a smirk as he said, "I didn't mean to sneak up on you. I'm just so relieved—"

She cut him off as she threw herself into him, wrapping her arms around his neck, careful not to draw attention to the crown she was holding. He nuzzled into her and kissed her softly on the jaw. The moment was too sweet to let go of, so she dug her fingers into his heavy jacket, clutching onto him tightly.

Though delight was filling her senses, something was missing. Anytime she had stepped foot back on Spring soil, her magic had flared. With her mind, she reached for the ancestral power of the land and found nothing. She drew away from Adrastus as a wave of nausea threatened to rear its ugly head. Her boots slipped on the icy ground as she took a few steps.

He gave her a knowing look as he explained, "Samael's magic is spreading faster than we anticipated."

She pressed her fingers to her temples. "How long was I gone?"

"A few hours." He watched her carefully as she paced in the frosty forest.

The adrenaline wearing off from her audience with the Elders left her feeling like a cornered animal. She stopped pacing. That was both good and bad. She hadn't lost significant time while she was down there, but that only meant Samael's curse was working much faster than they were prepared for.

Stubbornly, she raised her chin. "Well, I'm back now."

"And you come bearing gifts," he mused with a sly smile.

A heated blush crept across the bridge of her nose, and she moved to hide the crown behind her, but it was too late. He snatched it from her. His smile faded as his fingers roved over the smooth, sparkling metal. The twitch in his jaw gave way to her rising panic. She hadn't had the chance to talk to him about it. It wasn't that she wanted to be the one making decisions for their life together. But if she wouldn't have chosen in that moment, then they would have lost their opportunity.

"Dras, I had no choice." She winced and paused before amending, "That's not true, actually. I did have a choice."

"The debt?"

With a sigh, she responded, "Wasn't to take the crown. It was that I now belong to Elfhame."

His jaw twitched and shadows skidded across the whites of his eyes. They vanished as quickly as they had come, and she wondered if she'd imagined them. Calmly, he asked, "What do they mean by that?"

"That I can never leave. I can never return to Nevene."

Adrastus cursed under his breath.

Quickly, she added, "I already planned to stay in Elfhame with you, Dras. As far as debts go, this one's not so bad."

"Unless Samael succeeds."

Kelera bit her lip. She hadn't wanted to voice that part out loud. With a huff, she said, "I've already been over this with the Elders. What's done is done..." she trailed off as Adrastus closed the gap between them.

He clutched her arms tightly. "There's more. I can tell."

She gulped. "I and... any who come after, can never leave."

His face flickered with realization as he whispered, "Children. Any heirs you may produce will belong to Elfhame."

Kelera's heart skipped a beat. So much had been said during her time with the Elders that she hadn't allowed herself to linger on that part. She pulled away from him. "That's the least of our worries right now, Dras." Children were the last thing on her mind.

Seeming to take the hint, Adrastus moved on. "And what was it that they asked for in return for their blessing?"

"They simply requested that I search within myself and decide what I truly wanted."

"And this," he held up the crown, "is what you genuinely wanted."

"I want a world that is safe for the two of us. And for our friends and family." She inched closer and rested a hand on his arm. "I was afraid before that if I took the crown,

I would end up like Mabine, sacrificing everything for the good of the throne. But it doesn't have to be like that. We can make our own rules. There won't be a reason for me to leave Elfhame. We will defeat Samael and when it's all over, we will rebuild... together." Her breath hitched as she waited for him to respond.

His indifferent expression masked any emotion, spurring her to say, "I know we talked about a quiet life away from it all. It's a lot. I know that. And if," her voice cracked, "if you can't find it in your heart to rule, then I understand. If you don't think that the courts should be united, then I understand that, too. I never intended to force you into a life you don't want."

He silenced her with a kiss. It was fierce and said more than words ever could. Then he cupped her face in his hands as he declared, "I would give it all up. I would lay my kingdom at your feet if only to get the chance to witness your glory. Because the truth is, I cannot fathom a life that is not by your side."

Her heart soared with joy and relief. Tears welled in her eyes, and she kissed him again. Just as she had vowed to stand by his side against his brother, he was vowing to sit beside her on the throne. It was more than she ever could have asked for.

They walked hand in hand into the village. It had changed drastically since that morning when she had followed the council to the ash trees. Windows were boarded up to protect them from the cold and anything stalking about in the night. Small fires burned in piles of damp wood on the streets, in a sad attempt to keep chilled villagers warm.

Now that she was back in Elfhame and forced to face the Fae who resided there, she felt unsure of herself. What if she failed them? Even if they did defeat Samael, what would happen when they realized she planned to combine Elfhame under one rule? She knew of some who would support her, like their friends from the Winter village and the Guardians. But she wasn't convinced that everyone would be so open to the idea. Even after years of hearing about the prophecy, she was sure there would be at least a select few who resisted.

For now, the crown was tucked away in Adrastus' satchel as not to attract attention to them. They needed to return to the palace without any distractions. According to him, the palace was readying to march to the border to face Samael head on. Kelera wasn't sure it was the best idea, since they couldn't know for sure where Samael would be placing his forces. They had done a fine job of staying hidden in the shadows. Not even Gadreel's palace ravens were able to pin point their location.

Their efforts to get back to the palace without interference were shot down by a very angry Herald walking their way. Bothwell and council woman Anaya were in toe with looks of wild anticipation on their faces. Kelera gripped Adrastus' arm. She didn't want to announce her coronation here for all to witness. Not when she was such a frazzled mess. They could at least let her take a bath first...

Bothwell wrapped her in a hug, forcing her away from Adrastus. His eyes were warm with affection as he boasted, "I knew you could do it, Princess! I just knew it."

Herald snuffed, "Did you get the blessing?"

Bothwell shot him a scalding look as he released Kelera from his embrace. "Allow the girl the welcome she is deserved before you start interrogating her."

Herald got into Bothwell's face and snarled. "You may want to see a crown on her head, but we are out of time. Look around, you fool. Our army must march *now* and without the right person wielding Mabine's power, we are all lost."

Worried, Kelera glanced at Adrastus, only to find him watching the men argue with a raised eyebrow. Disapproving of his amusement, she pressed her lips into a hard line before opening her mouth to interrupt the fight. Neither man seemed to notice her as they continued to bicker.

Bothwell puffed out his chest. "You can try to weasel that power into your hands, but it will not work. The people will never follow you."

"If the girl doesn't want the crown, then it will not be for you to decide. It is up to the blood rites."

Adrastus barked with laughter, startling even Kelera. He pulled the crown from the bag and spun it around his finger. "There's no need for that, gentlemen."

Kelera felt a blush creep across her cheeks. To her relief, the villagers seemed to be too consumed with their own worries to notice the little tat their leaders were having. Adrastus offered the crown to her, and she took it with chilled hands.

Herald was distraught. His face had turned bright red all the way to the tips of his pointed ears. His eyes were glued to the crown as he asked, "Where did you get that?"

The hunger in his expression made Kelera hold it closer to her. "The Elders."

Anaya finally spoke. "They crowned you themselves?" Her eyes were two wide pools, reminding Kelera of the lake nearby that was surrounded by hawthorns.

When the Elder's magic had coronated her, she hadn't thought there was anything odd about it. But then again, she still lacked the knowledge of the Seelie's ways. The way everyone was reacting now—as if they were witnessing the impossible—told her that this was not a common occurrence.

"They told me if I wanted their blessing, then I would need to choose." She left out the details of the debt she had owed, and how she'd had no choice but to face the truth and accept that this was, in fact, what she wanted. Looking directly at Herald, she announced, "So. I chose. I accepted the crown and the conditions that come with it. My mother's power is, and will remain, mine."

As she spoke the words, her magic rumbled inside her. It wasn't like before. There was no threat of it overpowering her and unleashing itself on the world. It was like a friend patting you on the back to let you know they were there when you needed them. It gave her the confidence to continue. "Bothwell, if you could gather the council and court, I would like to address them."

He bowed deeply to her. "As you wish, Your Majesty."

Adrastus beamed down at her with pride.

Herald, however, shook with anger as he said firmly, "No."

Bothwell turned to him. "No? You dare speak to your Queen that way?"

Tired of people speaking for her, she handed the crown to Adrastus and stepped between the men, facing Herald with her head held high. Her voice was low and threatening as she said, "I did everything you asked of me. I went to the Elders. I received the blessing."

Herald seethed. "You are not worthy of it."

"It appears they thought I was worthy enough to crown me themselves." Magic itched in her hands, and she had to dig her nails into her palm to contain her temper. "Yet that still doesn't seem to be enough for you, Herald. I have given my heart and soul to Elfhame quite literally." A small crowd had gathered, and onlookers craned their necks to get a better look at their former King and the Princess who was brave enough to challenge him.

Herald bent down until he was nose to nose with her. His breath was hot on her face as he stated, "Then prove it. Prove you have the strength and ability to wield that power." He straightened, raising his voice in arrogant showmanship. "I challenge you, Princess Kelera, to the blood rites."

Bothwell interjected, "This is absurd! A rightful blood heir does not have to partake in the blood rites to claim what is already theirs."

Adrastus rumbled behind her, his shadows seeping around Kelera's legs toward Herald. They snapped, cracking into the icy ground, and Herald took an unsteady step back. For a moment, Kelera considered letting Adrastus teach Herald a much needed lesson. But the Fae gathered around them reeked of fear. It was heavy in the air like fog. If she allowed Adrastus to hurt Herald, then it would only feed their preconceived notions about the dangerous Unseelie Prince.

Using the bond, she pulled Adrastus' shadows back, drawing them into her until he relented. She shook her head at Herald. "This isn't the time. We need to stand together now more than ever." A few murmurs of agreement spread through the crowd.

Herald wasn't so inclined to see reason as he shouted, "I intend to claim what is mine!" His magic swelled around him, creating a gust of wind. It circled around his vicinity, forcing the crowd back. Lightning crackled at his fingertips and reflected in his eyes.

"You could, of course, deny my request, *Princess*." His smile was menacing.

She could reject the blood rites. Tradition gave her every right to do so. But what would that say to the people of the Spring Court that were gathered around them? That she was ill-equipped to rule them? That she couldn't handle the power her mother had passed to her? This one decision could influence their loyalty. Who would stand and fight for a Queen who hadn't proved herself? Maybe if she had been raised by Mabine... if the people had seen her brought up in her inherited position of power... but that wasn't the case here.

Adrastus whispered behind her. "The decision is yours, little thief."

Kelera nodded, calling forth the bright white light of the crown's power. She was careful not to summon the magic she'd been born with or the bound power that belonged to Adrastus. If she was going to fight Herald, she would do it with the very magic he lusted for. She would whip him into submission using her mother's power.

Herald struck first, sending a bolt of lightning in her direction. It narrowly missed her as she leapt and rolled to the side. The magic shot into the ground where she'd been standing only seconds ago. The icy ground crackled as sand erupted from beneath it, crystalizing into a hard, glassy substance.

Kelera wished she had read more about the blood rites during her time in the Winter Palace library. How many times had they been called into effect? How many lives had been claimed all for the power of a crown? Herald was as bad as Samael. Willing to turn on his own to get what he wanted.

She summoned the crown's power, emanating light from every pore on her body. It seeped through her arms and even from the top of her head. The Fae around her gasped in awe. She took in every one of their faces. Herald was fighting for himself, but she was fighting for *them*. That gave her more to lose.

With a roar, she lashed her power at him, knocking him to his knees. His jacket caught the brunt of the flame. He rolled wildly in the snow to put the fire out, leaving his arms smoldering and filling the air with thick smoke.

Before he could rise, Kelera bore down on him with her magic. She imagined the blinding light of the sun and cast it into his eyes. Herald yelped and flailed around the ground. Kelera took the opening, kicking him in the face as hard as she could. His nose crunched under the blow, and he hit the ground once more.

With his eyes still shut tight to keep out the light of her magic, he reached his hands out for her. She tried to break free from the grasp he had on her leg, but he had more brute strength than she did. He dragged her to the ground and climbed on top of her. A fist slammed into her jaw and her ears rang. Afraid of losing consciousness, she bucked and kicked, trying to get him off of her.

As he reared back to strike her again, she burrowed her magic into him. It went so deep she could feel the blood in his veins, like water flowing through a stream. He had her by the collar now and slammed her head into the ground. Her vision blurred as the frozen ground jarred her. Red, hot anger fueled her magic. She channeled it until it, too, burned.

Herald hissed in pain as she boiled his blood. She could feel it bubble and pop as she unleashed her rage through the hold that she had on him. Herald threw himself away from her as if trying to escape the pain, but it was too late. She would cook him alive if she continued on as she was. Her head spun from his assault as she stood.

Towering over his cowering body, she asked, "Have you had enough, Lord Herald?" Her chest was constricted between the fight and the use of the magic. She'd never used Mabine's power to this extent, and it was taking a toll on her. Exhaustion threatened to throw her into the abyss, but the onlookers in the crowd forced her to hold her composure. She'd come too far to fail now.

Herald cried out in agony as his blood threatened to boil him from the inside out. Realizing he may not be able to speak through the pain, Kelera let up slightly, drawing the magic down to a simmer.

Again, she encouraged him, "Concede."

His voice cracked as he said, "The... crown... is... mine..."

Kelera grabbed him by the collar of his jacket. Men like him and Samael never knew when to quit. She grabbed hold of his nose, now crooked from where her boot broke it. He wailed in agony as she twisted it. "Concede."

He whimpered as she released his nose and took a step back, leaving him in a crumpled heap. To the crowd she said, "Lord Herald, husband of the late Seelie Queen—*my mother*—has lost."

His voice was barely audible as he argued from the ground. "You haven't killed me. The blood rites state that—"

Kelera spoke over him. "I will not kill this man. That is something Samael would do. We are better than that. Lord Herald is free to go." She snarled at him, "But make no mistake, should you ever raise a hand to me and my claim to the throne again, then I will not be so inclined to show mercy." She called her magic back, taking with it the heat in his blood.

No one made a move to help Herald up. He fell once before finding his footing again, but Kelera had no sympathy for him. She had shown the people that she could control the Seelie crown's power and in the same breath, she had shown them her compassion.

Adrastus joined her, placing the crown on her head. They watched as Herald stumbled away, back in the direction of the palace. As the crowd cheered for her, chanting her name and new title as Queen, Adrastus leaned in and whispered, "Well done, Your Majesty."

Kelera rubbed her jaw where Herald had hit her. "Tell Bothwell to put a watch on him. I just humiliated him and you know how men like him respond to that."

Adrastus nodded and joined Bothwell. Kelera continued to watch Herald carefully as he crossed the village. Fae leapt out of his path and he pushed by in a fury she had only ever seen outmatched by Samael. They would need to keep an eye on him. A man as ambitious as Herald did not give in so easily. And even though Bothwell believed the majority of the Seelie would kneel to her, she knew first-hand that there were some Fae amongst the court who would only do so for Herald.

A chill whipped through the air, and the cheering from the crowd died down. Fae bowed to her before taking their leave to find warmth and shelter. Soon, the village was cleared of nearly all onlookers, leaving Kelera with the wind biting into her bruised face.

Now able to speak freely with her council, she asked, "Do you think he'll try something foolish?"

Anaya answered, "I have known Herald since he was a boy. I have no doubt he will—" a pinched gasp escaped her lips.

Startled, Kelera turned to her. Blood seeped from Anaya's stomach where an arrow had landed. Panic surged through Kelera, sending with it a jolt of adrenaline. It was another attack. Once again, they'd let their guard down and had been blindsided. Worse, the attacker was nowhere in sight.

Chapter Eleven

K elera watched as Anaya's face went gray, reminding her of Chaz, the Guardian who had taken the sand witch's barb in his gut to save her. Her head spun as Adrastus threw himself on top of her, shielding her from whatever archer was hiding. Bothwell did the same for Anaya, hovering over her with his hands pressed firmly against the wound.

Kelera's first suspicion was directed toward Herald. But he was in no condition to try for another round, and she had watched him fade out of view in the direction of the palace. There was no way he'd have had time to rally his allies. If it wasn't him, then it could only be... her stomach dropped as she considered the only other man who wanted her dead more than Herald.

Though it was only mid-afternoon, the sky had darkened with thick, stormy clouds. Unusual for even the Spring Court's storms, which usually appeared with fluffy light gray ones. This wasn't the natural order of things. This had to be Samael's doing.

The few villagers that still lingered outside were shouting and taking cover in their homes. Kelera knew it would do nothing to protect them against whatever minions Samael was commanding. Adrastus' shadows, however, did what they do best. They snaked around her, Bothwell, and Anaya, folding over them like a rounded shield.

His voice was rough as he commanded, "Stay here. I will locate the archer."

Kelera grabbed him by the collar of his jacket. "Like hell. You're not going out there alone."

"You are the Queen now, little thief. You must be protected at all costs." He ducked beneath the shadows before she could stop him.

When she reached out to push past them, her hand met a force like a stone wall. She pounded her fist on it repeatedly, summoning all of her strength to try to break through. Inside their shield, a blue light started to glow from where Bothwell's hands rested firmly on Anaya. His brow dripped with sweat from the strain of using his healing magic.

Kelera couldn't break the shield and risk exposing them to whatever danger waited on the other side. But she also couldn't let Adrastus go out there on his own. Calling on her power, she imagined a doorway opening. Something clicked and a space large enough for her to crawl through, opened to reveal the village.

With a start, she scurried through. When she turned, the door in the shadows had shut. Bothwell and Anaya were safe... for the moment. She scanned the village for any sign of Adrastus, but it was difficult to see through the falling snow. Smoke billowed above the buildings. Her heart skipped a beat when she realized what was burning. *The food stores.* She cursed under her breath.

That son of a bitch was taking out the provisions that would get her people through the frost. He would starve an entire realm to achieve his goals. She wasn't sure why anything he did anymore shocked her. She had to stop it before all the stored crops were lost. Thick snowflakes clung to her hair as she started down the road that cut through the cramped houses.

She reached for her magic, hoping it would bring her a sense of comfort, but it felt... dimmer, somehow. Like a flame that had been burning for too long. It gave her an uneasy feeling as she broke into a run.

At the very least, she had expected a few of the villagers to be outside attempting to save their food supply. But it was deserted. Using the snow to her advantage, she pulled at the element she needed. Water pooled above the ground like it was being held by an invisible bucket. Without hesitation, Kelera dumped it onto the burning building before it could spread to the next. Her stomach was in knots at the callousness Samael continued to show without remorse. Not only was he trying to starve her people, but he was willing to do so at the risk of innocent lives. If she had gotten there even a moment too late, the fire might have extended throughout the entire village, wiping out any who hid within.

By the time she finished, she was covered in ash and her hair was sticky with smoke. Now that the fire was out, she'd expected to see someone... anyone, coming out of the homes, but they didn't dare. A hush had fallen over the village. It was the sort of quiet that you experienced moments before the unthinkable happened. Like the fates themselves were holding their breath in anticipation.

The hair on Kelera's arms stood on end and she clutched her hands to hide the shaking fear. The ground rumbled as skeletal horses made their landing. Snarling Night Riders circled around her, trapping her at their mercy. Blinding light emanated from her fingertips as she slowly allowed her magic to present itself. She was holding back... she hadn't used the full force of her royal gifts on purpose yet and didn't want to repeat what had happened at her mother's feast. This time, the other Fae may not be so lucky.

One of the Riders, who appeared more ancient than the others, with tattered robes and a skeletal horse that no longer held any flesh on its bones, spoke first. "We are pleased to find you here, halfling." His armor creaked like a broken door as he looked around the village. "Where is your master?"

She raised her chin. "I have no master."

A Night Rider in untarnished armor and robes laughed. It still sounded human, which meant he must have been recently turned. What had this man done to be chosen for Samael's curse? The rest of the Riders stayed silent. Their eyes were shielded by their hoods, but she could feel their heavy gazes on her.

The ancient Night Rider seemed unphased by her response as he said, "We expected the bastard to be by your side. No matter. We will find him when we're finished here."

Screaming came from one of the homes and Kelera's heart leapt into her throat as she watched a Rider dragging a woman out of her house. He had a firm grip on her hair, and she left marks in the snow where her bare feet dragged along the ground.

The Rider pushed her to her knees just beyond the circle of his comrades. Just within Kelera's eyesight. It dawned on her that they believed they needed the leverage of an innocent life to get her to do what they wanted. That meant they were afraid of her. With good reason, too. Not only had she defeated one of their own before she'd ever learned to use her magic, but she had shown her hand at the Queen's feast.

Kelera kept her voice even as she asked, "What is it that you want?"

"For you all to cower at the High King's feet."

"You should know me better than that by now."

To his friends he chuckled, "Think of the favor I will gain when I bring the halfling whore to the King, screaming." Then more seriously to Kelera, he said, "Give up, or this woman will suffer in your stead."

The woman's face was rosy red from the cold and tears were streaming down her cheeks. She was no warrior. Though all Fae held magic, most had never used it to fight. She wouldn't stand a chance against the Rider threatening her life. It would be up to Kelera to ensure her survival. But she certainly wasn't about to hand herself over to Samael.

A small smile crept across Kelera's face. "You tell your High King that if he wants me, he can come get me himself."

Flames sparked at her fingers as she summoned her magic. She recalled the heat of the fire that had engulfed the Autumn Court manor and the scars that now graced Samael's face. She'd owed him that one after the scar he'd left her with. One of ice and one of fire. A mark for a mark.

The Night Riders were silent, and she hoped that it was shock that would be found beneath their hoods. Her magic was steady as it inched from her fingers onto the snow fallen ground. It melted in her power's wake, leaving little streams of water that muddied the earth underneath. The horses took a few uncomfortable steps back as the flames threatened to lick their legs.

While the Riders were distracted by the fire creeping toward them, Kelera focused on the man who held the woman captive. Before any of the cursed Riders could notice, she blew out a small breath of air, shooting the fire up the man's body. The woman saw her opening as he released his hold on her hair and she scrambled out of the way.

The Night Riders shrieked in shock as they watched their friend become consumed by Kelera's power. But more piercing were the agonizing cries coming from the Rider at her mercy. His chain mail sizzled under the heat of her flames. The rotting steel melted from his body, leaving him utterly exposed to her wrath.

The Night Riders tried to advance on her, but the circle of fire she'd formed around her kept them at bay. She never took her eyes from the Rider that she had targeted. His robes were nothing but dust and the armor had melted down to his skin. Though the sight of his twisted and decayed, cursed body sickened her, she did not look away. If she was going to take a life, then she would face it head on.

These men had come into *her* kingdom. They had attacked *her* people. And for that, they would pay. The man's body was nothing but rotting skin and bone, but as the fire burned through him, she caught a glimpse of the man he once was. Blemish free, pale skin and striking silver hair that flowed down to his waist. He had been beautiful once. Until his will and life had been stripped away from him.

Her magic faltered as she wondered if she could still save him. But as the flames began to die down, he turned to her with soulless black eyes filled with hatred. He bared what was left of his teeth at her and charged her way.

She raised her fist and clenched it in the air. The Night Riders wailed as the ground opened up beneath their comrade's feet, swallowing him whole. Without a second thought, she pivoted to face the remaining Riders with her fist still in the air. She opened her hand with her palm facing the land, but before she could close it into a fist again, the Night Riders ascended to the sky. Their horses screamed in agony from the sudden movement of their broken bodies, but even so, they rose.

They retreated before she could attack them further. The moment they were gone, her magic settled into her bones. There was no strain in containing it once again. She was in complete control. It filled her with a mixture of relief and satisfaction. Surprisingly, for once, everything had gone exactly as she'd planned.

The woman who had been threatened was standing in her doorway, watching her carefully. Even though the crown was not on Kelera's head, the woman curtseyed. It was so deep that she nearly sank to her knees. This was the first time any of the villagers had shown this much reverence to her since being crowned by the Elders. Kelera's chest swelled with excitement and pride. The reaction surprised her. She wasn't sure what she'd expected to feel after making her decision, but this woman was alive and well because of her. And she was grateful to Kelera for it. There was no lingering fear or distrust to be found.

Kelera bowed her head to the woman before turning away with a smile. She rounded the road that led back to Bothwell and Anaya and stopped short when she came face to face with Adrastus. His jacket was gone and his shirt torn. Blood coated his chest and Kelera scanned him carefully for any hint of injury.

His voice broke slightly as he reassured her, "It's not mine."

Thanking the fates, she leapt into his arms. He smelled like the tang of blood and sweat, just as he had the night that he'd defeated his brother in the pits. She nuzzled her face into his neck and kissed it. If it had been up to her, they would have remained like that, but he pulled back. Shadows danced in his eyes, and she fought the instinct to step back from the danger.

She gasped. "Dras, your eyes."

He blinked harshly and clenched his hands into fists. His magic whirled wildly through their bond, trying to cling to hers. But each time, its hold slipped away. The Elder's warning that he would have to overcome the darkness echoed in her mind, leaving a bitter taste in her mouth.

She placed a hand on his chest over his heart. "Adrastus, listen to me. You need to calm down. Breathe."

He followed her command, taking a deep, steadying breath. With each one he took, his magic eased into a steady ebb and flow. It settled enough for her power to wrap itself around it like a soft braid.

Once he was steady enough to speak, he said, "I told you to stay in the shadows."

She was quick to retort, "And I told you that I would stand by your side always." She paused, pushing her hair behind her ear. "I just had a little trouble finding you..."

He chuckled, lightening up a bit. "I found the archer. A mountain man from the Winter Court."

Pain flickered in his eyes and Kelera felt sorry for him. It couldn't be easy to be fighting the very people he'd spent his life trying to protect. Killing the Night Rider had been a simple choice for her. They were cursed, their souls long destroyed to make them into unwavering servants of the Unseelie crown. But the mountain men from the Winter Court and other Fae being forced to fight for Samael were not all bad. Many had no other choice. Facing them in battle would be much harder for her.

She bit her lip and rubbed his arm in a fruitless effort to comfort him. "Dras, the Elders warned me about your power. We need to find help before it overwhelms you. They said to... seek out old friends. Do you know who they could mean?"

His mouth twisted in confusion. "I don't..." The regret in his eyes was enough to break her heart. But he added, "I'll figure it out."

"Not on your own, you won't."

Giving her a reassuring smile, he promised, "I will ask Gadreel to help."

They stood in uncomfortable silence until Bothwell called out for them. When they reached him, some Fae from the palace were already placing Anaya on a stretcher. Her face had a blue pallor to it from the loss of blood, but her chest still rose and fell steadily, with a sure sign of life.

Kelera approached Bothwell. "Will she survive?"

He nodded solemnly. "I believe so. But if I had not been here to begin the healing process, then there is no way she would have." His eyes widened at the blood on Adrastus' chest. "Are you two alright?"

Adrastus grumbled. "Yes. But this changes thing. The people are more afraid than ever. Now that Samael has attacked so close to the palace, villagers will be flooding the gates in search of refuge."

Bothwell shrugged. "And refuge we will give them. It will be a tight fit, but we knew this could happen."

Kelera scoffed. "How can we keep them safe if the frost is damaging our defenses? The Wildwood is doing nothing to slow the Night Riders down. First the palace and now the village."

Bothwell cringed. "We are working on it. Now that you have the power you need, we can fortify the defenses." Kelera remained quiet, and he continued, "Was there any damage further into the village?"

Kelera shifted on her feet, thinking of the hole in the ground. Wary from the blood rites and now the fight with the Night Riders, she said, "Some." She gestured for them to follow as she walked down the road to where the Night Riders had attacked. There was some superficial damage to the buildings on the street, but nothing that couldn't be repaired. The biggest loss was the food storage, but even then, it had only wiped out one. Things could have been much worse.

What she was more worried about was the danger the open ground would pose to any passerby. She held her breath in anticipation, but found that it wasn't necessary. The hole was no longer there. Instead, there was lush, springtime grass where it had been. While the ground around it was still covered in snow and ice, the land that had swallowed the Night Rider was unmarked.

She gulped. "I-I don't understand. The earth was broken here. I tore it open with my magic."

Bothwell and Adrastus exchanged confused looks. There was no explanation for what had happened. Perhaps it was the Elder magic—the magic of Elfhame—that had repaired what was broken. But the awed faces staring at her from the windows in the village gave her a sense that it was something much more than that.

Chapter Twelve

K elera squirmed uncomfortably as her skin chilled against her mother's throne—her throne now—as the council argued below. Most had taken the news of her crowning with grace. Showing their support with sweeping bows and wide smiles. A few had settled on the sidelines, exchanging angry glances with Herald.

But she couldn't be bothered with their disdain for her in that moment. Bothwell had assured her that the Queen's guard was keeping a close eye on them after Herald's humiliating loss at the blood rites. Feeling that it was safe where Herald was concerned for the time being, Kelera could focus on the more pressing matter at hand. It was time to retaliate on Samael.

The self-proclaimed High King of Elfhame had resorted to an assassination attempt. But on who, exactly? Did he know that she was Queen now? It was only a matter of time before he did. But he had wanted her brought to him. That could be a bad sign. Who knew what sort of things he would have in store for her if she was his prisoner again? She itched at the scar on her cheek at the thought of it.

On the other hand, she couldn't imagine that he would send an incompetent archer to do the job. The sickening sound of the arrow breaking through Anaya's stomach sent shivers down her back. That arrow had met its mark with ease. Had Samael simply wanted to get the Queen's Council out of the way? Taking out the territory's leaders would be a surefire way to weaken the Seelie Court. Either way, the malevolent *High King* had made his move. Now it was Kelera's turn.

She made a point to pretend the audience, including Herald's supporters, didn't exist as she addressed the council members whose support she knew she could count on... and Adrastus.

He hadn't followed her to the throne. It had stung a little, since she'd hoped to have him within her reach. It would be comforting to feel his hand in hers right now. But she understood why he had lingered below. The council needed to adjust to the idea of her as their ruler first. There would be time later for him to take his place beside her.

He caught her eye and gave her a wink. Heat crept across her face. Was it proper for a Queen to flirt and blush in front of her entire council? Probably not. But she didn't try to hide it. She wouldn't end up like her mother, hiding and sacrificing. Perhaps if she was honest with them from the start about what she wanted, then they would understand her choices better. For a moment, she considered calling out to Adrastus to have him join her on the dais, but Herald's irritating voice rose above the rest.

"Enough of this talk. What is it that you intend to do, Your Majesty?" The words rolled from his tongue like an insult, and her nose flared in response.

"Well, Herald," she refrained from using any titles and smiled at the sneer on his face, then she continued, "When

I was traveling to the blackthorns, I came across Samael's guards." She rubbed her arm subconsciously where the ghost of a wound resided. The injury she'd gotten from the horrible creature that had attacked her after she'd left Adrastus. "They were searching for weaknesses in the border between the Spring and Autumn Courts. I believe if they are to march, that is where the bulk of their force will enter."

The council remained silent, hanging on her every word. It was vastly different from what she was used to. The men in the mortal court had ignored her, only listening when another spoke up for her first. Here, she, above all others, commanded attention.

With confidence, she proceeded, "If Bothwell can set up the maps, we can decide where to send our army. I would like to hear from the generals who are well acquainted with the area." She met Bothwell's eyes. "I need you to gather the officers so that they may present their thoughts."

The next topic would be a sensitive one. She braced herself as she said, "As you know, I have deep ties to the mortal realm. It is important to me that we succeed not just for Elfhame, but for them as well." The council members glanced at one another uneasily. She didn't let them deter her as she continued, "We can assume with some surety that King Tristan will ally himself to Samael because of the Winter Mountain raiders who attacked Nevene while carrying the Seelie emblem." She nearly winced at the memory of the Fae she and Gadreel had encountered on their way to save Adrastus.

Herald snarled, and she noted the way his nose hadn't fully healed yet. Up close, she could see the slight curve in it where the healers had attempted to reset it but failed. It appeared the wounds she'd inflicted on him had done nothing to bruise his arrogance as he asserted, "The mortals are nobody to us."

Anger rumbled in her chest and she spoke before he could continue. "My family and my friends mean everything to me." She raised her chin and addressed the rest of the room. "My father is the commander of the King's Knights. That should give us the support we need in order to sway them to our side. Should the mortals march on Elfhame, I will request a meeting with King Tristan and his officers. In the meantime, any mortals spotted in our territory are to be brought here *alive*." She would not have mortal blood spilled because of Samael's deceit toward them.

Herald rolled his eyes, and Kelera's power flared at her fingertips. Didn't he realize how lucky he was to be amongst them? If not for her mercy, he would be lying six feet under the cold, frozen ground. With a deep breath, she went on, "Additionally, Samael has scraped up every last able body he can in the Unseelie Court to fight for him. We must do the same, though with more grace and tact. I would like to start by calling upon the Guardians of the Wildwood."

Herald's laugh grated on her nerves. Worse was when he said, "The Guardians are not warriors. They flit about the woods fighting thieves and ghosts. They do not belong on the front lines with our trained soldiers."

His friends murmured in agreement. Bothwell was looking at Kelera with raised brows. Clearly, he had no intention of helping her through this one. It was time for her to show them she could rule on her own.

So she stood. The room fell silent as she proclaimed, "Lord Herald, you are here because I had the grace to allow it."

He pressed his mouth into a hard line and even his friends had the good sense to look down at their shoes rather than antagonize Kelera further. Word had spread quickly about the blood rites as the villagers poured through the palace gates, bringing their firsthand accounts of what happened between her and Herald. It wasn't long before the servants and courtiers were gossiping about how their new Queen had shown both strength in magic and in her restraint.

Assured there would be no more interruptions, she proceeded, "The Guardians of the Wildwood are true warriors. I have fought alongside them and I trust them with my life... and with *my realm*." One of Herald's supporters caught her eye as he sneered at her with arms crossed. She had no problem maintaining the confidence in her voice as she went on, "We will call them to arms. If they accept, then we will ask that they spread the word."

An older councilman asked, "Spread the word?"

Kelera nodded. "To any who will come to our aid. If we can convince the dryads and the forest giants... the creatures of the Wildwood, to stand with us, then we will have the numbers and strength we need to defeat Samael."

Herald's eyes were wild with outrage. He sputtered, "You cannot possibly think that we would allow the Lesser Fae to stand amongst the High Fae in battle! They are not trained. They are not powerful enough to—"

"They are the heart of this land. It is their choice, but if they say yes, then we will welcome them without prejudice. I do not know you and the extent of your abilities, Herald. But I have seen theirs with my own eyes. Any who are willing to fight with us and do what is right for the good of Elfhame will be honored. If you have a problem with that, then you are welcome to stand down."

Adrastus smirked smugly at Herald, who had, in turn, shut his mouth promptly. The council members on her side agreed loudly. Their approval echoed through the chamber, silencing any objections Herald's men might still have. The tension in Kelera's shoulders slowly dissipated. It was a relief to know that she hadn't gone too far. She had no desire to dishonor their ways here in Seelie, but she also wanted change.

If she was to rule, then she would not compromise her beliefs. She would not cave to political pressure as her mother had. Or allow the power to go to her head like Herald had. She and Adrastus would carve their own way in this world.

She called out to Adrastus, "I would like for you to convene with Ragnor, Jinx, and Tepin. Meanwhile, I would like to speak to Oliver and Gadreel in private."

Adrastus gave her a dazzling smile and bowed deeply to her. Giving him a task in front of the council was a show of hand. It told them all that she trusted him and that his role in the palace was more than that of a royal guest. It also settled the anxiety plaguing her. She trusted him above all others and knew he would not let anyone stand in his way as he carried out her orders.

She pushed her hair behind her shoulders and took to the stairs as gracefully as she could. If only her father could see her now. What would he think of his daughter raising an army and commanding it? She hoped she would have the chance to find out.

The glittering crown on her head felt awkward. She was afraid if she even breathed wrong, then it would topple off, making a great show of just how unprepared she was for all of this. And she had to refrain from reaching up for it when she moved.

The council immediately rose to attention, bowing as she passed by them. She hoped the heat on her cheeks wasn't visible to them. Picking up her pace, she crossed the room and looped her arms through both Gadreel and Oliver's. Gadreel snickered at her as they exited the throne room.

"That was quite entertaining, I must say." He nudged her in the side.

"I'm glad someone enjoyed themselves in there," Kelera grumbled. Her mood was becoming sour. Until Adrastus and the Guardians secured the additional force they needed, she wouldn't be able to relax. And there was still the matter of deciding on their strategy. Hopefully, the army's leaders would be as receptive as the majority of the council was.

Gadreel pouted. "I do plan to hold it against you for the rest of our lives for not inviting me to the blood rites. I'd have paid a handsome sum to see you hand that boar's ass to him."

Oliver smiled warmly at her and stopped as they came to her private chambers. "What do you need from us, Your Majesty?"

She released her hold on their arms and opened her door, gesturing for them to come inside. "Please, none of that. Just Kelera."

Gadreel wiggled a suggestive eyebrow at her as he eagerly said, "I hope you've brought us here to plan your coronation celebration." He waved a careless hand in the air. "I know the Elders already took care of the crowning, but it wouldn't be right to deprive us all from a party."

He plopped down on the sofa and kicked his boots off before setting his feet on the table. His lightheartedness was infectious, and she was starting to feel better just from him being there. Her gown rustled as she shifted it and sat on the floor across from him. Oliver chose a cushy chair nearby.

Kelera smirked at Gadreel. "There will be plenty of time for that later."

He pouted and leaned back on the pillows. He loved a good party and was renowned for his ability to make people forget their troubles. But Kelera didn't have it in her to celebrate until Samael was no longer a threat.

Oliver tilted his head. "What is it you truly need from us, Kelera? Whatever it is, ask freely."

"I need you to keep an eye on Herald. I don't trust him. Blood rites or not, he has favor in the palace and I'm afraid that those who support him will work behind my back to undermine my authority." The words felt strange coming from her mouth. She'd seen palace politics play out before—had even been at the center of it—but she'd never been at the *head* of it.

Gadreel drawled, "He's a snake in the grass. I've heard talk of him in Unseelie. From the rumors, you'd think he came from my father's court. He's been waiting years for the chance to take part in the blood rites. It's not surprising that he's in such a foul mood about losing to you."

Oliver agreed, "He's dangerous. The generals know him well and that gives him an advantage you do not have. I will keep an eye on the council members who wanted him on the throne. But you need to be careful when you go into that meeting."

She leaned against the wall and rubbed her temples. Maybe she shouldn't have sent Adrastus off so soon. Gadreel jumped from the couch to pour them all a drink, and she accepted it gladly. One glass wouldn't hurt.

She raised the crystal cup to her lips, but paused to add, "Gadreel, I trust you're looking into Adrastus' magic?"

"I'm doing what I can." His face fell into a frown and Kelera regretted being the one to wipe the smile from his face. Oliver reached for him, taking Gadreel's hand in his own and grazed his thumb along his knuckles.

Kelera smiled softly at the comforting gesture. "I know. I just wish the Elders would have been more helpful. We've all seen what happens when his magic overwhelms him."

Gadreel downed his drink and walked away from Oliver. His posture was rigid as he poured another, filling it to the brim. "That we do."

The room became unnervingly quiet, and Kelera reached for her glass again, but someone whistling from the hallway gave her pause. Curious, she sat up straight and asked, "Do you hear that?"

It was surprising because the halls had been fairly quiet. The courtiers resided elsewhere in the palace, offering her privacy and space away from the hustle and bustle of it all. But Oliver's face was wraith white and his hand inched toward his sword. Kelera eyed Gadreel to gage his reaction, but he seemed as puzzled as she was.

The whistling continued, echoing through the room so that it appeared to be coming from all directions. But that wasn't possible, was it? There was no one inside her chambers but the three of them.

Kelera laughed nervously. "Is this some sort of trick, Oliver?"

He held up a silencing hand as he stood. Kelera had half a mind to rise from the floor too, but as she debated the urgency, the door to her chambers burst from its hinges. Wood splinters clattered to the ground and before she could react, Oliver was already in front of her, sword drawn.

The creature positioned under the broken door frame sent the hair on Kelera's arms standing on end. Its elongated limbs dangled awkwardly as it stepped over the threshold. Long clawed fingers crackled and popped as they extended.

Gadreel dispatched his ice magic in the creature's direction. The sleek, sharp crystals aimed themselves at the monster's heart, but it swatted them away like an irritating fly. Kelera sidled up to Oliver's side. She wouldn't have others defend her when she was capable of doing it herself.

Oliver whispered to Gadreel, "Your ice magic will not work on it. It is of the Spring and your magic is no match for it in the heart of Seelie."

The creature stalked toward them slowly, as if unsure of what it was there to do. She raised her hands, allowing her Seelie magic to dance on her knuckles. But she did not act. Not yet. If this creature was Seelie, then it was one of her subjects. She would give it the chance to do the right thing before striking it down.

She summoned the dignity she imagined her mother had spoken with as Queen as she said, "Stand down. We have no desire to harm you."

Its strangely human eyes danced with laughter, but a guttural sound rose from its throat. Kelera's heart sped. Where were the guards? Had this thing harmed them? She stepped in front of Oliver and Gadreel, moving slowly.

"Did Samael send you? You must know that he does not have good intentions for you or your kind."

The creature's lanky body bobbed around erratically, and she worried about the reach it had with its oddly long limbs. Still, she didn't stop. Not until she was close enough that she believed her magic would be able to incapacitate it without harming Gadreel and Oliver.

Its voice sounded like a shovel being scraped on stone as it said, "The malevolent King is not my master. My master says you will be the end of all things. That you are the destroyer of our world." It flashed two sharp, dripping fangs, and Kelera took an alarmed step back.

"Your master has lied to you. For the last time, turn around and return to where you came from."

The creature shook his head, and Kelera's magic spurred to life as he lunged at her. A bright bolt of light, like lightning, shot from her and into the creature's stomach, catapulting him out the door and into the hallway. His body hit the wall with a thud.

Kelera took a cautious step toward him, but Oliver stopped her and said, "Allow me to go."

He bounded into the hall, holding his fingers to the creature's neck. Kelera and Gadreel joined him. Oliver looked up at them and shook his head. Kelera breathed a sigh of relief, knowing she wouldn't have to finish off an injured creature.

She urged Oliver, "Tell the guards to come collect him. Give him a Spring Fae's burial."

Oliver balked at her. "It tried to assassinate you. It doesn't deserve such an honor."

She knelt beside them and sought to make him understand, "It is my first day as Queen and I do not intend to dishonor Seelie customs. Not when we still need the Lesser Fae, like him, to stand with us. I do not blame him for his misguided belief that I am a danger to the Seelie Court. I intend to hold the one who sent him responsible for what just happened."

Gadreel hugged himself. All the optimism he'd had earlier had vanished. He sounded uncertain as he said, "Could it have been Samael?"

Oliver gave a solid shake of his head. "No. It could not lie when it said Samael was not its master. More than that, this is a Lesser Fae of Seelie. It would never allow Samael and his men to get close enough to find it. This had to be someone on the inside."

Kelera had no doubt as she said, "Herald."

Oliver's face was grim as he nodded. "I think so. He would have been the only one of authority to get this creature to do his bidding. And the guards... they're nowhere to be seen."

She stood abruptly, dusting off her gown. "Then there is only one thing to be done." She knew this command would win her no favor within the court. But there were more pressing matters to attend to. She would not spend her precious time looking over her shoulder for back stabbers. She placed her hands on her hips and shrugged as she said, "Arrest Herald."

Chapter Thirteen

Kelera bit her tongue as Bothwell paced the gardens. The sun had barely had time to rise before he'd sent for her with a guard escort big enough to pass for a small army. He'd been lecturing her for nearly half an hour now and she was having trouble focusing. She'd hardly slept the night before after the run in with the assassin. Two assassins in one day. That had to be a Seelie Court record.

Adrastus was sitting on a stone bench in the corner of the garden. He and the Guardians had been successful the night before, and the pride in their eyes when they came to her rooms to tell her had made her heart swell. They'd spread the word, and Lesser Fae were trickling through the palace gates by the cartload. They were all coming to stand with the High Fae, even at the risk of their wellbeing. She hoped the army was treating them well and made a note to go down to the tents to check on them.

Bothwell tapped his foot on the ground and chided, "Are you listening to a thing I'm saying?"

Kelera rolled her eyes at Adrastus and he chuckled. Then she turned to face Bothwell's wrath. "Yes, of course."

"You cannot arrest the King Regent."

"Former," she corrected.

"What?"

"*Former* King Regent. As in, not anymore."

Adrastus laughed in the corner, earning himself one of Bothwell's seething stares.

Kelera continued, "Oliver was a witness to the attack. He agreed that it had to have been someone of Herald's standing who sent that thing to kill me. And you saw him after I bested him in battle. He never had any intention of bending the knee to me after that. As an immediate threat, I have every right to arrest him until we could be sure."

"Some of the council members are in an outrage. This is no way to begin your rule."

Heat crept up the back of her neck. "Don't you think I know that?" she snapped. "The *only* reason I ever even came here in the first place was to stop Samael. And now, I find myself Queen of a land that up until a few weeks ago, was foreign to me. I am doing the best I can to live long enough to end this war."

Adrastus stood, and his shadows stirred around her magic like an oncoming hurricane. A sign that his own irritation with Bothwell was rising too. Kelera tried to settle down so he wouldn't feel the need to step in and say or do something that they'd all regret.

More calmly, she said, "If you're that concerned about it, then I will allow him to be sequestered to his rooms. I want him confined to his chambers with guards of *your* choosing outside. I don't want anyone there that could be in his pocket. And he is not to see any of his accolades. Until we can be sure it was not Herald, I do not want him roaming freely."

Bothwell nodded. "That is fair and just. I will see to it personally that Herald is questioned when the guards bring him in."

"For fair questioning," Kelera added. She wasn't sure if the Seelie Court believed in applying physical pressures to their prisoners and had no intention of allowing someone—even someone as horrid as Herald—to be tortured under these circumstances.

"Understood." Bothwell bowed. "Your Majesty." Then he fled the gardens, leaving Kelera and Adrastus to sit in peace.

Kelera huffed. "Finally."

Adrastus shrugged. "The man sure loves to hear himself talk."

"At least he's on our side." She tugged her hair back from her neck. It was exceptionally warm inside the palace with all the fireplaces lit, and the heat was drifting into the gardens that stood in the center of it. It was the only parcel of land that was safe from the frost at this point. Samael's magic was beginning to creep up to the palace gates. It was like a sandglass, tracking the time they had left before things escalated further.

Adrastus' eyes darkened as he said, "The Guardians fear their magic is declining with each piece of land that succumbs to the frost." His eyes were searching as he asked, "Are you feeling it, too?"

Kelera bit her lip, thinking of the delicate way her magic had felt before the Night Riders attacked her in the village. "I suppose I might have. My mother's power is so new to me. I guess I wasn't sure what I was feeling exactly. But it makes sense that if the land's magic is weakening from the frost, then the Seelie people's magic is weakening with it." She studied him. "What about you?"

"I still feel the steady rhythm of our bond. But..." His pause made Kelera reach for him. His muscles were tense under her touch as he continued, "it feels fragile. Like it could be snuffed out at any moment. And I worry that if it does, then there will be nothing left to contain the darkness."

Kelera caressed his cheek. She knew the darkness he was referring to. He relied on his Seelie magic, and hers, to ground the darker power he had inherited from his father. Without it, the shadows could overtake him. She'd seen it in his eyes when he was caught up in a fight or coming down from the adrenaline of a confrontation.

"We won't let that happen," she reassured him, though she knew he would not breathe easily until this was all over.

Adrastus pressed his forehead to hers. His voice rumbled like a distant thunderstorm, sending warm tremors down her spine as he purred, "I miss this. I've missed *you*."

She kissed his lips softly, then admitted, "So have I. But this will all be over soon and when it is, we will dance and go riding into the Winter village. And maybe we can even take a holiday to the Summer Court again!"

His face brightened. "It's a plan."

Kelera rested her head on his shoulder, soaking in the quiet moment. It was wild to think that she'd viewed him as her enemy when they had first met. And now he was her greatest ally. She trusted him completely. They'd proven their devotion to one another and though the worst was still to come, she had no doubt that she would be strong and capable with him by her side. Samael was going to regret ever underestimating the two of them.

Adrastus' powerful hands gripped her around the waist and he drew her effortlessly onto his lap. Warmth spread between her legs, but she glanced around the garden, nervous someone might see.

His breath was hot on her neck as he whispered, "There's no one here but you and I."

Shivers ran along her arms as he lingered at the base of her neck, planting kiss after kiss. His hands roved over her thighs. The only thing stopping him from going further was the thinly layered gown she wore. Secretly, she cursed that dress, wishing there was no barrier to hold them back. How very scandalous of her to let him touch her like this in the palace gardens. Before coming to Elfhame, she never would have dreamed of doing something like this. But would anyone even care if they did happen upon them? Elfhame was far more relaxed when it came to matters of intimacy.

And if anyone did see the two of them, would it really matter to her? She loved him and he loved her and there was no shame in that. A small moan escaped her lips as he gripped her firmly overtop her gown, scrunching the airy fabric with his calloused hands.

Her breath quickened, but hitched in her throat as the pounding of drums filled the air. Adrastus' hands pulled away quickly, and he lifted her from his lap, helping her to stand. Before she could question what the beating drums meant, he took hold of her hand and hauled her with him into the entryway of the palace.

Gadreel and Oliver were already there, surrounded by council members and courtiers. Their faces were drawn, and many were trembling. They didn't have to explain what the drums meant after all. She could tell just by looking at them. Samael had made his move before she'd had a chance to make hers.

Bothwell came into the foyer with what appeared to be every available guard in the palace. Even in the big open space, it felt cramped and stifling. Everyone was talking at once. For a moment, Kelera was so swept up in the panic of it all that she forgot it was *she* who was now responsible for quelling their fears.

She raised an authoritative hand, and a hush fell over the crowd. Addressing Bothwell, she commanded, "Tell me what has happened. Leave no detail out."

He clasped his hands tightly together. "Word has come that Samael's men are attacking in the southwest corner of the Wildwood. We do not know their numbers or who is leading them. All we know is that a few solitary Fae were able to escape the storm. They came here to warn us."

Adrastus spoke low, so only she could hear. "We need to act now."

She whispered back to him, "But if we take the whole of our army, then that would leave the palace and northern villages unprotected."

"Then send me." His jaw was set, and she knew he'd already made up his mind. He would not stay at the palace when his brother was out there.

Kelera raised her voice to the others. "Adrastus and I will take two units of soldiers to stop them. That should leave the palace and the north with a sufficient defense should Samael attack from more than one front."

Adrastus seized hold of her arm and turned her to him. "I will go. You stay here."

She ignored him and looked directly at Bothwell. He would surely have his own opinions, but he was a loyal subject. He would not fight her on this. She stood straighter and said, "We will leave immediately."

Bothwell bowed. "Your Majesty." Then he turned to the guard to give the command. Their orders were to inform two of the officers to prepare their men to march.

Adrastus was still trying to argue, but Kelera stopped him. "We do this *together*. I want the Guardians to accompany us as well." Adrastus opened his mouth as if ready to disagree, but Kelera called out, "Oliver. Gadreel." They came running to her immediately. "I want you to stay behind. You and Bothwell will take charge in my stead. Together, I trust that you will make choices similar to mine."

Bothwell shuffled his feet as he approached them. "Your Majesty, there is one more matter to attend to before you go." She nodded, and he continued, "Herald has escaped. I was working with the guard to track him down when the Fae from the attack arrived." He was avoiding her eye, and it was hard to tell if it was from the shame of misplacing their prisoner or if he was afraid of how she would react to the news.

Herald was a threat, but the more immediate danger was Samael and his army. She tried to think of what an experienced monarch would say. "Tell the guards to keep looking. Should a threat arise here in the palace, then they are to abandon the search to defend the Fae that are here."

Bothwell straightened. "Understood."

As the people in the foyer dispersed, Adrastus was staring daggers into the floor. She inched closer to him before saying, "I'll be okay, Dras. We knew this moment would come."

He pushed his dark hair back and nodded. "Let's get to it then."

Soldiers stood at attention as Kelera and Adrastus walked down the rocky path. They saluted her with their armor shining in the early sunlight. The Queen's crest on their chests taunted her. This would be her first battle as Queen. Fighting against bounty hunters and Night Riders with Adrastus had been one thing. Before, she had prayed to the stars that the fates would keep him safe, and they had pulled through each time by the skin of their teeth. But now the fear would extend to these men and women as well. They were there to stand with her. To fight for her.

Now she understood all too well the sort of pressure her father often felt as the commander of the King's Knights. He'd always done it with such grace and dignity. His men were his family, and they trusted him. She tried to channel that sort of strength and courage as she passed by each soldier.

She met each one of their eyes, trying to memorize their faces. When this was over, she would dine with them in the barracks. She would learn their names. Adrastus strode confidently at her side and she noticed a few of them glance unsteadily in his direction. He would have to join her when she went to see them after this. They needed to learn to trust him, too.

Though she'd decided to forgo any armor—worried it would be stifling when she tried to use her magic—she was wearing sleek black pants and a leather vest over her blouse, donning the Queen's crest. She fiddled with the vest, pulling it down toward her hips.

When they reached the end of the line where the Generals waited for her, Adrastus stopped and drew her toward him. He reached into his satchel and pulled out her crown. With a lopsided grin, he said, "You forgot something."

Yes. It seemed she had. When she'd gone to change out of her gown, she had set the crown on her bed. In a rush, she'd left without it. But here it was, shining like a beacon in Adrastus' hand. Reluctantly, she took it from him and placed it on her head, tucking it into the thick braids that were holding her hair away from her face.

He smiled more deeply now. "There. Now, you are ready." He tilted her chin up with a gentle hand. "They must know who you are now. *You* were chosen by the Elders as the champion of Elfhame. Wear that crown proudly. Show Samael just how high you've soared."

All at once, her nerves settled. They had been preparing for this moment. Samael had started this when he'd taken her best friend from the comfort of their home. But things had changed. Kelera had changed. Elfhame was her home now. And she intended to claim it as her own.

Chapter Fourteen

The Wildwood near the southern border was nothing like Kelera remembered it. Snow crunched under the boots of her army. It was the only sound within miles. Had she really only been in these woods days ago, celebrating her birthday and Beltane? It was unsettling to think that this was the very forest where she and Adrastus had made love on soft grass, with a spring breeze drifting through the air.

They had moved quickly past the slumbering giant rocks and through the river that was now covered in a thick layer of ice. She tried to focus on Adrastus' steady presence beside her rather than the pit in her stomach. Should she have had her army stationed on the borders to begin with? If she had commanded them to march sooner, then they wouldn't have the disadvantage of walking through the dense fog in search of Samael's men.

Between the clouds and the heavy, blinding fog, she couldn't see more than an arm's length in front of her. Adrastus had taken to reaching out with his shadows, guiding their way and making sure they didn't walk right into the Unseelie camp. The biggest threat at this moment was an ambush. Her body was as rigid as the twisted tree branches and she couldn't shake the sense of being watched.

The Unseelie had strong magic and there was no telling what sort of effect the frost had on them and their abilities here in the Seelie Court. For all she knew, Samael's curse would amplify their strength even in a territory that wasn't their own. There would be no reason for them to stand face to face in order to attack. They could just as easily do it from the tree line.

Jinx stepped forward, peeking between Kelera and Adrastus. There had been a time when Jinx and the other Guardians of the Wildwood opened up to her, showing their vulnerable sides. Jinx had even confided in her about his desire to find true love. But none of that vulnerability showed now. Instead, he, Ragnor, and Tepin were as intimidating as they'd been the moment she first laid eyes on them in the Summer Court tavern. They were warriors, bound for glory amongst the Wild Hunt. And she was grateful to have them on her side.

His jaw twitched as he said, "I don't like the looks of it." He clucked through his teeth and shook his head solemnly. "Anyone could get the jump on—"

"Jinx," Kelera warned, "don't even say it." He'd gotten the name for a reason and even though she didn't care much for superstitions, she knew better than to tempt the fates.

Jinx pretended to lock his lips with his fingers and dashed around to the front of them.

Ragnor stepped in line beside him and peered into the fog. "Jinx and I will scout it out first." He chuckled as he added, "Three eyes are better than two, after all."

Jinx touched his eyepatch gingerly and feigned a hurt expression. Kelera had to stifle a laugh and opened her mouth to scold him for the joke. Before she had the chance, whistling filled the air and soldiers at the rear grunted. Their bodies were obscured by the fog, but the thuds as they hit the ground gave evidence that they'd been struck down. The generals began barking orders at their men and the sound of steel being unsheathed drown out the whistles.

Adrastus shoved Kelera to the ground and her eyes widened as an arrow dove into the spot she'd been standing, cracking the icy ground around it. Archers were in the trees. They needed to shield the men. Adrastus was already two steps ahead of her as he cast his shadows around the soldiers nearest to them. But there were so many men with them that it couldn't possibly reach them all.

She grabbed his hand. "Use my magic to extend the shield."

As he sucked in a deep breath, she felt the pull of her power answering his call, flowing through her hand and into his. There would be no way for her to know if it was working, since the fog obscured her vision, but it didn't matter. They were sitting ducks and needed to push back on their attackers.

Shouting and steel clashing sent a jarring wave of adrenaline through her. She steadied herself by leaning into Adrastus. Men were screaming in pain and crying out in anger all around them. And here she was, frozen in place. How could she have thought she'd be capable of leading these men into battle?

She braced herself as a man bundled in a heavy jacket with a scarf wrapped around his face barreled through the fog and headed for her. He plunged his sword at her, but shadows twisted around the steel before it could hit its mark. Kelera shot Adrastus a look of gratitude. He was grappling with a tall man with ease, evading each swing of his blade.

She returned her attention to the man who'd attacked her. The scarf had slipped from his face and was trampled under his feet. A heavy pressure settled in the pit of her stomach as she realized there was nothing Fae about him with his rounded ears and tired stance. He swung his sword and crouched into a position of attack. Kelera's magic blazed to life like small fires on her fingertips. The flames wavered in the chilly air and she wasn't sure how long it would hold.

The man's eyes went wide, and he whispered, "Demon."

This man was frightened of her magic. Even though she was using only a miniscule of her power. He wasn't Fae, after all. He was human. She scanned around her, squinting to get a better look at the men Samael had sent to ambush them. They were rugged, wearing styles similar to the Autumn Court, rather than the armor of King Tristan's soldiers and knights.

If these men were from the mortal army, then why were they not prepared? Why did they come wearing the clothes of Elfhame commoners? Her gaze bore into the man before her. She inched closer to him, and he held his sword out in front of him in warning. It pointed at her heart, but she didn't stop. She needed him to hear her over the chaos of battle.

Raising her voice, she asked, "Where are the Unseelie?"

Were they hiding somewhere in the tree line, waiting for their moment to attack? It would be foolish of Samael to send in mortals to face an army of magic wielding Fae. Even if their power was dampened by his frost.

The man stuttered, "I-I don't know. They were supposed to be here."

She tilted her head and tried to ignore the unsettling feeling in her chest as she said, "Samael has tricked you. He has led you all to slaughter." Though she couldn't figure out why. She scrambled to think of reasons, recalling the many times she had listened in on her father's meetings with his knights. It might be a diversion of some sort. Or a chance to test the mortal's strength against the Fae before sending the full force of them into battle...

The man shook his head with wild denial and wiped at his brow. "No. They-they're coming."

Kelera glanced back at the fight. Seelie Fae were cutting down anyone in their path as their magic targeted anyone who did not carry the Queen's crest... her crest. The mortals would never survive this. True, she would leave here with the loss of some of her men, but it wouldn't be a devastating defeat in number.

She took another step toward the trembling man and said, "Look around. You have already lost this. Get your men to lay down their arms and no more of you will be harmed."

His eyes filled with frightened tears. "That is not my call to make."

Kelera's irritation flared. "Then *I* will make the call." She tried to find Adrastus, but the fog was too thick. He was gone. Her stomach dropped. She shouted, hoping he could hear her—praying he was okay. "Dras, they're all mortal! Samael and his men are not here!"

There was no answer. Only a few confused Fae glanced in her direction, but the mortals were relentless in their attack. Magic struck them down one by one. She had to think of something, and fast. This would be a massacre.

She realized the mistake she'd made, turning her back to the man a moment too late. His sword tore into her shirt, nicking the skin. With a hiss, she called on the vines buried deep beneath the snow, slamming him into the ground. His head bounced on the icy earth and his eyes rolled in the back of his head. Fury made the vines tighten around him. She could command them to grab his neck. To squeeze the life from him.

"No," a thunderous roar came from the fog.

Holding the vines steady, she looked up from the man to find Duke Cunningham's familiar sharp, angular face staring at her in shock. He held a bloody sword in his hands and his hair was wet and matted to his face from sweat and snow. With a careful step, he held the sword away from him, reaching out to set it on the ground.

Kelera narrowed her eyes. "Where is Samael? Where are the Fae who stand with him?"

Cunningham's eyes flicked to the man on the ground. He ignored her questions and surprised her with his plea. "Please, release him, Lady Kelera."

She gritted her teeth. "It's Queen Kelera, now." Memories of him shoving her through the mob of villagers who called for her blood returned to her. He'd thought her nothing more than dirt when he'd arrested her and thrown her in the Nevene dungeons.

His eyes bulged as he took in the crown resting on her head. But still, he said, "I beg of you. Let my son go."

His son? Kelera peered down at the whimpering man. Now that she had him at her feet, she could see that he was younger than she first thought. Even more so as tears streamed down his face.

She leveled her gaze at Cunningham. "I will release your son if you will call off your men."

The worry in his eyes was replaced with burning rage as he countered, "You *owe* me. For allowing you to leave the palace without harassment."

He wasn't entirely wrong. Had he not kept his mouth shut, she and Gadreel would have had to shed blood to escape the palace. He had kept his word, stepping aside so they could flee. Just another debt she had racked up.

She swallowed the lump in her throat and took a step back. Holding her hands up in defeat, she allowed the vines to snake back into the ground. Cunningham's son scrambled to his feet and ran to his father's side.

Kelera snarled at Cunningham, "Tell your men to retreat before it's too late. They do not stand a chance against the magic. Whatever aid Samael made you believe would be here is not coming."

Cunningham looked toward the fog where the sounds of battle still echoed. A vein twitched in his temple as he nodded. Then, without a word of thanks for sparing his son, the two of them ran into the fog, disappearing from Kelera's view.

A heavy sigh escaped her, and she prayed he would heed her warning. Now she needed to find Adrastus. She reached deep within her, concentrating on the feel of his magic wrapped around her own. If she could focus, maybe it would lead her to him.

With her eyes closed tight in concentration, she took a step into the fog. Pain lanced through her head, doubling her over. She opened her eyes, but there was nothing, Only blinding white light. Something had hit her. She reached out for something to steady her, but it was too late. Her knees jarred as they slammed against the ice solid ground, and she drifted off to the sounds of war.

Chapter Fifteen

Crackling fire woke Kelera from the abyss. Her eyes struggled to focus on the snow-covered trees spinning above her. She let out a groan as the pounding in her head worsened. Where was she? It was impossible to tell at this point because of the spreading frost. Stars sparkled in the sky like the metal on her crown that was no longer resting on her head. It was night. How long had she been unconscious?

A man's voice that she didn't recognize called to her from across the fire, "Lady Kelera, welcome back to the waking world."

She clenched her fists, willing her magic to come, but there was nothing. Well, not nothing. Cold chains burned her skin as she moved. It gave her a sickly reminder of the chains that Samael had subdued Adrastus with. Frosted restraints that prevented him from protecting himself with his power.

Ignoring the chill from the enchanted metal that was biting into her wrists, she shimmied to a sitting position. Shadows were cast over the men's faces, but she could make out rounded ears. No pointed tips. That meant she'd been captured by the mortals. Men who she'd once considered her people. Unfortunately, they had come prepared. The magic dampening chains were Samael's idea, no doubt.

Sitting up straight to maintain her dignity, she faced the men and asked, "Who are you and what are you planning to do with me?"

One of the men spat in her direction. The rest of them ignored her. She pinched her lips together, trying to resist the urge to lash out at them. Once upon a time, she had been one of them. Living in their court, trying to fit in.

With all the civility she could muster, she tried again. "I am your prisoner. At the very least, you can tell me who you are."

A young man who couldn't be more than a year or two out of his teens answered, "We are from the third regiment of King Tristan's army."

The third regiment meant lesser trained soldiers. She knew as much as the daughter of the Knight Commander. They were the men sent in first and usually the least likely to ever return home from battle. Samael was smart, sending in men he no doubt deemed expendable. But why send any of his numbers to the slaughter? What sort of move was this?

She longed to reach for her head to stop the pounding. It was causing her vision to blur every so often. Blinking a few times, she asked, "Are you taking me to Samael?"

The men exchanged uncomfortable glances. There were only four of them. Enough for her to take on if she could access her magic... or get her hands on a sword. It had been a while since she had last used one, but surely it was like riding a horse. It was something trained into her muscle memory after years of practicing with her father's knights.

Her heart skipped a beat as she thought of Sir Aldric. "My father. Is my father in Elfhame?"

The men shifted awkwardly. It was the young one who spoke for them again. "King Tristan has demoted him. He is no longer the Commander. His knights are here in Elfhame, but he is not."

Kelera didn't know whether to sigh in relief or huff in anger. It was comforting to know that her father was out of harm's way, but if he wasn't leading his men, then who was? And would they stand with her as Dodger had promised?

Thinking of Nevene, she dared to ask, "And what of Lord Alexander? Has Tristan released him?" If he hadn't heeded her father's warning, then there was a good chance she would have to face her traitorous ex-fiancé again. Something she wouldn't relish.

Another uncomfortable silence and then the young man answered, "Dead."

Kelera's face hardened. "How?"

The adam's apple in the young man's throat bobbed. "No one knows. King Tristan released him after your escape. Next morning, he was found in his room with blackthorn berries shoved into his mouth."

Berries... Samael's favorite calling card. When he'd taken Cierine, he had left them on Kelera's pillow. Later, he'd taunted her with them on her breakfast plates. She held no sympathy for Alexander and his ill fate after his betrayal. She'd warned him that allying himself with Samael would only end in disaster. If only he'd listened.

She studied the men's faces. They were all fairly young, with rosy cheeks. Their shoulders were slumped, and they had a look of sorrow about them. It was likely that this was their first time to ever see battle, just as it was hers. And they'd no doubt lost friends back in the fog. If she could convince them what a mistake it was to align themselves with Samael, then she could make it out of this without shedding any blood.

Cautiously, she said, "You need to release me. My people will come looking for me and when they do, you do not want to be caught in the crossfire."

One of the men scoffed and kicked at the fire with a blood splattered boot. "We have our orders."

Kelera snarled, "From who? King Tristan or King Samael?"

These men had no idea what they were dealing with. If they were shaken from that one battle, then they were in for quite the surprise when the full force of Elfhame clashed against one another. King Tristan was a fool to bring his men here, and worse... to trust Samael as an ally.

The man with the bloodied boot spat back. "We don't take orders from the Fae. King Tristan is here to make the Seelie pay for what they did to us."

Kelera shook her head and laughed. "King Tristan has been played for a fool. Samael orchestrated those attacks. You are fighting for the very Fae who slaughtered our people."

The man moved faster than she expected. He fisted the front of her blouse in his hands and she heard the fabric tear. His eyes were filled with rage as he stated, "We are not *your* people, halfling."

He raised a hand as if to strike her and she flinched. The satisfactory smile that spread across his face made the hairs on the nape of her neck stand on end. Determined not to give him any more satisfaction, she leaned in close to him. "That's *Queen* halfling to you, soldier." Surprise flickered in his eyes. She had his attention now, so she continued, "The moment Samael has Elfhame in his clutches, he'll come for you and your families next. He'll tear the blackthorns from the roots, opening the veil for any creature to pass through freely. There will be nothing left to protect you. If you thought the recent attacks on the Nevene villages were bad, then you're in for a rude awakening."

He released her and stumbled back a few steps. All eyes were on her. They were white with fright and for good reason. She spoke nothing but the truth. Samael would ravage the mortal lands. He would turn them into his own personal playground. The scar on her face was evidence of how Samael liked to play.

To drive her point home, she added, "Look at what he did to you all back there. Where were the reinforcements he promised? You think he didn't know you would all be slaughtered if he didn't send the Unseelie Fae to help you?"

The young man gulped and said quietly, "They should have been there."

Kelera tilted her head as she looked at him. She, too, could feel his heartbreak. Softly, she stated, "I never had any intention of killing mortals. We went there expecting the Unseelie. I had no idea..."

The revelation hit her like a wave. That was it. Samael had known that the mortals would be outmatched by magic. If the Unseelie had been there, then the playing field would have been leveled and the mortals would have aided with their steel and their numbers. But the Unseelie hadn't been there. Now anyone who heard the tale of the battle would believe that the Seelie had unfairly massacred the mortals. It would be the final wedge between her and King Tristan.

The brilliance of it brought unwelcomed laughter from her throat. She dug her nails into her palms and swore. "That son of a bitch. He knew this would happen. That it would be just the thing to fuel you all in the war against Seelie." The men looked at one another with clarity. They might have been inexperienced in battle, but they weren't stupid.

The young man scratched the back of his neck and, to his friends, asked, "What if she's telling the truth?"

One of the other men bit his lip. He was older than the rest, which surprised her that he'd been paired with the third regiment. He studied her face as he spoke. "I know your Pa. He's a good man and what King Tristan did to him wasn't fair. His knights might be here in Elfhame, but they are still loyal to him." Then to his friends, he said, "If she's right, then we can't just hand her over..."

Yes. That's what she wanted to hear. She pushed further, saying, "Then let me go. Return to camp and find out for yourselves. Dig around, see what Samael is really up to. Surely the truth will come to light."

If her father's knights were still loyal to him, then that meant they would be loyal to her when the time came. But it wouldn't be enough. She needed these men to seek the truth and spread the word through their ranks. If the mortals abandoned Samael and joined her army, then it would turn the tide further in her favor.

The older man opened his mouth to respond, but thunderous hoofbeats echoed through the sky. Kelera struggled against the restraints and she shouted to the men, "You need to free me, now!"

Only two types of Fae rode their steeds amongst the stars: the Wild Hunt and the Night Riders. Regardless of whose side these men were on, they weren't safe around Samael's horde of cursed Fae who did his darkest bidding. She needed her magic if she was going to protect them. Samael clearly didn't view the mortals as important allies. There would be nothing to keep these men safe.

They ignored her, drawing their swords and circling around to try to catch sight of the intruder. A horse whinnied from above and two of the men went tumbling to the ground as the rider landed in front of them.

The steed stomped his hooves into the earth, tearing through the snow and icy dirt underneath. Starlight glistened in its wake. Its beautiful midnight black coat was sweat streaked and Kelera's heart soared. There was no smell of decay or sign of rotting flesh. This was a steed belonging to the Wild Hunt.

The man who sat atop the healthy horse stared down at her with vibrant purple-blue eyes. Though his skin glowed like starlight now, his sweet smile was as recognizable as it had been when she'd first seen him in the tavern with the Guardians. Chaz was here. Warmth radiated through her body, and tears stung her eyes. Chaz had given his life in the Summer Court to save her own, and there was no doubt in her mind that he was there to save her once again.

His sword blazed with moonlight as he unsheathed it and pointed it at the young mortal man. Kelera tried to stand, but stumbled with her hands still behind her back. She fell to her knees and cried out, "Chaz, no! I do not want them harmed."

His mouth gaped in surprise. "They have taken you prisoner, have they not?"

She shrugged, "Yes. But I have a feeling that they will do the right thing and let me go." She shot a pointed look at each of the men. They were so stunned that none seemed to be able to find their words. She'd been just as fascinated and frightened when she'd first come face to face with the Wild Hunt. They were otherworldly, even for Fae. Far more ancient than anything else that roamed the earth. Their ranks were made up of the dead, yet they were still full of life.

The young man nodded slowly and sidestepped to her, careful not to turn his back on Chaz and his sword. Kelera turned, giving him access to her hands. His fingers trembled against her wrists as he unlocked the chains.

The moment they fell from her, her magic bloomed. It made her gasp as it danced freely once again. Adrastus' was still there too, comforting with its chill against her power's warmth. He was alive, that much she could tell. Though he was probably beside himself, knowing she was missing.

Chaz didn't lower his sword, still eyeing the mortals warily. His voice was strong and sure as he spoke. "Woden sends his regards, Your Majesty. He has sent me to retrieve you."

The man with blood on his boots interrupted, "We had our orders..."

Chaz wrinkled his nose in distaste. "Your orders do not concern me. And they no longer concern her." He gestured for Kelera to come to him. She stepped up to the horse, and he extended a hand to her. She couldn't help the butterflies fluttering in her stomach. He expected her to ride a horse of the Wild Hunt... in the sky? She'd done many new things since coming to Elfhame, but flying had not been one of them.

With his help, she mounted the horse behind Chaz. The men were shifting around nervously on the ground, a couple still gripping their swords. She pitied them. There was no telling what sort of lash back they would receive for returning without their prize. Would King Tristan be able to protect them from Samael's wrath?

Gently, she urged, "Consider what I have told you. I promise you it is the truth. Samael planned those attacks so King Tristan would turn to him for help. Now he wants to use you like pawns in this game of his. You are so much more than that. Know that when the time comes, we Seelie will welcome you into our ranks."

The older man nodded. "We will not take what you have said here lightly."

Chaz spurred his horse, and with a jolt, they lifted from the ground. Soon, the mortals below were nothing more than dark dots on a snowy landscape. Magic shimmered all around her, kissing her skin softly like a warm whisper. Every nerve in her body vibrated under the strength of it. She clutched Chaz tightly, afraid she might fall at any moment.

It was quieter than she'd expected. Even at their fast pace, the magic allowing them to fly seemed to block out the sound of the wind. Chaz barely had to raise his voice for her to hear as he asked, "Are you alright, Your Majesty?"

"Yes, just a little shaken. I'm more worried about the men we lost today." She bit the inside of her cheek and tried to quell her nerves.

"I am sorry to tell you that the battle was not what you thought it was." Chaz's voice shook slightly.

"I feared as much. It seems Samael might have used it to solidify the mortal army's anger toward the Seelie." She dug her fingers into his jacket as the horse dipped down to turn. The trees were coated in thick white snow, but she could tell by the full shapes of the tree tops that they were the evergreens of the Spring Court. The mortals hadn't taken her very far, after all.

Chaz tensed under her touch as he said, "It was more than that. Villages surrounding the palace have been attacked. The battle you led your men into was a distraction from something far worse."

The hatred that filled her in that moment was like poison darkening her heart. Her entire body began to shake with fury. Through gritted teeth, she asked, "Where is Adrastus?"

The horse turned again, bringing them closer to the palace. War cries filled the air, breaking through the barrier of magic keeping them in the sky. It sent shivers down her spine, and her magic itched at her fingertips.

Chaz pointed with a gloved hand. "He's down there."

"Take me to him."

The sweet tang of blood filled her mouth, and she realized she'd bit her cheek too hard. Samael had tricked her. And now he had brought the battle to her front door. She would make him pay for the lives lost today. She would make him pay for all of it.

Chapter Sixteen

Kelera had never witnessed anything this bloody. The savagery she had watched in the Winter Palace fighting pits paled in comparison to the brutality the Unseelie Fae were using against the Seelie. Killing blows from both ice magic and barbed weapons were dealt swiftly. Even the battle that Kelera had led the small portion of her army into earlier that day was nothing compared to the fury she was looking down on in that moment. She gripped Chaz tightly as he spurred his horse downward. Below her, the battle was fully visible—untouched by the fog Samael had sent into the last one. Every broken body could be seen lying on the ground. Each blade wielded, and each magical attack flashed clear as day.

Chaz called out, "Ready yourself! Once I drop you, I must rejoin the herd." The Wild Hunt, which he was referring to, wasn't far. They were doing what they could to hold the Night Rider's back from the battle below. Acting as the first line of defense between the monstrous men and the Fae who already had their hands full with the Unseelie.

Still, through all the carnage, the Unseelie's numbers seemed far too small. Where were the mountain men that Samael had coerced into fighting for him? Or the mortals that he had deceived into joining his army?

Chaz's horse knew exactly where to take her, as if by instinct. Adrastus was near the palace walls, fending off any Unseelie who were experienced enough to make their way through the thick of the battle. His raven hair was matted to his blood and dirt-streaked face. Had he come directly from one battle to the next? Surely it was doing a number on him and his magic. She'd hardly noticed him relying on their bond, which meant he was unleashing the full terror of his power without hesitation. That was a very dangerous game for him.

The horse landed on the hard earth with a thud, nearly jarring Kelera from its back. She slipped off with a grateful smile in Chaz's direction. The words didn't come, but she hoped her look said it all. She hoped to see him once this was all over. Nobody had ever mentioned what might happen to the Wild Hunt if they were slain in battle. They were already dead... Would the Elders welcome their souls beneath the hollow hills?

Shrugging off the uncertainty, she ran toward Adrastus. He was no more than a few yards away and the Fae around her were lost in their blood thirst. They barely noticed her. She dodged a few assaults, careful to remember the defensive maneuvers her father and Dodger had taught her. Before any of them could strike again, men she vaguely recognized from the Queen's Guard were there to block them. It startled her. She'd grown so used to having only a select few in her corner that she could trust, yet now there was an entire army there to face the danger with her.

She knew the moment Adrastus spotted her. His eyes went wide and his magic, bound to hers, tightened. It was like a hand grasping at her and pulling her closer. Her heart sped with each running step she took. Once the gap between them was closed, he grasped her face between his hands. His eyes were dark with the shadows that threatened to take over, but it wasn't worry that she felt as she looked into them. Instead, it was relief. She placed her hands over his and leaned into his touch.

He was breathless from fighting as he spoke. "I was so worried when we lost you in the fog."

"I'm here now."

Her heart ached at the pain in his voice as he said, "I went after you, but there was no trace. That is when the Wild Hunt came to tell us of the attack here." Grunts and deadly screams echoed around them as he continued, "Chaz promised to find you. They all insisted I was needed here. That it is what you would have wanted..."

"It was," she soothed him. "One of us had to be here to lead our people."

He grimaced, deepening the scored flesh where Samael had scarred him. "I worry that there will be another ambush we don't see coming. This can't be the full force of Samael's army."

"My thoughts exactly." Kelera bit her lip as she scanned the road which was now turned into a battlefield. "Has there been any sign of him?"

Adrastus whipped his shadows at a Fae charging their way. They snapped against the man's mind, sending him to his knees in a daze. His eyes were devoid of emotion as he stared up at the sky and mumbled something incomprehensible. She eyed Adrastus, searching for any sign that he might be losing control over his Unseelie magic, but could see none. Nor could she feel anything strange in their bonded power. Still, it was not like him to use his abilities to enter one's mind so freely.

Adrastus shook his head. "No sign of Samael. The coward could be watching from a distance, waiting to see how this one will play out."

Maybe. But the mortal men had been eager to deliver her west. If Samael was here at the Seelie palace, then surely they would have headed north instead. Before she had a chance to voice her theory with Adrastus, something sharp sliced along Kelera's arm. With a hiss, she reached for it and found blood on her hand. Just a flesh wound, thank the Fates.

Adrastus pulled her into him as another flash of ice soared by. A hit that would have been far more damaging had she not moved. A familiar laugh, like Yule-time bells, chimed a few feet away. Queen Beatrice waved at her with slender fingers and nails as sharp as claws. But it wasn't her presence that shocked Kelera to her core.

It was her face. The Queen of Unseelie, and mother to all its princes except for Adrastus, had been frightfully beautiful the last time Kelera encountered her in the Autumn manor. But now, her flawless skin and regal demeanor were replaced with burns reaching from under the dress she wore to the top of her head. Her pale blonde hair had been scorched and fried from her scalp, leaving patches of blackened skin to contrast against what was left.

Kelera felt no guilt at the sight of her. Beatrice was a malicious, foul creature who preyed on those below her in status. She'd tortured innocent people, sending them to the pits to be slain for nothing more than minor insults. No. Kelera felt no pity for the fire she had started in the Autumn Court. All she had done was reveal the monster that was within Beatrice all along. Now the world could see her for what she was.

Kelera waved back, and Beatrice stiffened. A man hiding beneath a black hooded cloak placed his hand on the Unseelie Queen's shoulder and she relaxed slightly. Adrastus let out a frustrated growl as the man removed the hood to reveal himself. Kane, too, had succumbed to Kelera's fiery wrath that night. His mouth was twisted with scars from the wounds that the healers had been unable to fix, and he leaned on his left leg as if it pained him to put weight on the right. How much of his savage body had been injured in the fire?

Kane whispered into his mother's ear and a slick smile spread across her face. She called out over the sounds of battle, "My son, the High King of Elfhame, has sent us to claim what is his."

Adrastus huffed out a laugh. "Too afraid to come claim it himself?"

Kane took a step forward as if to engage with Kelera and Adrastus, but Beatrice held her arm in front of him, bringing him to a staggering halt. Kane was his mother's puppet. He would do nothing without her say so. But if Kelera and Adrastus could kill Kane, it would weaken Samael's magic. The brothers were bound, after all, and *what was bound may not be broken except in death*. Even if it only slightly weakened Samael, it would be worth it.

In an effort to draw Kane out, Kelera taunted, "You don't look so good, Kane."

He spat at her. "You tried to kill us, but you failed."

She let out a genuine laugh. He was and always had been a fool. "I simply wanted you to feel the pain that others have suffered at your hand. Though your deaths would have been preferable, I must say that seeing you like this is rather satisfying as well." It was liberating to speak her mind without holding back. She had her power, Adrastus, and an army at her side. All Kane had was a tyrant and a self-centered Unseelie Queen at his.

Adrastus took a step toward his brother and stepmother, stalking like the predator that resided deep within him. Kane clenched his fists, but Beatrice seized hold of his arm, digging her nails in. To Kelera's frustration, it gave him pause.

So, she continued, "I wonder how you would fare now in the pits, Kane. Do you really think you stand a chance against Adrastus and me? I knew you were stupid, but..."

That did it. Kane shoved his mother away and limped toward them in a fast paced jog. Adrastus snarled as his shadows clashed against the ice magic that shot from Kane's hands. While Adrastus and his older brother faced off against one another, Kelera cut around the side of them. Drawing her magic from the land, she called on the roots to take hold of Kane's feet. But the land's power was growing weaker with the incoming frost. It was taking too long for the vines to answer her call.

Abandoning that idea, she drew on the power of the rising moonlight, imagining the tides it controlled. Rushing water ran along her skin, flowing from her and into Kane. It knocked him from his feet with a heavy thud.

Beatrice screeched, summoning ice to attack Kelera. But Adrastus' shadows were already there, shielding her. They wrapped around Kelera, Adrastus, and Kane, blocking out Beatrice and the raging battle around them. It sounded like arrows hitting a shield as Beatrice tried to break through the barrier to get to her favored son.

Kane roared as he slammed his massive body into Adrastus' knees, taking him down with him. Kelera's chest tightened as the two of them grappled on the ground. Arms and limbs were striking out, making it impossible for Kelera to use her magic for fear of hitting Adrastus with it by accident.

Instead, she did the next best thing. Letting her instincts take over, she jumped into the fight. An elbow hit her hard in the corner of her eye, jarring her for a moment. But soon she had her arms around Kane's throat. With all her strength, she squeezed like a snake trying to break its prey.

Kane clawed at her, tearing into the skin on her shoulders and neck, but she didn't relent. Adrastus regained his bearings, facing her and Kane. He reached for his boot and the flash of steel caught Kelera's eye. He gave her a curt nod, and she released her hold on Kane. With precision and speed, Adrastus put the blade to his brother's throat and cut. Kane let out a gurgling sound, grasping at the wound, but it was too late. He fell to the ground without another sound.

Shadows danced in Adrastus' eyes more than before. Kelera knew he had no love for Kane, but it was still his brother. That was two brothers dead now at their hands. She reached for him, placing her hand on his cheek and drawing his attention away from Kane's lifeless body. The shadows dissipated slightly, enough to catch a glimpse of the brilliant shades of green again. It would have to do for now. There was still a battle to face.

As Adrastus expelled a heavy sigh, the shadow barrier returned to him, allowing Beatrice a view of what had transpired. Her hands flew to her mouth, and she ran to her son with an ear-piercing scream. She shook Kane, trying to wake him.

Kelera had no room in her heart for remorse. Not for them. Calmly, she stated, "It is no use, Beatrice. He is gone. Surrender now, and we will take you to our dungeons *alive*."

She had never seen pure hatred in someone's eyes before, but as Beatrice looked at her, there was something far darker and more sinister than shadows residing in them. Kelera took a careful step back and her magic swelled at her fingertips. It flowed out in a ball of light, illuminating the area around them. She would not hesitate to put the Unseelie Queen down.

The cries of battle quieted in anticipation of the two Queens standing off against one another. Kelera could feel the hush of the two armies like a deep breath being held in. Adrastus' magic danced around hers, begging to be released with her own power. Beatrice had never been any kind of mother to him. She'd let her sons terrorize and hurt him. She had even turned her back on Gadreel because she did not think he was as strong as the others. This was the woman who had birthed and raised Samael to be the entitled, torturous monster that he was today.

Queen Beatrice hissed through clenched teeth, "You little bitch. You have taken my sons from me, and now I will take something from you." She puckered her lips together and blew out a frosty wind.

At the same time, Kelera unleashed her power on the hateful woman. Beatrice's body convulsed and her arms twisted into sharp, unnatural angles. She let out a wicked laugh that sent the hairs on Kelera's arms and neck standing on end.

Adrastus grunted, falling to his knees. He pressed his hands into his stomach and pulled them back to reveal blood covered in a light blue frost. His eyes rolled to the back of his head and he dropped to the ground, unconscious. Kelera's vision went red with rage. Beatrice's magic had met its mark, but it wasn't Kelera. She had promised to take something from her... Adrastus.

With an enraged cry, Kelera snatched hold of the magic that was holding Beatrice at her mercy. She clenched her fists, driving it into the Unseelie Queen. As it penetrated her skin, it turned to fire, burning Beatrice from the inside out. Sparks licked her skin, filling the air with the putrid scent of searing flesh. The wicked woman screamed and begged for mercy, but her words were drowned out as the fire reached her mouth. Her skin turned black as it cracked and split, revealing the fire beneath like an ember.

Men from the Unseelie army shouted for retreat as they noticed Samael's mother succumbing to Kelera's retaliation. Kelera, however, did not stop the assault until Beatrice's body burned away, leaving nothing but ashes behind.

Kelera swayed on unsteady feet once it was finished and collapsed. She clawed her way on the cold, solid ground until she made it over to Adrastus, who was already surrounded by Seelie Court healers. The Seelie army was cheering in response to the Unseelie's retreat, but it was all just noise to Kelera. There was nothing for her to celebrate.

She wedged herself in between the healers. The cold air burned in her lungs as she choked the words out. "Tell me he's alive."

A healer tore Adrastus' jacket from him with quick and expert hands. Judging by the lack of trembling, this wasn't his first time on the battlefield. "There's a pulse. But he's in bad shape..."

Kelera leaned down, getting as close to Adrastus as the healers would allow. Her voice broke as she pleaded, "Dras, Dras, please wake up." His breathing was shallow, like the soft flutter of a bird's wings. Guilt gnawed at her as she planted her hands on either side of his face. Perhaps it wasn't just his magic that was a danger to him. Kelera had been so brazen with taunting Kane and Beatrice that she had let her guard down. She should have seen where the attack was aimed.

Adrastus' breathing was ragged. Each breath he sucked in creaked like a door on a broken frame. A pained sob escaped Kelera as she rested her forehead on his. She couldn't lose him. Not now. Not like this. Everything around her slipped away as she prayed to the stars. *He cannot die. I can't do any of this without him.* She kissed him deeply, savoring the taste of him on her lips so that no matter what happened, she wouldn't forget. When she pulled away, she lingered over his mouth and a tear fell from her eye onto his cheek.

Before she could wipe it away, someone grabbed hold of her shoulders and tried to pull her away, but she grabbed tight to the neck of Adrastus' shirt. She shook the hands from her, but they just came back again, drawing her away from Adrastus. Hot tears streamed down her cheeks.

She shouted at the healers, "Save him! Your Queen commands it!"

Someone whispered in her ear in a comforting voice, but she couldn't make out the words. All she could do was focus on the presence of Adrastus' magic, still weaving into her own. As long as the bond still held, she knew he was going to be alright. Her heart felt as if it were tearing in two as several Fae guards lifted Adrastus onto a canvas stretcher and carried him toward the palace.

She leapt in their direction, determined to stay by his side, but Gadreel stepped in front of her. His brow was furrowed in concern as he said, "Kelera, there is still work to be done. I will go and look after him, but you have a duty to your people." He gestured to the soldiers, looking at her expectantly.

She swallowed the lump in her throat and fought the urge to throw up. None of this mattered to her right now. Duty, responsibility... she hadn't wanted any of it without Adrastus by her side. But the battered faces looking to her for direction gave her pause. They had lost friends and family today. They had shed blood for their home and their people.

Her mother had warned that it was Kelera's turn. But until now, she hadn't fully comprehended what that would cost her. Mabine had given up love, freedom, even her own daughter. Pain and risk were the price of ruling. Was Elfhame collecting on that price now? Would it snatch Adrastus from her in one fell swoop? She clutched at her chest, where her heart was threatening to shatter into a million pieces.

The pounding in her head almost drowned out Gadreel's words as he beseeched her. "Kelera. They need you. *We* need you."

Her turn, again, the words echoed in her mind. But she was not alone. Gadreel... her friends... they were still here with her. Gadreel was wrong, though. They didn't just need her. She needed them just as much. It was time to trust the healers to do their job and save Adrastus. And it was time for her to do her duty.

She pushed her shoulders back and whispered, "Gadreel, do not leave Adrastus' side. He *must* live." Then to the guards standing nearest to her, she commanded, "Gather the Queen's Council."

Never before had she understood exactly why her mother had given up her chance at love, all so she could bear the crown. Even with this small glimpse into what it meant to be Queen, she was not ready to admit defeat. Today, they had won the battle and dealt a major blow to Samael. His family was gone. But Kelera's was not. Gadreel was here with her. Her father was safe in Nevene. Adrastus would live, and they would win this war.

Chapter Seventeen

The Seelie Court meeting was a symphony of loud opinions. To put it simply, it was a mess. No one could quite agree on what should be done next. The council was as divided as ever. Some believing they should attack Samael immediately, and others firm on their objections that they should use every able-bodied Fae to fortify the palace.

It left Kelera frustrated and hopeless. Not to mention, incredibly out of her depth. Samael's attack had depleted their numbers. Many had fallen on the battlefield or were injured, and unable to return to arms. With attacks from the Unseelie coming in one after another, they would have no time to heal all of their men before the next.

Kelera had no patience for any of it. Nor could she formulate a plan to offer them, with Adrastus at the forefront of her mind. Every few minutes, her eyes would dart to the doors, waiting for the healers to barge in with an announcement. Her mind whirled, unable to decide if it would be a good or a bad thing. Every sound that came from the direction of the entryway left her with either a sense of dread or a glimmer of hope. Would they enter to tell her that he'd recovered and was asking for her? Or would they enter with solemn faces to announce his death?

Kelera's blistering headache worsened as the council dispersed to attend to the needs of the villagers gathered within the palace gates. Bothwell and Oliver were already meeting with the generals of her army to ensure they would be ready to march. This was it. The moment she'd been dreading. They would take their men to Samael to face off in what would hopefully be the battle to end all of this.

A few courtiers raised their hands as she passed by in an effort to grab her attention. But she'd given enough of herself for the time being. Her boots pounded on the marble floors as she hurried to the infirmary. To Adrastus.

Guards were posted at the entrance and stepped aside quickly, bowing to her as she swept by them. The stone door was cold on her hands, reminding her of the spreading frost, but she continued on, determined not to allow herself to be deterred.

Gadreel was sitting at Adrastus' bedside with a green pallor to his skin. When he spotted her, he laid Adrastus' hand gently on his stomach and stood. Injured Fae were placed neatly around the room on soft white beds, each arranged in rows that made it easy for the healers to scurry about. Kelera sucked in a ragged breath when she saw Adrastus laying helplessly on silky featherdown pillows. At first glance, you'd have thought he was just another Fae soldier whose luck had run out on the field.

His eyes were closed and his sweat soaked brow was furrowed. Someone had pushed his hair from his face and covered him with a soft fur blanket. She knelt at his side, taking his hand in hers. Memories of the lake danced in her mind. The fear of losing him came flooding back. After all they had sacrificed, they found themselves in the same position as before. It wasn't fair.

Gadreel lingered behind her. His voice was soft as he spoke. "The healers say he will live."

She chewed nervously on her lip. "When will he wake?"

"That is up to him. My mother's," his voice broke, "magic was strong, but it was no match for a Prince of both Seelie and Unseelie. Adrastus is vigorous and with his Seelie magic to help the healing process, your healers were able to withdraw most of the effects."

Kelera looked at him incredulously. "Then why is he not awake?"

Gadreel shook his head sadly. "I do not know."

Kelera sighed and ran her hand through her hair. "I cannot go into battle without him. I can't do this alone."

Gadreel knelt beside her and nudged her gently in the side. "You are not alone, Kelera."

A small pang of guilt struck her heart. Gadreel had only ever tried to help. And she was not the only one who was worried. Adrastus was his family... the last of his family, aside from Samael.

Suddenly feeling like an insensitive fool, she said, "How are you doing? With the loss of your mother and Kane?" Though she would have struck both of them down again if given the chance, she still imagined Gadreel was mourning in one way or another.

He shrugged. "I gave up on them a long time ago. Adrastus has been the only true family I have ever known. Until you, that is."

Kelera's heart warmed. He was right. She'd come to them as a frightened girl whose mother had abandoned her. Adrastus and Gadreel were men who had struggled to find a semblance of love in their father's court. They had all filled a void for one another and because of that, they had made a family of their own.

She wrapped her arms tightly around his neck. A small sob escaped her as she said, "I'm so afraid of losing him."

Gadreel patted her hair with one hand while holding onto her with the other. His steady embrace seemed to be the only thing keeping her sane right now. And his words were soothing as he said, "I know. I know."

***

There was a loud clatter across the room, stirring Kelera from sleep. She wiped at her mouth as she lifted her head from Adrastus' sick bed. Gadreel was leaning beside her, resting against the mattress, and still sleeping peacefully. She scanned the room for the source of the commotion to find that a healer had dropped a tray of herbs and was scrambling to put them back into their jars.

With a sigh, Kelera turned to check on Adrastus. He was no longer slick with a feverish sweat. His eyes were closed gently, and his face was smooth and soft aside from the growing stubble. He looked peaceful, like the night they had slept beside one another for the first time in the Summer Court. They'd been so frightened then. Running from the bounty hunters Samael had sent after them.

She'd come to the Spring Court knowing things were going to get worse before they got better. But she never imagined she'd be sitting in the infirmary praying to the fates that they gave Adrastus yet another chance at life. Were they pushing their luck? Was it simply their fate to die in this war?

Peeking at Gadreel to make sure he was still sleeping, she whispered to Adrastus, "I don't know what to do, Dras. Our men are set to ride to the Spring and Autumn border at sunrise. How am I to face Samael without you?" She paused as tears welled in her eyes and laid her head on his shoulder. "How am I to face *life* without you?"

"You don't really think I'd let you have all the fun, do you, little thief?"

She shot up with a start to find Adrastus staring back at her. The gasp that escaped her lips echoed loudly in the room, drawing the attention of the healers. They started toward them, but Gadreel was already standing with his hands out. He ushered them to the other side of the room, and Kelera was grateful to have the moment alone with Adrastus.

She kissed him fiercely, and he let out a grunt. Pulling back, she whispered, "Oh, no, I didn't mean to..." She blew a strand of hair from her face and granted him a sympathetic smile. "Does it hurt?"

"Just a bit." He smiled back weakly.

"I'll go get the healer." Kelera pulled away, but he grabbed her arm.

Drawing her into him, he kissed her deeply. One hand ran through her hair, brushing over the tip of her ear. He moaned, but this time it did not sound pained. It was a hungry one. One that she knew well by now. She returned the kiss, parting her lips to welcome him. Heat warmed in the very bottom of her stomach, and she ached to feel his touch rove lower.

"Ahem." A woman appeared on the opposite side of the bed in Kelera's eyeline. Silver bracelets dangled from her arms, clinking against one another as she clapped her hands together.Kelera reluctantly pulled back from Adrastus, adjusting her vest and brushing her hair away from her face. Adrastus chuckled and laid his head back on the pillow. Perhaps the interrupting woman wouldn't notice, but Kelera could see in the twitch of Adrastus' jaw that he was frustrated by her presence. Either way, she went to work checking his breathing and pulse. Her hands glowed in a warm orange light as she checked him over, and Adrastus sighed in relief.

At Kelera's questioning glance, the woman explained, "Just a little pain alleviation to help with the wound. We were able to close it up, but you'll have to take it easy—"

Adrastus sat up, causing the woman to take a few uneasy steps back. His words were clipped as he stated, "Not a chance."

Kelera's heart sped. "Maybe she's right..."

His voice softened as he spoke to her. "You said it yourself. We need to do this together."

On instinct, she opened her mouth to argue, but thought better of it. He'd made up his mind and she couldn't very well command him to stay put. Not after demanding that he allow her to make her own choices. If he wanted to ride into battle with her, then there would be no stopping him. And they needed to go in as a team without the tension of a fight between them.

Kelera raised her chin and directed her words at the attendant. "Please retrieve Prince Adrastus' things."

She dipped into a curtsey. "As you wish, Your Majesty."

Adrastus groaned as he pushed the covers off of him and placed his feet on the floor. Kelera offered a hand to help him up, but he declined. It wasn't surprising that he would want to do things on his own. That was okay, as long as he knew he could count on her, so she remained in place in case he changed his mind.

Once he was dressed and armed, Kelera walked with him to the door. At first, he was unsteady and off balance. It didn't help the pit in her stomach to watch him moving so slowly. But she said nothing.

Gadreel, however, had no such reservations. He blocked the exit and stood nose to nose with Adrastus. His voice was low as he warned, "No."

Adrastus rolled his eyes. "Out of my way, brother."

Gadreel shook his head. "You are not well. You need to rest."

"I'm rested enough." Adrastus tried to side step around Gadreel, but his older brother stepped with him, mirroring his movements.

Gadreel turned to Kelera with pleading eyes as he said, "You can't let him do this. He'll get himself killed."

She placed a supportive hand on Adrastus' shoulder. "I will not order him to stay if he doesn't want to. We are equals and I trust his judgment."

Gadreel swatted angrily at the air and stepped aside. Adrastus pushed through the doors and picked up his pace as he walked down the hall. Kelera gave one last apologetic look at Gadreel. She didn't want him to be angry with her, but he had to realize that Adrastus needed their support more than their protection.

Palace attendants and courtiers jumped back to avoid Adrastus' determined stride. Kelera had to jog to catch up to him and called out to him, "Dras, slow down!"

He spoke over his shoulder to her. "We've wasted enough time. You said the men march at sunrise. Look around."

She wasn't sure how she hadn't noticed it before, but warm sunlight streamed through the open ceiling and large airy windows, dancing between marble columns. How long had she been asleep? Someone should have woken her sooner.

Bothwell was waiting for them at the entryway. Kelera was surprised to see him suited up for battle as well. She shook her head when she reached him and said, "No. You're not coming."

Bothwell shot Adrastus a snotty look. "He gets to come, but I am commanded to stay?"

Did all the men in her life have to be so stubborn? She explained, "If Adrastus and I do not make it back, then you must be here to lead."

Adrastus excused himself to speak with the generals, allowing Kelera and Bothwell a moment. She smiled gratefully at him. It would be natural for the two of them to lead together. They each anticipated what the other needed without having to say so. Butterflies fluttered in her stomach at the idea that things here could work out after all.

Bothwell, baffled, said, "Lead?"

Her attention snapped back to him. "Yes. There are few I would trust with the task. Gadreel is an Unseelie Prince with no claim to the Seelie crown. Oliver, though capable, does not hold enough standing with the council. You are the only one I would feel comfortable leaving the crown to if I were to die in battle."

Bothwell's face softened. "It is in moments like this that I see so much of her in you."

"My mother loved you Bothwell. And she knew you loved her. I believe this is the choice she would make too."

Bothwell nodded and bowed deeply to her. "Your Majesty."

She patted him on the shoulder and turned away. The guards opened the doors as she stepped up to them. Her breath hitched in her throat at the countless faces staring back at her from outside. Fae, both men and women, were there, armed and ready for battle. Even Lesser Fae from the villages were there from the Summer and Spring Courts. Their faces were bright and hopeful as they laid eyes on their Queen. Most of them were seeing her for the first time, and she fought the urge to smooth down her hair. Maintaining a perfect appearance would do nothing to bolster their spirits. What they needed was to see their Queen for who she really was.

She would ride into battle alongside them. They were ready to defend their people and their land. Even if it meant losing their own lives. As incredible as it was to see them all there, what really caught her off guard were the creatures gathered in the courtyard with them. Solitary Fae who had spent centuries living alone in the woods were scattered through their ranks. Witches with spider web wrinkles around their eyes and dryads with leaves intertwined in their hair were clothed in bark armor. They were all there because she had called.

Adrastus placed his hand on the small of her back, drawing her closer to him. His breath was warm against her ear as he whispered, "They're all here for you."

Her voice came out child-like as she said, "What if I fail them?"

He kissed her on the temple. "We will see to it that you do not."

Generals began barking out orders and organizing their ranks. The Lesser and Solitary Fae fell into line with them, mixing the army until it looked like something out of the storybooks Kelera had read as a child. She recalled hand painted pictures of the creatures of Elfhame gathering for revels in which they would trap mortals for eternity. How different she had viewed them all back then. Now she truly knew them and even loved some of them.

The Guardian's, led by Ragnor, looked dazzling in their bark and vine-colored armor as they stepped up to Kelera and bowed. Jinx smirked at her, squinting his eye, and said, "Don't look any different to me, little lady."

She shoved him gently in the shoulder. "That's cause I'm not."

His eye widened. "Is it true that you commanded the land to swallow a Night Rider whole?"

A blush crept across her face. "Yes."

He hooted. "You've got to show me that one!"

Her shoulders tensed as she asked, "Did you see Chaz?"

Ragnor smiled broadly and tugged at his beard. "We saw him ride in with the Wild Hunt. It was..."

Tepin finished, "Remarkable."

Kelera couldn't help but smile, too. She knew how much their friend meant to them. And how amazing it must have been for them to see with their own eyes that everything they'd strived for all their lives was worth it. That when their lives were claimed in battle, they would be welcomed into the ranks of the Wild Hunt, destined to watch over the realm for all eternity.

Ragnor clapped his hands together. "Though we are always happy just to see your beautiful faces, we come bearing gifts!" Putting his fingers between his lips, he let out a loud whistle.

The ground quaked, throwing Kelera into Adrastus' side. Soldiers shouted in alarm, closing their ranks to defend against the forest giants appearing beyond the gates. Their bodies towered over the stone walls, and Kelera didn't blame her men for feeling threatened. She, too, had been terrified the first time she'd encountered them.

But for her, it was like seeing an old friend again. They had been the first to bow to her. Knowing who she was before she did. They'd sensed Mabine's power transfer to her and had already pledged their allegiance through that show of respect.

Jinx was vibrating with excitement, clapping his hands together and bouncing on the balls of his feet. "That's not all. Wait for it..."

Ragnor and the others took the lead, heading out through the palace gates. Kelera's army waited for her to pass before following behind. A few of the villagers hesitated, and she turned back to give them an encouraging smile. Soon she and the full force of her army were standing outside the palace gates, staring up at stony giants. They were only slightly shorter than the forest giants, but they made up for it in the bulkiness of their build.

Kelera felt dizzy. "These... they..." She couldn't find the words in her disbelief.

Ragnor puffed his chest out proudly. "We wanted it to be a surprise. The giants awoke from their slumber. Ready to fight for their Queen."

The massive boulders they had passed on their journey to the Spring Palace were standing as real and alive as any other creature. Smooth stone curved inward on their faces, giving the appearance of large hollow eyes as if an artist had expertly carved them into a human likeness. Even their arms were chiseled into strong muscular forms. It was both terrifying and remarkable.

She stared in awe, unable to take her eyes from them as she said, "It was just a story, though."

Adrastus put his arm around her and gave her a small shake. "In Elfhame, there is always some truth to the stories." He loped over to the giants, circling around them in child-like awe.

Turning to her army with newfound confidence, she proclaimed, "I know you are all afraid. It would be reckless of you not to be. Today we face a threat born and bred of the very land we defend. Samael will stop at nothing until he destroys everything that is good and right in Elfhame. But *this* is where his reign of terror ends. Together, we defend our land. It's power. Our people. Today, we finish this!"

The crowd roared in response and the forest and stone giants shuddered in what she could only assume was agreement. Adrastus let out a loud war cry, raising his fist in the air, and Kelera knew that this was their moment. It was the beginning of the end.

Chapter Eighteen

The air grew colder the further they went from the palace. Signs of frost became more prevalent. It shimmered on the naked tree branches in a solid, thick coating. And soon snowflakes were drifting from the sky. They clung to Kelera's hair, which she'd braided back, showing her ears proudly. Though she couldn't deny her ties to the mortal realm or the love and respect she had for her father and friends there, today she would be the very image of Seelie royalty.

When she'd first arrived in the Winter Court, Samael had dragged her through the Unseelie Palace, parading her around as a weak halfling. A girl ignorant of Elfhame's ways. And although she still had much to learn, today she would face him as a Queen. Strong and confident. And proud of the Fae blood running in her veins.

Adrastus and the generals had discussed a plan for both the forest and stone giants. If they traveled with the main army, then Samael would hear them coming. That is why they decided—with Kelera's approval—to send them around to flank the north and south sides of the border. It could even work as a beneficial distraction if Samael sent a portion of his men to challenge them.

Kelera released a gentle sigh thanks to her generals. It was a relief to be surrounded by soldiers who had trained their whole lives for something like this. As capable as she believed herself to be in a fight, Kelera had never been taught the art of battle. Anything she'd picked up had been through the odd book she came across in the library or from overhearing her father's men talking in the barracks.

The prospect of coming face to face here in Elfhame with the Mortal Knights that she'd befriended in childhood made her jittery. Dodger had pledged to help her when the opportunity arose. But the rest of the mortal army would be more difficult to sway. Especially after the recent slaughter at the Seelie army's hands. She shook her arms out, trying to stop her palms from sweating.

Adrastus, observant as always, bumped her shoulder with his arm. "Calm and collected, little thief. Calm and collected."

She side-eyed him, noting that he was no longer limping. His back was straight, and he carried himself with his usual confidence. Looking at him, one would never know he'd been injured just hours ago. Seelie healing powers truly were a marvel to behold.

The Spring Court's trees were covered with a soft blanket of snow as they neared the border. As nervous as she was for the fight they were about to face, she hoped she was right about Samael's position. It had been too risky to send scouts ahead. If Samael was in fact at the Autumn border, then they needed to take advantage of whatever element of surprise they could by meeting him there. He was overconfident. It was simply his nature. And it was a weakness Kelera planned to use against him.

The Seelie Fae marched silently behind and beside them. Their stealth was impressive, especially as they reached land coated in frost. They stepped carefully, as not to make any crunching sounds under their boots.

Kelera leaned in to whisper to Adrastus. "We have to be getting close." She reached her power deep into the soil and felt a steady but weak pulse of the land's magic. "Samael's magic has ravaged the land here."

"Aye. I can feel it." Adrastus scanned the shadows in a copse of trees they were passing. Just beyond, Kelera knew the Hawthorns, and the lake were waiting. If anything happened to them, then perhaps they could get to the healing waters. That is, if the Lady of the Lake was willing to help them again. Kelera had barely gotten her to agree the first time.

The veins in Adrastus' neck twitched with tension. She wanted to say something to comfort him, but knew it would be fruitless. He stopped in his tracks, holding a fist in the air to alert the army to do the same. Kelera slipped on a slick spot of icy dirt and grabbed onto Adrastus to stop from falling.

Breathlessly, she whispered, "What is it?"

"Do you see that?" He pointed ahead to the tree line where the Spring Court evergreens met the bare Autumn Court trees.

Her heart sped as she spotted a thin veil of fog. When she let out her breath, it came in a fleeting, misty cloud. She took a nervous step forward and felt the temperature drop significantly. It was like being in the Winter Court again with a bitter cold that seeped into your bones. Samael was here. He had to be.

Her generals silently signaled for their army to fall into formation. One of them, a burly man with a braided beard who looked remarkably similar to Ragnor—so much so, she wondered if they might be related—stepped up to her. His lips were down turned and pressed tightly together as he looked her up and down.

A puff of frost came from his mouth as he said, "Your Majesty, I will send my men ahead. You and Prince Adrastus can take up the rear."

Ignoring his condescending tone, she replied, "Or your men can stay back while Adrastus and I take the lead." He opened his mouth to argue, but she spoke first. "I will not send my men into possible danger while I remain behind, tucked away safely like an expensive vase. I came here to lead and to fight, and that is precisely what I intend to do."

She didn't wait for a response as she seized Adrastus' hand and drew him toward the thick mist. After the ambush in the southeastern corner earlier, she wasn't about to take valuable fighters into yet another one. With Adrastus at her side, they would be more than capable of fending off an attack long enough for her men to come to their aid.

Stepping into the mist filled her body with a painful chill. Adrastus shuddered beside her, but said nothing. They both knew what this was. Samael's magic had consumed the land. Trees, shrubs, even the ground on which they walked were dead. There was no snow, but rather a barren, frosty wasteland. If his magic continued to spread like it was, then there would be nothing left of Elfhame. No way to farm. Nothing for the animals and other Fae creatures to live off of.

There wasn't even a hint of magic in the depths of the earth. No matter how far Kelera pushed her power into the land, she couldn't find it. She bit her lip and tried to steady her rapid beating heart. But the further they trudged, the more furious she became. What sort of kingdom would Samael have left to rule if he destroyed it? He must have truly gone mad. And how did one defeat a mad man?

A deafening roar echoed in the mist, parting it enough for Kelera to see a dozen or so mountain men rushing toward them. Adrastus used his shadows to push them back in defense. Knowing she could not call on the land's magic,

Kelera summoned the fire that lingered beneath the surface of her skin. It erupted against a few of the men who had dodged Adrastus.

Once the men were incapacitated, a horn blew from the west. From Samael's camp, no doubt. In turn, Kelera shouted for her army. It was time for them to join her. This was what they'd been waiting for. Their footsteps were no longer silent as they advanced toward the sound of the horn. Before she knew it, bodies were clashing violently against one another.

She felt dizzy as her eyes flitted from one side of the battle to the next. *Focus*, she thought to herself. Keeping track of Adrastus was the most important thing. Second only to finding Samael. It wouldn't be surprising to find the treacherous *king* taking up the rear of his army. Better to let his men fall first, and step in only when he knew he had the upper hand. She growled in frustration as she shot a bolt of light at a man coming up behind Adrastus with his sword drawn. The Unseelie soldier crumpled into a heap on the ground. But her mind was already on the next attacker.

One after one, she used her magic to take down anyone who dared come near her and Adrastus. He was handling himself beautifully, casting shadows into the minds of men bold enough to try their hand at a fight with a Dark Prince of Unseelie. How easy it was to forget that he shared his father and brother's power.

In her peripheral vision, she saw a large man advancing on her. She summoned a glowing heat at her hands, but paused when she realized it was Ragnor. With a gasp, she drew the magic back in.

"Are you insane? I could have killed you!"

Ragnor's head was bobbing as he glanced around the forest. "Our magic is too weak here. Many of the villagers are being forced to fight with weapons they are not skilled in. Even the army is struggling."

"Shit," she paused to think. If they didn't do something fast, then more lives would be lost. Casualties were to be expected, but it was going to be hard enough to live with the regret of that. The guilt of taking her men into a fight they couldn't win was unthinkable. She could think of nothing other than finding Samael. If she could kill him, then his army would no longer have a king to fight for. With Beatrice and Kane dead, there would be no one left to lead the Unseelie but Adrastus.

"We have to reach Samael!" she screamed to Adrastus.

Ragnor added, "We'll cover you!" He whistled, alerting Jinx and Tepin to their sides.

Adrastus joined them, too. With a firm nod of his head, he clutched Kelera's elbow, engulfing the two of them in his shadows. The veil was thin enough for them to see where they were going and to make out the faces they passed. The ferocious sneers and pain in their eyes seared into her mind. As they raced, the Guardians defended them from attacks on all fronts. Their moves were effortless, like they'd been made for this exact moment.

The ground quaked as both the forest and stone giants fought against the army to the left and right flanks. They were doing real damage. Squashing anyone stupid enough to get near them. Even the dryads were holding their own against the Unseelie. The beautiful, scantily clad women she had seen in the trees when she'd entered Elfhame looked like avenging Valkyries, tearing apart their enemy. There was a strange beauty to it.

They made progress through the battlefield, finally reaching a point where there was nothing but the twisted limbs of the Autumn forest. A few more steps brought Samael into view. He was standing on a large mound with his father's twisted crown on top of his head. The horns on it reached to the sky like foreboding towers. From this distance, his eyes looked like black, soulless pools. His regal face was held up with pride and a sickening smile was spread across his face, flashing his white teeth. He would have been mistaken for something inhuman and untouchable if it weren't for the rotten skin where she'd burned him. He was no immortal.

Samael might be the frost that threatened the world. But ice melted under a fire's touch. And she was exactly that. She was the wildfire that would set all his dreams ablaze. Adrastus let out a frightening guttural growl, startling her to a slower pace. Her stomach tightened as she caught sight of his eyes. They were clouded with his shadows and focused solely on Samael.

"Careful, Dras," she cautioned and tugged at his Unseelie magic through their binding. It resisted like a rope pulled taut. This wasn't good.

His shadowy blockade bumped into her back, forcing her to walk faster. Her heart was racing, and she tried to regain her focus. She'd be no use to Adrastus if she wasn't prepared to fight with him. They were bound and she would have to trust that it would keep him grounded and pull him back from the void if things went too far.

Ragnor roared, "Down!"

Just in the nick of time, Kelera grabbed hold of Adrastus, forcing him down to the ground. He barely seemed to notice as his body slammed into the hard earth. Kelera's head whipped around to see what had warranted Ragnor's warning. Above her, hoofbeats crashed against the shadowy shield, but it held strong.

A Night Rider glanced back at them with a sneer and yanked at his skeletal horse's reins. The horse spun, turning toward them at a full gallop again. Kelera braced herself for another strike, but Ragnor and Tepin were already in front of them. They roared as they aimed their swords at the steed and plunged them in. The horse screeched and skidded across the ground, throwing the Rider from its back.

Kelera shook Adrastus. "Drop the shield! We need to help them!"

His voice sounded distant as he responded, "No. We need to get to Samael."

Kelera pushed against the shadows, but they held firm. Adrastus pulled her up roughly by the collar of her vest and dragged her away from the Guardians. She stumbled across the uneven ground, unable to take her eyes from Ragnor and his men. The Night Rider was ancient with his tattered robes and paper-thin skin. Yet he was still strong and blocked the Guardians with ease.

She made a desperate attempt to talk sense into Adrastus. "We need to go back! They need our help!"

He ignored her, focused only on his brother standing upon the mound. No matter how hard she fought against his hold, he did not relent. This wasn't like him. The Guardians were his friends. In his right mind, he would never leave behind the people he cared for.

Still watching Ragnor and the others, she yelled, "Adrastus, damn you! Listen to me! They need—" her throat closed up as the Night Rider's rusted sword sliced into Ragnor's neck. Her friend dropped to his knees with steaming blood dripping down from his throat. A scream tore from her and she clawed at Adrastus' hand. "Let me go! Jinx and Tepin need us!"

Adrastus might as well have been in another world. He didn't even glance at her or back at the friends he'd left behind. Jinx and Tepin didn't let the shock of their loss deter them. In perfect unison, they descended on the Night Rider, tearing at him with a ferocity she'd never seen before. They each swung at one of the Rider's arms. They didn't stop until they had severed the flesh and deteriorating muscle enough to tear them from his body.

Kelera watched in heartbreak as their friends lost themselves to a wild rage. She kept her gaze on them until she could no longer see through the tears in her eyes. Then, with a ragged breath, she whispered the prayer she'd heard only once before, hoping she got the words right, "May you ride atop the stars. May you be given a steed amongst the warriors of the afterlife, destined to claim your place beside Woden and his sword. May you find glory in the afterlife as you did in this one."

Wiping away the hot, angry tears, she started to jog, passing Adrastus. Only then did he release his hold on her. She didn't dare look back at him for fear of what she would see in his eyes. His hatred and need to destroy his brother were ruling him. And if that is what it took to end Samael and this war, then she, too, would let it fuel her.

Chapter Nineteen

The heat of Kelera's power rose like a spiking fever. Witnessing her friend's death had snapped something inside her. Ragnor sacrificed himself to protect her—to make sure she reached Samael. So many lives were being given in the name of this war. On both sides. It was disgusting and infuriating. Samael had cursed men's souls, had dragged families from their homes, and was killing the land slowly all for a crown he had no right to claim.

When they arrived at the last line of Samael's defense, nearest to the mound, she growled at Adrastus, "Drop the shield." She tried to ignore the scratchy pain in the back of her throat and the angry tears threatening to fall as she waited for him to do as she bid.

This time, he obeyed. The shadows slithered back into his hands, but they clouded his skin, not settling into him fully. He wanted to break his brother, and she could not blame him for that. She couldn't even truly blame him for leaving their friends behind. His power was wild—a mix of Seelie and Unseelie. No one had ever taught him how to control it, but rather, he was encouraged to nurture its volatile nature at his father's behest. Her only hope now would be that she could save him from himself when this was over.

At that moment, however, Samael was their priority. The malevolent self-proclaimed King's eyes flickered in excitement when he caught sight of them. "Brother, you aren't looking so well."

Kelera glanced at Adrastus. The shadows in his eyes were more erratic than ever, and his complexion was a sickly gray. He didn't retort against Samael, but continued to stare daggers at him. She worried he would snap at any moment. If he did, there may not be a way to bring him back.

Samael proceeded to goad him. "I can remember, growing up, you always held your own against one of us. But when you were outnumbered... now that was a different story." Frost snaked from Samael's hands, creeping toward her and Adrastus.

Adrastus bared his teeth and a low rumble rose from his throat. His voice was strained as he said, "You, Kane, and Ammon never did like to play fair."

"You're right about that, little brother." With a broadening smile, Samael snapped his fingers in the air. Men shouted as they marched forward, standing between them and Samael.

Kelera took in their garb and held back the bile threatening to rise in her throat. They sported shining armor and the crest of Nevene. Samael chuckled. The horrible man deserved credit for his devious plotting. It would be excruciating for her to fight against the people she'd grown up alongside. Worse, Adrastus—especially in the state he was currently in—would not hesitate to destroy them all.

The only way to protect these men would be to draw Samael out. Kelera cupped her hands around her mouth and yelled, "Hiding behind mortals now, Samael? Sort of pathetic, even for you!"

To her pleasure, he clenched his fists at his side in response. When it came to Samael, the easiest way to get under his skin was by chipping away at his ego. It was short-lived, though, as he gestured for someone to join him on the mound. King Tristan walked boldly to Samael's side and Kelera felt a stab of betrayal. She'd known he had been tricked to the Unseelie ranks, but seeing it with her own eyes was something that struck a chord. She'd been raised in Tristan's court. He'd watched her grow up. Her father had taken her to his coronation where she'd marveled at how grand her new king was. No matter how much she thought she'd let go of the girl who sought his approval, she still lurked beneath the surface.

Samael spoke loud enough for Kelera to hear. "King Tristan, if you would do the honors. Order your men to bring me the halfling and kill my traitorous brother... No need to be gentle."

"No!" An all too familiar mess of red hair came running to Tristan's side.

Kelera's knees went weak in shock. Cierine was here. In Elfhame. This couldn't be happening. She should have been home in Nevene, far away from the danger. What was Tristan thinking, allowing his only heir to accompany him to war?

Cierine's cheeks were rosy from the cold, even though she was swathed in layers of fur. She clutched King Tristan's sleeve. "You can't, Uncle. I'm begging you, don't do this!"

Kelera looked at Adrastus for help, but he continued to eye his brother. She could practically feel the hatred in his magic as it stirred around her own. If she was going to sway King Tristan to her side, then she would have to do it alone.

"King Tristan, listen to the Princess!" Kelera shouted to him. "It was Samael who attacked the villages. I saw it with my own eyes. Your knights were there! They witnessed it."

Tristan seemed to shrink as he gulped and looked over at a large group of men. Kelera followed his gaze and spotted

Dodger at the head of them. She hadn't noticed him before because of the helm he wore, but it was off now, and he was clutching it tightly in his hands.

Dodger's voice was rough from the cold as he stated, "As we told you, Sire. Lady Kelera aided us in stopping the attacks at the border. We spoke the truth." There was venom in his words as he added, "*Sir Aldric* spoke the truth."

Samael crossed his arms over his chest and repeated, "Give your men the order, King Tristan."

Kelera licked her lips in anticipation. She had to convince King Tristan before Samael lost his patience. "The battle yesterday morning... I was there! Samael tricked you into believing his men would be joining yours, didn't he?"

King Tristan exchanged a look with one of the young soldiers who had taken her hostage. She felt an ounce of relief. He'd been true to his word, after all. They'd told Tristan about what had happened. That relief was replaced with disappointment. Why hadn't Tristan put more stock in what his men had to say? She recalled Cierine's kidnapping and how he'd dismissed Kelera so easily. He'd taken the word of his council over her. And then again, when she'd returned to Nevene, he'd listened to the real traitor, Alexander, and had locked her in the dungeons. He was a weak-minded man. Not fit to rule. Perhaps he and Samael deserved one another. But the mortal men fighting for him did not. They deserved so much more.

Samael snarled, "Enough of this." He grabbed King Tristan by the back of the neck. "Command them, or I will."

Tristan's wide eyes met Kelera's, and she saw genuine fear there. She gave him a small shake of her head and mouthed *no*. Tristan's hand trembled as he began to raise it in the air to give his men the order. But before it reached the height of his shoulder, he stopped and lowered it.

Samael shook his head in disappointment. "Very well." With a snap of his fingers, ice penetrated the side of King Tristan's head, driving through his ear and into his skull.

Kelera wanted to scream, but no sound came. The only thing she could hear were Cierine's horrified cries.

Kelera's chest hitched as she watched Tristan hit the ground with a sickening thud. They'd had their differences, but she'd grown up in his home. Had been there when he was a rebellious young prince and had seen him crowned when he came of age. The day's losses were growing by the minute. How much more could she take?

Samael turned to her with his hand raised. Fueled by grief, Kelera summoned her magic, but Adrastus beat her to it. Before Samael could kill her best friend, Adrastus' shadows snapped out like a snake, severing two of Samael's forefingers and his thumb from his hand. They fell to the ground, and he directed his attention to Adrastus. There was hardly even a glimmer of pain reflected on Samael's face. Was he truly that blinded by his ambitions that even injury wouldn't slow him down? The thought, mixed with the sickly sight of blood dripping on the snow with little puffs of steam nearly doubled her over with nausea.

Mortal soldiers dove out of the way as the Princes of the Night's shadows clashed against one another. Kelera took a few running steps toward Cierine, but Dodger already had a hold of her. He shouted to the Mortal Knights as he dragged her to them, "Save the Queen!"

They obeyed, making a protective circle around their new ruler. Kelera tried to wrap her mind around what had just happened. King Tristan was dead. Cierine was now the Queen of Nevene.

Kelera screamed at them, "Get her out of here!"

Shielding her with their bodies, they backed away from the battle. Only then did Kelera feel ready to rejoin the fight. Sweat beaded Adrastus' brow as he held strong against Samael's magic. Killing Kane and the bond they'd had may have weakened Samael slightly, but it wasn't enough. He still had the power of the Unseelie crown.

Wind blew wildly around them and the sky darkened. Within seconds, eerie clouds blanketed the sky, blotting out the sun. The first sign of a blizzard. When she turned to look back at how her men were faring against the Unseelie, it sent a spike of adrenaline through her. Many had fallen. Others had abandoned their magic and were now relying on their weapons. There was no Seelie power to be found here. And for many, without the land's strength, they had nothing to draw on. They were becoming as defenseless against magic as the mortals.

Even with Samael defending himself against Adrastus, he was still strong enough to spread his frost through their world. Flurries splattered across her face. Heavy snowflakes matted in her eyelashes.

Were they going to die here just as Ragnor, Tristan and so many others had? She clutched her locket. The Elders were wrong. She wasn't worthy of the hope they and the Fae of Seelie had placed in her. How could she save them when she couldn't even save the man that she loved from the darkness inside of him?

A chill shattered through her body, sending her to the ground, moaning in agony. She reached for her magic, but it flickered like a candle flame in an open window. Adrastus wrapped his shadows around her, blanketing her in his protection. The man she knew and loved was still in there somewhere, and her heart ached as she tried desperately to grasp onto that hope.

Chapter Twenty

The blizzard was getting out of hand and Samael's men blotted out any view Kelera had of her army. If she was struggling with her magic, then that could only mean they were as well. She clenched her eyes shut to prevent the snow from blurring her vision. The pained screams of death and destruction shattered her mind like a blow to the head. Those were her men and women out there.

She thought of the many times she had watched her father with his knights. He always put them first. There was no battle worth sacrificing them for. This was no different. Did she want to be the kind of leader Samael was? Or did she want to be the sort of leader her father would be proud of? If she was ever to face him again with her head held high, then there was only one choice to make here. They had to pull back if they wanted to live long enough to regain their strength and try once more.

With a quick glance at Adrastus, she righted herself. His shadows were holding steady against Samael. Slowly, they inched in closer to him. But it wasn't enough. Adrastus' eyes were completely glazed over now, and it was as if nothing else in the world existed except for him and his brother.

Kelera cupped her hands around her mouth and shouted to her army, "Retreat! Your Queen commands you to retreat!"

The command echoed in the voices of her men, spreading across the battlefield. "Retreat!"

Kelera pushed through the snow until she reached Adrastus. Behind her, the Seelie army was falling back into the Spring Court tree line. The Unseelie, sensing their victory, held back, allowing them to leave. Kelera cocked her eyebrow in surprise. The Winter and Autumn Fae looked as weary as she felt. In the heat of battle, it was difficult to remember that they were not all there by choice. That they had been forced to fight for a mad king's cause.

She tugged on Adrastus' sleeve, shielding her face from the force of his magic as it roared from his hands. "Dras, we have to go. We will get another chance, I promise." It was tricky to make promises in Elfhame. But in this instance, she had every intention of honoring it. She would not let this defeat determine how their story ended.

Adrastus grunted under the strain of holding off Samael's icy power. But it didn't look like he had any plan of heeding her words. There was only one way for her to stop him. Using the bond, she reached deep inside and snatched hold of his magic. It had been flowing like a river's rapid current through her veins, but with all her might, she took dominance of it and yanked.

Adrastus resisted, attempting to pull it back to him. With a heavy breath, Kelera drew it further into her, imagining it taking root in the pit of her stomach like a great ash tree. Her power wrapped itself around his like vines, solidifying her grip on it.

On the outside, his magic weakened. Kelera allowed enough slack for it to hold Samael's attack off, but it buckled under her command. Adrastus snapped out of his trance long enough to notice her presence. He blinked rapidly, but his eyes still did not clear of the shadows.

His voice was raspy as he said, "Little thief?"

Firmly, she declared, "We are leaving. Now." She raised her hand, blasting a bright white light of power in Samael's direction. It was enough to give her and Adrastus the opening they needed to disappear into the trees.

To her relief, Adrastus ran steadily by her side, keeping pace with her even though his long legs could take him much farther and faster than hers could. He gripped her hand tightly as they ducked and dodged fallen tree branches. All dead and withered, as if they'd experienced a blight.

Further into the Spring forest, they came to a large barricade. Seelie soldiers popped over the hastily build wooden walls with bows in hand. The archers aimed at Kelera and Adrastus, making them skid to a sudden halt. Kelera held her hands up and stepped slowly into the soft sunlight, which was less obstructed now that the battle had ended.

The archers let out loud whistles and a massive group of armed guards pushed through the rickety gate. Kelera didn't release a sigh of relief until they ushered her and Adrastus inside. Her sides cramped from the run and she bent over to catch her breath. Adrastus stood silently at her side, making her nerves grow. What was going through his mind? Did he even remember the battle?

Generals swarmed Kelera, spitting out information and numbers. Their opinions on what had gone wrong. How many they had lost. The number of injured. And worst of all, questions about what their next move was and how soon they would return to battle.

She had to admit they had done an impeccable job of building a camp between the battlefield and the palace. It would have been foolish to go back to the palace, where

Samael could have the opportunity to bring the next battle to them. But this camp was not nearly as fortified. The wood they'd used to build the wall was rotting and damp. If Samael really wanted to get to them, then there wouldn't be much to stop him.

They had to act fast. Eager to be free of the outspoken men who were vying for her attention, she demanded that they draw up a plan and bring it to her in her tent. They would discuss the best course of action then.

She turned to Adrastus. "Do you think Samael intends to attack again today? Or will he allow his men to rest for the night?" It was hard to tell with Samael. He was ambitious and didn't care about his men. But he was also smart. He had to know that the Unseelie would need to rest and regain their strength before fighting again, right?

Adrastus didn't respond. Instead, he stared off at the distance, not seeming to focus on anything in particular. Her cheeks flushed with heat as her officers shot nervous glances between one another. They could tell something wasn't right with Adrastus. She needed to get him into the tent before anyone dared suggest anything dangerous. If they knew his Unseelie magic was overtaking his mind, then they might try to expel him from the camp. They would make her choose between him or them.

She added quickly, drawing the officers' attention back to her, "Act with haste. I do not want Samael to have any more advantage over us than he already does. As soon as the men are fed and rested, we must go back out there. Any who are willing and ready to fight will be called to the gates at sunrise."

They nodded in understanding, but a few of them cast one last wary look at Adrastus. Kelera stepped between them without thinking. Nothing would make her betray him. She swore to never leave him behind again. Once free of the men, she grabbed hold of Adrastus and ushered him into the tent adorned with the Queen's crest.

She closed the flap behind them and secured it with a tie. Adrastus stood awkwardly in the middle of the makeshift room, as if clueless about what he should do. Kelera lit three tall candles on the small wooden table someone had placed beside the bed for her and grabbed hold of his chin. She drew it down to look into his eyes. They stared right through her, coated in shadows.

"Dras?" she asked with more of a bite than she intended.

No answer. His mouth was turned down slightly, and his brows were knitted together. What was going on inside his mind that had him so out of it?

She tried again, "Adrastus. Talk to me. I know you're in there somewhere. You need to be strong. Fight it." Her body ached with exhaustion, but she stayed firm. "Ragnor is gone. Taken from the living. From us. King Tristan has been executed. The mortals are in disarray, our army is battered. And I need you with me, Dras. Do you hear me?"

When he didn't answer again, she changed her approach. Standing on her tippy toes, she placed a light kiss on his mouth. Still no reaction.

Huffing out a frustrated sigh, she released her hold on him and took a step back. Their bond had been strong enough to stop him on the battlefield. But it wasn't enough to snap him out of this strange daze.

The flap tore open, and Kelera turned quickly, placing herself in front of Adrastus. If they were coming for him, they would have to go through their Queen. A head of stark white hair ducked into the tent. Gadreel lacked his usual luster as he stepped inside. He kept a safe distance between her and Adrastus. And concern clouded his eyes as he took in his brother's demeanor.

Defensively, Kelera said, "He'll be fine."

Gadreel shook his head. "I thought the destruction I saw out there in the healing tents was bad. But this," he gestured to Adrastus, "is *bad*, Kelera. This is the thing I've feared the most."

Kelera backed closer to Adrastus until she was close enough to reach a hand around to him. "Gadreel," she warned, "we will snap him out of it. It will all be okay."

Gadreel's eyes widened. "Look at him. He's trapped inside his mind. It's only a matter of time before something sets him off. What if he hurts someone? What if he hurts *you*?"

Kelera clenched her jaw, then replied, "We saved him before. I was able to break the curse. We can do it like before." It sounded like Gadreel had already given up. But he wasn't there on the battlefield. Adrastus had shielded her, even in his stupor. He'd snapped out of it long enough for her to get them both to safety. He wasn't lost to them. He couldn't be.

Gadreel tensed. "Kelera, I found someone that may help. I hoped it wouldn't come to that... but I need you to keep an open mind."

Her words were laced with fire and ice as she said, "Then what are you waiting for? Retrieve them. Now."

Surprise flickered across his face, and he took a cautious step back. He paused for a moment and responded cautiously, "It may take some time."

Kelera glared at him. Then, with a nod, he turned to exit the tent, leaving her and Adrastus alone. She pushed him gently on the shoulders, steering him to the bed. He sat obediently with his hands on his lap. They were clenched into tight fists and the magic bound to hers felt just as taut.

"I'll be back." She kissed him on the forehead and laid him down on the bed. Tucking him in safely, she whispered, "Stay here. Rest. I will return soon."

Her breathing was erratic as she left the tent, securing it shut behind her. Turning to the guards posted outside, she commanded, "No one is to go into this tent. Understood? If Prince Adrastus wakes or if Prince Gadreel returns, alert me immediately."

They nodded in unison, and it gave her enough confidence to head to the healer's tent. As much as she wanted to stay with Adrastus, she had a duty to her men as well. She needed to see to it that they were being cared for. And they needed to witness her standing tall, now more than ever. If she showed the turmoil she was feeling on the inside, then they might lose any fighting spirit they had left.

As she made her way across camp, she stopped to speak with men and women from the Seelie army. She checked on the solitary Fae who were camped near the other Lesser Fae. They were all mingling with one another. Men with antlers protruding from tufts of hair on their heads swapped cards near a warm fire. Dryads lounged lazily on hammocks, speaking with dashing Summer Fae who had scales along their arms.

Even the High Fae were sitting and eating or drinking with witches and stout bogies. If they'd had their differences before, they weren't present here and now. Fighting alongside one another would do that. It created bonds that could not be broken.

Friendships like the one she and Adrastus had made with the Guardians. A sob slipped from her lips. Ragnor. By the fates. She'd been so worried about Adrastus and overwhelmed with plans for the next attack that she hadn't allowed herself to think of Ragnor's downfall in detail. Images of his gruesome demise filled her mind, and it was all she could do to keep walking.

A Seelie woman with flowing raven hair was hurrying to one of the tents with a tray of pitchers. Kelera jogged to catch up with her. Her voice shook as she asked, "The Guardians? Jinx and Tepin... have you seen them?"

The woman's mouth popped open in surprise and she gave Kelera a clumsy curtsey, nearly spilling the pitchers in her hands. Kelera reached out to right the tray before it could fall. The woman gave her a grateful, halfhearted smile and said, "Two of the Guardians returned. They are being patched up as we speak. The third though..."

Kelera didn't wait for her to finish. She already knew the fate of the third Guardian. She bolted to the healer's tent and was confronted with the destruction caused by Samael's army. The soldiers outside had looked worn and tired. Many had been coated in blood and sweat, but they still had life in them. But the Fae in this tent were teetering on the edge. They were beaten and wounded. Some made pained noises, but others were silent. As if they were waiting patiently in line to reach the hollow beneath the ash trees. How many here would meet the Elders by the end of the night?

Kelera stifled a cry and caught hold of one of the healers. The man's expression changed from determined and focused to relieved. He smiled. "Your Majesty. I heard you had returned but seeing you with my own eyes brings me joy like you couldn't imagine. The injured could benefit from a boost of morale."

She sucked in a swift breath. "I will visit each one. But first, have you seen the Guardians? Two of them came in and—"

"Over here, Your Grace." He led her to a dark corner where Tepin and Jinx were lying.

Once he was gone, Kelera knelt between the two beds, reaching out a hand to each of her friends. They sat up, shocked by her presence, but before they had a chance to speak, she started, "I am so sorry. I failed you. I failed Ragnor. It's my fault."

Tepin and Jinx gave each other a wild look. Jinx barked out a laugh so loud Kelera was convinced he'd lost his mind. Tepin chuckled too. She couldn't comprehend it. Had they, too, lost their minds on the battlefield?

She stammered, "I d-don't understand."

Tepin gave her a lopsided grin and his dark eyes crinkled at the corners. "Firstly, there was nothing you could have done. If Adrastus had released you from the shield, then it would have only put your life in jeopardy, along with ours."

Jinx spoke in agreement. "Our job was to clear the way for you, and that's what we did."

Her heart felt like it was breaking. "But Ragnor..."

Tepin held up a bruised hand. "Ragnor fought valiantly and was rewarded for it."

Kelera pinched the bridge of her nose. He'd been killed. Violently. How was that a reward? They continued to stare at her, as if waiting for her to catch up. Realization dawned, and it was as if a weight was lifted off her chest. She whispered, "The Hunt."

Jinx laid back on his pillows with his hands behind his head and said, "Indeed. Saw it with my own eye. Rag received his steed and sword. He rides with Woden here on out." There was a hint of jealousy in his words and now it was Kelera who felt like laughing.

Instead, tears of relief streamed down her face. Her friend lived on with the most prestigious protectors of the land. He had achieved his lifelong dream and now rode with Chaz and the Wild Hunt. She should have known. But the chaos of it all had overshadowed the realization.

After a brief reunion with Tepin and Jinx, she excused herself to make her rounds in the tent. She took her time speaking to each Fae even if they were lost to unconsciousness. She hoped they could all hear her words of thanks and encouragement. But by the end, the words felt hollow to her. They'd been defeated, and it was hard not to blame herself for it. She was their Queen. It was her duty to ensure their victory.

Kelera wiped the sweat from her brow as she slipped out of the tent. It was getting late and her stomach grumbled with hunger. Adrastus must have been hungry by now as well. So she grabbed two bowls of steaming stew from the cook and walked to her tent. The mixture smelled delicious, but it was mostly broth. With Samael's frost eating away at the land, they were forced to ration their reserves. Meat and vegetables would be hard to come by and if they didn't defeat Samael soon, her people would starve.

When she reached her campsite, she stopped abruptly. Gadreel, Oliver, and a familiar elderly woman were waiting for her. Her heart raced as the woman turned to her and smiled. Spiderweb wrinkles crinkled around her narrowed eyes. The witch. The one who had recently haunted her dream. The woman's knotted, tangled hair was longer than the last time Kelera had seen her in real life. Twelve... no. Thirteen years? Was that how long it had been since the witch had tried to steal her away to take her to Elfhame?

The witch spoke with a voice that sounded far younger than she looked as she said, "Hello little fire starter, it has been a long time."

The bowls of stew dropped from Kelera's hand, splashing its contents against her boots. She bared her teeth and readied her magic. This woman was no friend to her. And Kelera did not doubt that she was here now for Adrastus.

Chapter Twenty-One

Kelera couldn't believe what she was seeing. After all these years, the woman who had tried to lure her back to Elfhame was here. The very same one who had threatened her and her father with the prophecy. The old crone had no business here in Kelera's camp. And she certainly had no business being this close to Adrastus when he was in his shadowy state.

Through clenched teeth, Kelera said, "You are not welcome here."

The woman gave her a bold smile. "You should be thanking me."

Power flashed at Kelera's hands, dancing along her fingertips. "Thank you? For trying to take me away from my father as a child?"

The woman batted at the air and shrugged her shoulders. "I was simply seeking to do your mother a favor. She was frightened of the prophecy. But if you would have come with me to be returned to your rightful place, then you would have been prepared for this." She gestured beyond the gates and to the tent with a slender arm. "You would have been prepared for *him*."

Kelera balked. Was she referring to Samael or Adrastus? Unsure of the answer, and unwilling to ask, she simply stated, "I did not need your help then and I do not need it now." She pushed past the witch and Gadreel. He stumbled back into Oliver, who caught him with graceful hands.

She sighed with relief when she saw Adrastus resting peacefully on the bed. But the shuffle of boots grated on her nerves as the three unwelcomed guests staggered in. She knelt beside Adrastus, brushing his hair from his forehead and spoke over her shoulder, "What are you still doing here, Gadreel?"

"I am trying to help, Kelera."

"I told you, it's going to be fine." The words sounded empty, even to her. Nothing about this was okay. She was in over her head. With the war. With Adrastus. All of it. But the witch was like a nightmare come to life. She'd frightened Kelera as a child. So much so that she had made a promise to her father to never use her magic again. Seeing her now brought back too many awful feelings. How could she trust her to help with Adrastus?

Gadreel knelt beside her and she softened as he put his arm around her, drawing her into him. She'd been putting on a brave face in the camp, scared that if her weakness showed through the cracks in her facade that everything else would come crashing down. The generals agreed that they should leave at first light. But how could she endure this battle knowing that Adrastus was losing himself to the darkness he'd always feared?

Gadreel's voice was soft as he said, "We are here to help, Kelera. I love him too and I would never do anything to harm him. Please, listen to what she has to say."

Kelera whispered angrily, "The Elders told me we would need to rely on friends to give light to his darkness. What makes you think we can trust *her*?"

"Because she is here. Just talking to me marks her as a traitor in Samael's eyes."

"And if she is here *because* of Samael? Who's to say he isn't the one who sent her?"

Gadreel groaned in frustration. "What other options do we have?"

Adrastus stirred slightly. "Kelera?"

By the stars, he was awake. And talking to her! She leapt toward him. "I'm here, Dras!"

He scrunched his brow in pain. "Ragnor and the others... What have I done?"

Ignoring the knots in her stomach that still lingered at witnessing Ragnor's bloody end, Kelera reassured him, "Jinx and Tepin are alright. I was just with them."

A tear streamed down his face, following the trail of his scar. "Ragnor?"

She bit her lip, reluctant to answer. "He fell to the Night Rider's sword." The pain of begging Adrastus to go back for him was still fresh in her mind, but Adrastus was the type to allow guilt to eat him up. There was no need for her to voice what they were both already thinking.

Softening at the shame on Adrastus' face, she quickly added, "He rides with the Wild Hunt now. He is with Chaz. Tepin and Jinx saw it all happen."

Adrastus mumbled something and buried his face in her hands. His shoulders shook, and she strained to make out his words, but could only catch bits and pieces. "So sorry... Monster... Destroying my mind..."

Gadreel turned and gestured for the witch to come closer. Kelera watched her with guarded eyes. She would give the old woman no indication that she desperately wanted someone to aid them. Not until she knew what the witch had in mind.

The woman struggled to kneel to the ground with a hand supporting her hip. Adrastus looked up in surprise, but didn't appear to be afraid of the woman. Perhaps he'd had more experience in dealing with solitary Fae like her. But Kelera knew that they were outcasts in society. Sent away from their homes and forced to wander because of the unstable nature of their magic.

The witch cocked her head to the side and spoke to Adrastus. "All is not lost, boy."

He leaned forward. "You can stop it?"

"No."

His face fell in a look of despair, and Kelera had a mind to boot her out of the tent. If she couldn't save him, then why was she here?

The witch amended her statement, "But *she* can." She tilted her head in Kelera's direction.

Kelera wanted to shake her for playing coy. "How?"

The witch spoke thoughtfully. "Your magic is already connected through the binding ceremony you performed in the Summer Court. But as a Prince of Unseelie, his power is attached to his father's royal bloodline. It is potent and unstable. The only thing that has been keeping it in check was the balance each of your Seelie magic was giving it."

Kelera pushed her hair from her face, doing anything she could to keep from losing patience. She snapped, "May I remind you that we are running out of time?"

The witch ignored her and continued, "Between the frost that weakens the Seelie magic and the amount of Seelie power it took the prince to heal from his recent wound... If he goes back into battle and uses his Unseelie magic at its full strength, then the binding will not be enough to protect his mind."

Kelera took a deep breath in, willing herself not to knock the witch on her ass. "Then what is it you propose?" She knew as well as they, that Adrastus would not sit the battle out. Nor would he hold back the full force of his power if it meant ending Samael's life.

The witch spoke with a superior tone that made Kelera want to slap her. "There is another ceremony that would bind his magic to the Seelie crown. He would not be able to wield it, but it would make him stronger in other ways. It would give him strength and agility. It will also tip the scales of his warring magic in the favor of the Seelie. And if I am correct in my belief, it will connect him to it like an anchor. Tethering him to you. Just as the binding ceremony bound your magic and souls, this one would bind your hearts. Giving your light to his darkness in the most powerful way," she paused, shooting a haughty look in Kelera's direction before continuing, "thus rendering his Unseelie magic the weaker of his two sides."

Goosebumps covered Kelera's arms. She couldn't deny the similarity in what the Elders had told her, claiming she *had the ability to shine a light on that darkness*. But this sounded too good to be true. Too simple. The binding ceremony they performed while on the run from Samael and his bounty hunters had been dangerous. But she'd do it again in a heartbeat. Whatever it took. Adrastus, however, gave her pause. His eyes were narrowed as he stared at the woman and there was a twitch in his jaw.

Kelera didn't understand what was holding him back. She encouraged him, "Dras, we can do it. This could be the answer."

He took her face in his hands. "Do you understand what she's suggesting, little thief?"

Kelera searched his face for an answer. When she found none, she replied, "A binding ceremony. Like the one we did in the Summer Court..."

The witch's cackle rippled through the tent. "Oh, silly halfling child. It is not *that* type of binding ceremony. It is..."

"A wedding ceremony," Adrastus finished.

Kelera could do nothing but stare at them all in disbelief. From the lack of surprise she found on each of their faces, it was obvious that they had known what the witch was going to suggest.

She took a few steps away from them all and cleared her throat. "So, you're saying either Adrastus and I bind ourselves in marriage or else he will lose himself to the darkness?"

The witch smiled in satisfaction. "That is precisely what I am saying."

Kelera marched up to the woman with her head held high. Best that she remind the witch that she was speaking to the Queen of Seelie. "And it is no trick? No ploy with strings attached?" The witch shook her head. But Kelera wasn't convinced yet. She needed more. "Why come here and help us? You are a solitary Fae. You owe loyalty to no court or crown. Why would you help us?"

This time, the witch didn't respond with smugness. Her eyes narrowed, and she flashed blackened teeth in a sneer. "Because the Unseelie King took something from me long ago. Something I can never get back. I want to see him suffer for it." She hesitated, softening a bit before adding, "Besides, I never have been a fan of harsh winters. I much prefer the heat of summer."

Her words, though simple, had meaning behind them. Perhaps solitary Fae did have loyalty to the courts, after all. A remanent of their past—of the homes they'd fled long ago. Had she been born to the Summer Court? Had she called it home before time and hardships had turned her into what she was today?

Regardless, it gave Kelera a sense of peace. She and Adrastus had already performed a ceremony that bound them for life. Some would claim that the binding was stronger than even marriage. And this was different, wasn't it? She *loved* him. It had been her intention all along to spend the rest of her days with him if they succeeded against Samael. If the power she'd inherited from her mother was the only thing that could quell the darkness he battled with once and for all, then wasn't it worth it?

She nodded to Adrastus. "I'll do it. I'll marry you."

His eyes went wide in surprise, and he glanced at the small audience—Gadreel, Oliver, and the witch, all smiled softly back at him in encouragement.

But Adrastus didn't return the smile. Instead, he waved a hand at them as he bristled, "Out."

They responded immediately, obeying the man who was, after all, royalty in his own right. Gadreel lingered at the tent's entrance and glanced back once more. A mix of emotions played across his face, making it hard for Kelera to read him. Was he worried Adrastus would say no? She hadn't considered the possibility of it or the humiliation that it would bring her. It had been bold of her to assume that he would want to marry her. Just because he loved her and wanted to be with her... The tent felt like it was closing in on her as Gadreel left them alone.

Adrastus' back was turned to her, and his silence was deafening. He was questioning them. He had to be. But why? She took a step forward. If he was too stubborn to reveal what was on his mind, then she would be the first to speak. "Dras, I don't see what has you so—"

He rounded on her in frustration. "This isn't how it was supposed to go."

"I know things didn't go the way we wanted on the battlefield today, but if we do this... if we can do something to protect you from overwhelming yourself when we go back out there, then we can do what we came here to do."

"It's not that." Shadows danced over his cheeks and the bridge of his nose in the candlelight. It reminded her of the first time she'd seen him in the Autumn forest when nothing but moonlight lit their way.

"Then what? Are you frightened that you won't be as strong without your Unseelie magic at full strength? Because

I've seen your Seelie power and it is just as capable of standing against your brother. You don't have to rely on the shadows—"

His frustration reached its limit as he nearly shouted, "The marriage! The proposal. Or lack thereof. This isn't how I imagined it would go." He ticked the list off on his fingers as he said, "Defeat Samael. Solidify your position as ruler of Elfhame. Make it safe for you and everyone else. Only *then* could I find a way to ask for your hand in a manner worthy of you." He was breathless as he finished.

Kelera's heart fluttered in her chest like a bird trying to take flight. A warm blush crept across her face as she asked, "So, you do want to marry me?"

He exhaled heavily. "That's what you took away from my speech?"

"It was the only thing that mattered." She closed the gap between them, reaching up to place both hands over his heart. "What better time than now to declare our love to the world? If it works like the witch promises, then you will remain *you* out on that battlefield. I almost lost you to the Night Rider curse, and I can't do that again, Dras. I can't watch you slip away."

"Kelera, I do not want you to marry me out of fear." He caressed her hands from the tips of her fingers down to her wrists. There was both strength and tenderness in the touch and it made her weak in the knees.

"Surely, you do not believe that's what this is. I accepted an engagement out of duty and fear once before, and it almost cost me everything." She thought bitterly of Alexander and his betrayal and shuddered. "I would never put myself in that position again. I would marry you for love. Because I want to be with you. To rule with you, because I trust and admire you. Saving your soul is just an added bonus." She gave him a wink.

He chuckled as he leaned in to kiss her. "That's a hell of a proposal, little thief." His fingers grazed the points of her ears as he cradled her head in his calloused hands. The moment might not have been what she imagined, but then again, things with Adrastus never were.

She pulled away slightly and peeked up at him. "So, you'll do it?"

He ran his hands through her hair, tangling his fingers in her wild waves. "Of course I will."

***

Kelera struggled to contain the butterflies dancing in her stomach. As she walked down the frosted path leading to where she would find Adrastus, she masked her exhilaration beneath a subtle smile. The last mask she would ever wear, she promised herself. And in this instance, it was for the benefit of those around her. The loss of friends and family was still heavy on all of their hearts after the battle with Samael. But still, any who could stand had come to the makeshift altar to see their Queen married.

As she rounded the crowd of Fae, her father's absence sunk in. Had they been in Nevene, he would have stepped in to walk her down the aisle to her future husband. Her ribs felt tight, restricting her breath. She tugged at the collar of her vest with a shaking hand. A few of the Fae who were blocking her view of Adrastus gave her small, hopeful smiles.

Bothwell wove his way through them. "Kelera, are you alright?"

She blinked away the tears threatening to fall. "It feels like something's missing. I just need a moment to catch my breath."

He studied her for a minute. "You're feeling the absence of family."

"How did you—"

"I'm wiser than I look," he joked, then held his hand out to her. "Having a father walk his daughter down the aisle is a tradition here in Elfhame as well. I know I am not your father, but I would be honored to stand in his place for the day."

Kelera's heart warmed at the gesture. Bothwell had been her mother's most trusted and loyal friend. And the visions under the hill were enough to show her the love they had for one another. It was Bothwell, after all, who had delivered her safely to her father all those years ago. Though it wasn't quite the same as having her own father there to give her away, it was an honor that he was offering.

She placed her trembling hand in his and he wrapped it through his arm. He patted her hand, comforting her enough to continue walking. The crowd parted as she stepped forward, giving her a full view of Adrastus.

Even dressed in his filthy battle jacket, he was magnificent. The white blanket of snow at his feet contrasted against his stark black hair, making him look like a dark winter prince. She gripped Bothwell's arm tighter, suddenly feeling self-conscious about her dirty vest and sweat-stained shirt. But when Adrastus' eyes caught hers, they shimmered like light hitting fresh snow.

When she reached him, she turned and kissed Bothwell's cheek. He blushed as he placed her hand in Adrastus' and backed away to join the onlookers. Adrastus beamed down at her and mouthed, *I love you*. Her cheeks flushed and her pulse raced as she took her place across from him.

Adrastus held her hands as they stood before Gadreel. He and Oliver had done a fine job finding scraps of wood from the surrounding oak trees for the arbor. With the help of others, they had twisted the branches and withering vines together to create a beautiful archway for them to stand under. To Gadreel's dismay, there had been no flowers to gather for a bouquet. They had all wilted under Samael's frost.

Kelera didn't care about the floral arrangements, though. Once upon a time, she had dreamed of the perfect wedding with a lace dress and a big celebration to follow. Similar to the one Cierine had had. Never in her wildest dreams did she picture marrying a Prince of Unseelie in the middle of an army encampment with a winter storm approaching. She'd never considered that her reception full of dancing and feasting would be replaced with a war.

And yet, she was happy. Truly, utterly elated. Adrastus was flawed and sure, he pushed her to her limits at times—usually charming his way out with that dimpled smirk of his. But they had been through so much together and no matter how bad things got, they only came out of it stronger. They relied on each other in a way Kelera had never seen other couples rely on one another. And in their time apart—when she'd returned to the mortal realm—she'd realized just how much she loved him.

That is why, now, under the light of the dawn, she was speaking the words rooted in Elfhame tradition. As Gadreel tied a scrap of green cloth around hers and Adrastus' hands, a jolt of power shuddered down her arms. It flowed through the soft pads of her palms and into Adrastus.' The power that belonged to him but resided in her veins from their previous binding, expanded, filling all of her senses.

Shadows swirled around their hands, following the path of the ribbon. With a flush of warmth, Kelera's magic met it, glowing brightly as it twisted around the shadows. The dark, smokey tendrils of his Unseelie Power turned white. It was as if her magic was lighting the shadows from within. Gadreel was muttering something, but she couldn't concentrate on the words. The power coursing back and forth between her and Adrastus was too overwhelming.

Focusing on her breathing, she did her best to relax her body and allow the magic to do what it was meant to. The witch had warned them of what to expect, and for that, Kelera was grateful. Adrastus' solid hold on her hands seemed to be the only thing keeping her grounded in the moment. She was lightheaded by the time the spell set in.

She choked back tears as Gadreel pronounced them husband and wife. Adrastus swept her into a kiss, much like she'd seen at mortal weddings. This was not the wedding she had envisioned. One in which Tristan's court all attended to watch her and Alexander say their pre-written vows. There would be no grand reception and she had not worn a beautiful gown.

But none of it mattered as they walked hand in hand back to their tent. They had bound their magic, their souls, and now their hearts. Nothing could break that. *Not even death.*

The rosy, pink light of dawn peeked through the cracks of the canvas tent, casting a soft glow on the bed where Adrastus was waiting for her. He'd shed both his jacket and his pants, leaving him looking like a marble statue. Kelera slipped from her own clothes and stood before him. He reached for her, placing his powerful hands on the small of her back.

She trailed her fingers over his body, noting each scar, both old and new. As she traced them, she couldn't help but wonder what stories lingered behind each and every one of them. She wanted to know everything about him. All of his triumphs and defeats. But there was so much uncertainty—a battle that still needed to be fought—she feared she'd never get the chance.

Her voice was hoarse as she said, "If we don't survive this—"

Adrastus placed a finger on her lips. "Stay in this moment, little thief."

She grabbed his hand, kissing the finger that still rested on her lips. Staying present in this moment with him would be her wedding gift to him. So, she allowed the rest to slip away, thinking only of the way her new husband smiled at her—as if she were the most magnificent thing he'd ever laid eyes on.

He lowered his hand and drew her into him. She settled over him, lingering just high enough to tease him with the promise of what she had to offer. Pressure built below her naval as his hand made its way between her thighs.

He let out a soft growl as his fingers slid along her skin, meeting its mark. Her body melted into his touch until he rolled on top of her. The scent of sweat and blood filled her nose and she could hear Fae preparing for battle outside of the tent.

They would have to join them soon. Choosing to make the most of their time, she tilted her hips toward Adrastus in a silent signal for him to take her. He swept into her, meeting her desire with his own. And just like that, she felt more complete than she had in her entire life.

Adrastus was the missing piece to her, and she was his. The fates had intended them to collide with one another, and what had been born out of that was something far greater than a marriage of convenience. She would have married him whether or not his magic was a threat. It wasn't about that for her.

As she looked into his stunning green eyes, she saw every-thing she had ever hoped for. Let people think whatever they wanted about their union. This was so much bigger than their prejudices and fears. The Seelie would come to know him and once they did, she had no doubt they would accept him just as she did. After all, who better to rule and unite Elfhame than a Seelie Queen and a Prince of Unseelie?

Chapter Twenty-Two

With her new husband by her side and a refreshed army at her back, Kelera had never felt more empowered. Even with Samael's massive force within view, hope swelled in her chest. She had seen to it that the men and women fighting for her were rested and well fed. Samael's force, on the other hand, looked as if they were the walking dead.

The Unseelie Fae standing across the field were a haggard-looking bunch. Their faces were gaunt and even from the Spring forest, she could spot the dark circles of exhaustion around their eyes. Samael had torn down the trees on the Spring and Autumn border, opening up the space that would host their final battle. And from the looks of his men, he'd forced them to do all the work.

She gritted her teeth and turned to her army. They were doing a fine job of hiding their fears and insecurities as they stared down the Unseelie with a ferocity she had never witnessed before. Adrenaline vibrated through her as the commanders shouted words of encouragement to them.

Adrastus grabbed her shaking hand and squeezed. Her gaze met his in silent solidarity. She was still floating on air after their time together in the tent. When euphoria had seized them both, they had left the bed with a kiss. One full of promises. Promises of what could be if they succeeded today.

Samael's voice carried across the field as he shouted to his men. Rather than look emboldened by their leader's words, they flinched with fear. She felt a tinge of sympathy for them as she studied their faces. They clearly had no love for their king. If only there was a way to sway them to her side. To get them to lay down their arms.

Adrastus pointed to the tall man who stepped up beside Samael. Golden hair and a chiseled face. Herald. Kelera was caught off guard at the sudden tightness in her rib cage. After the attempts on her life, she shouldn't have been surprised at the betrayal. But here it was anyway, rearing its ugly head and leaving her feeling vulnerable and foolish.

If anyone in the council or court had doubted his traitorous intentions before, they would not be able to deny them now. Heat rose to Kelera's face. It sickened her to see the man who had shared a life with her mother, who had shared her bed... standing beside the enemy. The Elders were right when they said not all Seelie were good. Even though she had believed it when they told her, it was painful to witness it firsthand.

Under her breath, she said, "He'll pay a price for this."

There was a hint of pride in Adrastus' voice as he responded, "Spoken like a true Fae."

Kelera shot him a half smirk. He'd once told her a debt to Unseelie cannot go unpaid. She had been the one to pay that price. But today, she would be the one to collect.

Mira stepped up beside her. Her cheeks were wet with the morning dew, and she looked incredibly out of place. Still, she did not tremble as she observed, "The mortal army is not here. Do you think Samael is planning another ambush?"

Kelera narrowed her eyes. Samael enjoyed his games, but something in her gut advised her that he was ready for this particular match to be over with. She'd surprised him the day before when she blasted him with her power. Perhaps even frightened him.

She shook her head. "I think this is his final move. Today will determine the fate of Elfhame."

It was odd, though. Where had the mortals gone? With King Tristan dead, there was no one left to lead them into battle. Samael had gotten what he wanted. With Tristan out of the way, he should have been able to claim the mortal court for himself. But what of Cierine? By birth right, she was now Queen. Kelera's stomach felt heavy and fear for her best friend jolted through her. Had he done something to her? If he'd hurt her, Kelera would tear his heart from his chest.

A horn trumpeted from the Unseelie lines, and Mira turned to whisper something to Diana. The two of them embraced. It was a passionate kiss of lovers parting. Burdened with the possibility of never being reunited with one another again. Kelera looked away, wanting to give the women their moment.

She, however, didn't kiss Adrastus. *No goodbyes*. That's what he had told her in their tent after the ceremony. Goodbye meant accepting that they might not make it home. They would not allow themselves to believe for a second that they may not be reunited in the end.

Kelera raised her sword. The one her father had gifted to her when she was young. There was no doubt in her mind that it would bring her luck and courage. As she lifted the gleaming blade to the sky, her army roared. Even the stone giants and tree-like men cried out. It was a fearsome sound that shocked the very earth beneath their feet, rocking the Unseelie a few steps back.

Adrastus said under his breath, "See you on the other side, little thief."

And with that, she swiped her sword downward, signaling for her army to attack. Their war cries were wholehearted as they ran full speed in the direction of their enemy. They swept past her in a blur. Their instructions were clear. They were to hold off the Unseelie for as long as possible. Defend themselves to the fullest, but take prisoners alive if possible. She had no desire to slaughter half of Elfhame. If anyone could be turned to their side, then she would welcome them with open arms.

She and Adrastus, however, held back. Samael was their concern. Get to him. Kill him. End this before any more lives were lost than necessary. Getting to him would be the trickiest part. That is why two forest giants stood on either side of them as they crossed the field. The Unseelie were either too frightened of the enormous bark covered men, or they were knocked away as easily as a hand swatting at a fly.

Samael was standing on his mound of earth, just as he had been the day before. Kelera scoffed. At least he was predictable. She and Adrastus were silent as they walked. Samael had spent his life shaping himself into the perfect predator. But today, it was his turn to be the prey. She was a huntress. Skilled and precise with the power of the crown strengthening both her magic and Adrastus'. Since the ceremony, his Unseelie power—his shadows and ice—had felt like waters after a storm. Calm, but deadly.

They reached Samael's last line of defense. Night Riders stood like a shield wall at the bottom of the mound. Their cloaks were soaked with sweat and their steeds bounced on anxious feet. She smiled at them. She'd defeated them enough times by now that they were starting to lose their nightmarish appeal.

As planned, she whistled loudly, signaling to Woden and the Wild Hunt that she and Adrastus had reached their destination. Hoofbeats pounded in the sky as the Hunt burst through the snowy clouds and circled above. Ragnor caught her eye and gave her a flirtatious wink. Her smile broadened and relief flooded through her. He and Chaz were the first to attack. They rode low enough to slash two of the Night Riders with their shining swords.

Samael scowled. With a snap of his fingers, a small group of the Night Riders ascended to the sky, meeting the Wild Hunt in battle. The remaining Riders stood still, ready to protect their master. It was a problem, but only a minor one.

Shutting her eyes in concentration, Kelera imagined a cavernous hole under their feet, big enough to swallow them whole. The earth rumbled in response, but it was not like the first time she'd done it in the village. The ground here was so hard, it was like chipping away at ice. She peeked through her lashes to see Samael's hands extended.

She snarled, "He's fighting my magic." Her breath caught in her throat as she tried to speak through the strain of it. "Freezing the ground..."

"Then we fight ice with fire." Adrastus took hold of her hand and their Seelie magic sparked like they were using a flint to light a campfire.

Sweat dripped down her back. "His magic is too strong here."

Adrastus reassured her, "We are stronger, Kelera. You know we are."

As she tried to regain her confidence, Samael yelled to his Night Riders, "Bring them to me! Alive!"

Metal scraped against bone as the Night Riders slammed their spurs into their steeds. With pained cries, the horses stampeded toward her and Adrastus. If they engaged in battle with them, then they would have to abandon their attempt to thaw the ground. They would have to take all of them on at once.

Having no other choice, Kelera released Adrastus' hand and drew her sword. A Night Rider with hollowed cheeks and scabs along his forehead rode between her and Adrastus, separating them. With a curse, Kelera spun around to regain her bearings.

The Night Riders were closing in, but a hard, feminine voice stole their attention. Kelera's heart fluttered at the sound of her best friend shouting over the chaos of battle. Cierine's golden pony danced around as she spoke. "King Samael, you are hereby found guilty of regicide! A heinous crime that will not go unpunished."

Then the most wonderful sight appeared beside her friend. The pooka who had risked itself more than once to help Kelera dug its hooves into the ground. When her eyes rose to the rider, a wave of elation hit her. Her father took his place beside Cierine. His shirt was soaked through with sweat, but his eyes were hard and determined. He sat tall on the pooka's back with his sword drawn. The sword that matched her own in every way except size.

Samael tilted his head from side to side in a steady rhythm, as if weighing his options. He rested his maimed hand on his hip and tapped it. A wave of nausea rolled inside of Kelera's stomach as she noticed the blackened skin around his severed fingers. Signs of frostbite she'd only seen in the healer books in the Nevene library. She felt dizzy at the thought of him healing himself with his ice magic. It was barbaric compared to the purifying healing powers of the Seelie Court.

Kelera's racing heart drowned out all the noise until Samael chuckled from the mound. He was still safe from her wrath as his Night Riders stood between them, and he didn't look the least bit nervous at the arrival of his prior allies. Instead, he wore the infuriating sneer she had seen so often in the Winter Palace. The one that revealed just how ready he was to see the carnage unfold.

Cierine didn't let it stop her. Her red hair was free from its clasp and flew wildly around her. It whipped around the crown she now carried on her head. Tristan's crown. Kelera couldn't help but stare in awe. King Tristan had been young when he was crowned. Though Cierine was next in line for the throne, he still could have produced an heir. Kelera never thought she would see the day when her best friend would take the Nevene crown.

And she looked absolutely stunning under it. Like she'd been made for this. Maybe she had. Fate, after all, had a funny habit of unfolding in the unlikeliest ways. Kelera knew that now.

She hung on Cierine's every word as she continued to speak with authority, "As Queen of Nevene of the mortal realm, I hereby pledge my allegiance to Queen Kelera!" The mortal army shook in anticipation, with their weapons already drawn. Cierine raised her own sword high in the air.

The battle had stilled slightly at her speech. Unseelie and Seelie alike gave pause as they waited to watch the tides of battle turn. Even Adrastus was stone still and seemed to be holding his breath as Cierine declared, "Samael, malevolent Prince of Unseelie, you have subjected my people... and your own, to your mistreatment for long enough." She paused and looked out at the battlefield. "Abandon him and his vicious visions of the world. Do what you know in your heart is right. Stand with Queen Kelera as I do."

Kelera's eyes darted from one Unseelie soldier to the next. Most of their faces were emotionless, like the mask of indifference she herself had worn many times. But there were a few who allowed signs of their true feelings to slip through. A nose flare or a twitch in their jaw.

Samael laughed bitterly. "You think I am frightened by a *mortal* queen and her grand words? For that's all they are. Words. Perhaps we should allow our actions to speak for us instead." He extended his hands above his head and the clouds darkened in response. They spread across the sky, blotting out any ray of sunlight. The temperature dropped, chilling Kelera down to her bones.

His Night Riders screeched as hail began to fall from above. It plummeted below, hitting any who were unlucky enough to be in its path. Adrastus' shadow magic tugged at her power, instinctually trying to place a shield around them. But it buckled under the Seelie suppression. To allow it the freedom it needed to protect them, Kelera imagined the protective binding untangling like a fishing line being loosened. The shadows seeped from Adrastus, rising above them in a thin veil.

Kelera studied his eyes. They were clear as the Summer Court sea. Still, she asked, "All good?"

Adrastus gave her a relieved smile. "Better than ever."

It was working! The strength of the royal Seelie magic was allowing him to access his Unseelie power, but was still keeping it dimmed enough that it wouldn't overpower him. Relief didn't begin to cover what she was feeling.

The Night Riders proceeded to antagonize them, but before they could do any real damage, Cierine's army charged. The full force of the mortals was enough to distract the Riders. Kelera grabbed hold of Adrastus and pulled him through. They ducked and dodged as the cursed Fae fought off Cierine's army and the Wild Hunt that had come to her aid.

When they reached the mound, Samael welcomed them with his arms dramatically held wide. "Ah, my brother, and his *whore*."

"Wife," Adrastus corrected.

Samael's eyebrows shot up in shock. "Wife? You're telling me you married this halfling *queen*?" He spat the word in a mocking tone, and Kelera clenched her jaw in response.

She cocked her head to the side and challenged him. "Jealous?" She shivered at the memories of the times Samael had pressed his body against hers and of the threats he had made. But she wasn't about to let it show.

He narrowed his eyes. "You are an imposter. You may wear the Seelie crown, but at the end of the day you are still a scared little girl playing dress up." He paused, then cooed, "But don't worry, when I claim this realm, I will claim you with it. I'm sure I can find something more fitting to dress you up in."

Adrastus clenched his fists, but interrupted coolly, "It is over, brother."

Samael rolled his eyes. "Look around. The mortal bitch's speech did nothing to sway my men. Even with the force that you have here today, you cannot defeat me. My magic has torn its way through the earth down into the heart of Elfhame. There isn't a thing you can do now to change that. This world is mine."

Kelera glanced back at the battle and was met with a wave of nausea. Fae on both sides were falling to magic and sword. Her army was fighting valiantly, but they were tired. Their movements were slower than before, as if their limbs were weighing them down. Any magic they tried to wield sputtered and faltered. They were not used to fighting with their swords and it was wearing on them.

When she wasn't looking, Dodger and her father had taken to the battlefield and were leading the mortal men. Only this time, they were fighting alongside the Seelie. Kelera should have rejoiced at the sight, but in the end they would be no match for the Unseelie. It would only add to the number of lives lost because of her.

She swallowed the large lump in her throat. She couldn't draw on the land or help the Seelie and mortals struggling behind her, but she still had the magic she'd been born with inside her. Magic that was linked to Adrastus until death. With that and the power of her mother's crown, *she* could turn the tide of this war herself.

She returned her gaze to Samael. He was wicked and unworthy. She had faced the Elders. They had chosen her for this moment. And she was going to revel in every second of it. With determination, she summoned the power made stronger by the inherited magic passed through centuries of royals. Burrowing it deep into the ground—through the frost and the ice, down into the warm center where the Elders and the dead resided—she spread it along the roots and through each grain of dirt until it touched everything within her reach.

Her eyes darkened with brilliant shades of red and gold—a sign of the power of Elfhame and the Elders showing through—as she extended her consciousness into the world around her. It reached out, extending her influence throughout the realm. Sharing in the power held by all who were born of the land. Like opening a curtain, she connected with its creatures. The fenrir, giants, and wildlife were all a part of her and she them.

A flood of emotions rushed through her as their anger and anguish filled her soul. She knew what they longed for. Every wish they'd ever made, every silent plea to the Elders... it all echoed in her mind as loud and desperate as if she had made them herself. She knew what they needed to do.

Her eyes met Samael's, and she found pure fear. The sort of fear he'd delighted in making others feel all these centuries. A smile spread across her face. His Night Riders were the only thing standing between them, and now she had the numbers they required to destroy them.

Recalling the pain and torment the cursed Fae had caused, she channeled her anger at them. Then, licking her lips and never breaking eye contact with Samael, she whispered to her new soldiers, "Kill."

Chapter Twenty-Three

The chaos Kelera had set in motion rivaled that of anything Samael ever could have done. Her call to the creatures of Elfhame had rang loud, echoing through the land like a siren calling to a fleet of ships. Animals and Fae beasts she had only seen mentioned in story books swarmed the battlefield.

They fought against the Unseelie with vigor and courage, tipping the odds in her favor. Fangs met flesh, tearing and slashing until there was nothing but white bone left. Large birds with flaming tales slashed through armor. Even smaller Fae—brownies, goblins, pookas, and many she couldn't put a name to—joined in the fight. They worked together in unison to thwart the Unseelie forces, taking on even the biggest mountain men.

Samael's voice quaked with rage as he turned to Herald and commanded, "Kill my brother. I will deal with the bitch."

Herald was stone-faced as he wielded two glistening axes at Adrastus. With ease, Adrastus dodged each deadly blow. A glow emanated from his hands as he whipped his magic around Herald's wrists, knocking the gleaning blades to the ground. With Herald and Adrastus engaged in hand to hand combat, Kelera focused on Samael.

The blizzard worsened above their heads, sending shivers down to her bones. The heart of the storm was here, with Samael. And it was Kelera's duty to quell it. She ignored the sting of her hair whipping at her face and the grunts of Adrastus and Herald behind her.

Samael's body wavered slightly, slipping halfway into the shadows. *Coward,* Kelera thought bitterly. She wouldn't allow him to give her the slip. Using his own storm against him, she summoned water from the sky. It slammed against him like a wave crashing against a rocky shoreline. Something cracked as he hit the ground under the weight of it. She hoped it was the sound of a bone snapping. The worse this hurt him, the better.

She shouted at him, hoping he was conscious enough to hear. "Surely it should not be so easy to beat down the *King of Elfhame*!" It was her turn to mock.

His icy white hair had come undone from his braids and matted to his face. Water dripped from him, turning to tiny tear shaped icicles and shattering as they touched the ground. Kelera didn't wait for him to make a move. This time, she summoned fire from the sun. It resisted her, struggling to connect with her power through the circling storm.

Samael swayed on unsteady feet. "I should have smothered you in your bed that night."

Kelera recalled the night he had slipped into her room and taken Cierine. She shrugged. "It would have saved you a lot of trouble. But that's your problem, isn't it, Samael? You can't resist a chance at power. You saw me as a tool. A thing you could use to make yourself grander. But instead, you played right into fate's hands."

He responded with shadow magic. Kelera cried out as it knocked her down. The thick, black shadows overwhelmed her, pounding her into the earth and forcing her chin into the frost. Ice cracked under the pressure, shooting pain from her face down to her neck.

Ignoring the sting of it, she stayed focused on her goal. Her palms were slick with sweat as her magic finally grasped a firm hold on the power of the sun. Its heat skimmed along her arms, up to her chest, and into her heart. Just as she had connected with the creatures of Elfhame, lending them the strength of her birth given magic, the sun shared its mighty force with her.

Hot, white light surrounded her, forcing the shadows away from her and casting a glow on the battlefield. Everything went silent and for a moment, it was as if she and Samael were the only two beings in the entire realm. He slashed desperately at the light with his shadows. But they sizzled as they touched the heat surrounding her.

Still, the snowstorm raged beyond her light. It wasn't enough. She needed more. As she stood, she reached further, stretching her power to the heavens. Twinkling starlight tingled against her magic and she knew it was precisely what she required. She sucked in a breath, pulling the power of the Elfhame stars. The stars she had adored since the moment she came to this realm. The stars she and Adrastus made love under. They were hers and she was theirs. They belonged to each other, just as she and Adrastus did.

It all belonged to her. Not Samael. The realm was never his to take. Fate demanded it. Her entire being burned with fire, but it didn't hurt as she would have expected. Every nerve in her body buzzed. She tugged all of it into her, pooling it into her chest, around her rapidly beating heart.

Samael wasn't ready to concede. She couldn't blame him. He had no idea what she was summoning into her. No one did. No one but the Elders who had made their promise all those years ago.

The world will succumb to frost and be reborn in fire.

She was the fire. And it was time to release the flame. The hail and ice falling from the sky faded with each ounce of Elfhame magic she pooled into her. The world darkened as if she were taking it all away. Every sliver of light. Every breath of life. Until there was nothing left.

Her breath hitched in her throat, and for a moment, the world turned upside down. All fighting below the mound ceased as everything around them became blanketed in starlight. Herald grunted, and she turned to find Adrastus drawing his sword away. His knees hit the ground as Herald's lifeless body fell. But there was no pain in Adrastus' eyes. She sighed in relief, realizing he wasn't hurt. He was only kneeling. For her.

Everyone was kneeling to her, both Seelie and Unseelie alike. All except for Samael. He was staring at her as if he would devour her whole if given the chance. Like a snake waiting to snap at its prey. He reached out with trembling hands and cursed when his magic didn't answer his call. But it couldn't. Didn't he understand? She was holding it. She was holding all of it. The magic of the living and dead flowed through her and it was exactly what she needed to fulfill the prophecy.

She'd been born with a flame inside of her. It had driven her to explore as a child, to wonder about the world and the creatures most people in the mortal realm could not see. It had emboldened her in the Winter palace and had connected her with Adrastus. Her power had scared her at first. She hadn't wanted to be the fire that would consume the world. But fire, much like her power, did not mean destruction. Rather, it was creation... a rebirth.

She reached out to the starlight with a careful hand and thought of all the truths that had been revealed to her since coming to Elfhame. Adrastus and the Fae of this land were not the monsters she had believed them to be. The mortals were not her saviors. Perfection was not the answer to her happy ending. And her mother had abandoned her out of love, not hate.

Staring into the starlight, she thought of her love for Adrastus. Of her parents' love for one another, no matter how brief. And of the love for her friends who had remained by her side when it mattered most.

When her fingers met the soft glowing light, it burst. With that one touch, all the blanketing starlight erupted. A scream escaped her as a wildfire swept across the land. It stretched as far as the eye could see, devouring the foliage, animals, and Fae in its path.

Her worst nightmares were playing out before her eyes. But the heat of the fire was so much worse than it had been in her dreams. It scorched her skin without even touching it. Agonizing terror and regret rocked Kelera to her knees, sprawling her out in front of Samael. The fire raged around them, casting an eerie glow along his rawboned face. He narrowed his gaze at her and grabbed her by the hair. Memories of being dragged through the unpredictable Winter palace halls flooded back. He knelt down in front of her and smiled deviously. She reared her head back, then slammed it forward into his smug face. His hold on her released, giving her just enough time to crawl away from him.

When he reached for her again, Adrastus rammed his knee between his eyes. Samael's nose crunched under the blow, and he fell back in a daze. Adrastus leaned down, offering her his hand, but before she could take it, fire knocked them apart. A deafening hiss pierced her ears as wind rushed past her and the world turned black.

The field was unnaturally quiet. The harsh absence of noise brought tears to Kelera's eyes. She imagined it was what a baby heard before being thrust into life. Or was it the sound of death? Maybe both...

It was touch that returned to her senses first. Soft grass that reminded her of childhood when she and Cierine would roll down the highest hills they could find. And warm sunlight on her face like the first day of spring.

Sight came next as the haze in her eyes lifted. Bright skies, clear and dazzling blue. It was like she was seeing color for the first time. She rolled to her side and looked out at the Fae armies. Her heart soared to see them alive and untouched by the fire that had swept over them moments ago. They, too, were waking from a stupor. Murmurs echoed in the clearing and she followed their gazes to the trees around them. On the side of the Spring Court, evergreens held tall and proud with leaves in full bloom. On the autumn side, vibrant orange and red foliage fluttered in the calm breeze.

There was no sign of frost. Everything was more alive and stunning than they had ever been before. Adrastus leaned in close, resting against her. His mouth was gaping in awe. Kelera was as shocked as he was. It had worked. She had stopped the frost, and more than that, she had restored the land with new vigor.

Men she didn't recognize stalked toward her and tossed rusted swords at her feet. Strong, muscled horses stood close behind them and it took her a moment to realize who they were. Though their robes were still torn and ragged, the Night Riders no longer looked like the walking dead. Their faces were pale, but not sickly. Their irises were a dark blueish-purple and blinked rapidly, as if regaining their sight for the first time in a long time. These were no longer the same cursed monsters who had haunted her waking dreams.

Kelera whispered in disbelief, "The curse... its broken..."

Adrastus cleared his throat. "You did it, little thief. I knew you could do it." He let out a loud whoop. It spread through the armies, both Fae and mortal, and they echoed his excitement with cries of elation.

Even Samael's army celebrated, laying down their weapons in relief. Samael... Kelera gasped and turned to where he'd been thrown by the fiery gust of wind. His dark jacket was singed, and smoldering as he struggled to rise.

She and Adrastus stood together, towering over him. Her hatred for him had dimmed at the sight of her victory, but it didn't change what he had done. Or what he would do if granted the opportunity again. One thing she knew for certain was that he would never stop. If she allowed him to live, he would haunt their lives forever.

Adrastus knew it too from the look of him. His jaw was set as he glared down at the brother who had tormented him his whole life. His glamor dropped, revealing the horrifying scars Samael had given him as a child. And it solidified Kelera's resolve.

She raised her chin and spoke loud enough for the armies below to hear. "Samael, son of Unseelie, Prince of Shadows. You are accused of atrocities against your people. And of patricide and treason. How do you plead?"

Samael struggled to his knees and spat blood at her feet.

Adrastus ignored him and turned to the gathered Fae. He gestured to her as he declared, "Queen Kelera, daughter of Seelie and honored wife of Unseelie, has claimed victory today. The renewed land of Elfhame that you see around you now is a reflection of its rightful heir. Will you claim her as your sovereign ruler?"

Shouts rose from the crowd, "Aye!"

"Long live the Queen!"

"The prophecy is fulfilled!"

Soon everyone was crying out in favor of her. Butterflies fluttered in her stomach, replacing the stone-like feeling she'd had since first entering their realm. Adrastus beamed at her, his eyes sparkling in the sunshine. She wanted to wrap her arms around him, but remained where she was.

This was her kingdom's moment as much as it was hers and she wanted to stand tall and proud for them.

Adrastus pointed to Samael, still speaking to the crowd. "Then what say you? Is this man guilty of these crimes?"

Again, the Fae roared in agreement. Their boots stomped loudly on the ground. Even the giants who had risen to aid them rumbled in unison. And so it was decided. Samael would at long last pay for his crimes.

When Kelera looked down at him, she didn't find defeat on his face. Instead, he grinned at her. She stiffened in response, irked by his vanity. Did he truly think she wouldn't be able to finish what she started? Adrastus joined her, taking hold of her hand. His fingers grazed her knuckles, but rather than the comfort his touch usually brought, she found their magic sparking between them. The power braided itself together like a rope. It tightened and solidified, providing them the edge they would need to end the life of a king.

Samael pushed himself to his feet and spat on the ground. "You think the two of you can kill me?" He raised his chin, turning his face so the sunlight shined on his burn scars. "You have tried and failed." He spread his arms wide in a grand show of confidence. Murmurs spread through the crowd as he challenged her and Adrastus. "But you are welcome to try again."

Adrastus shook his head and laughed, startling Kelera. He showed no sign of fear or anger. It was a genuine smile. One that brought out the dimple in his cheek. His voice bellowed as he said, "Your confidence is admirable, brother. But like our father, your hubris is your downfall. You think yourself untouchable, but no one is above the natural laws of Elfhame. Your grasp at endless power has brought us all to this very moment, just as the Elders foretold."

Samael snarled. "I warned father that bringing you to us was a mistake. That you would be too weak to do what needs to be done for the good of Unseelie. Kill me, and you will ruin us all."

Kelera interrupted, "*You* are and always have been the problem, Samael. Today, your reign of pain and suffering ends. Today, Adrastus and I stand united before the fates, ready to release Elfhame from your horror."

"You horrible little bitch—" Samael's words were cut off with a guttural growl as Kelera and Adrastus unleashed their magic on him. His eyes widened as he looked down at his stomach where their power had met its mark. The wound sparked and, try as he might, he could not stop it. He pressed his hands over the gash and called on his shadows.

They were released from inside of him in thick tendrils, but the moment they touched the Seelie magic, they sizzled away. Samael bared his teeth and tried to open his mouth to speak, but nothing came out. The power Kelera and Adrastus drove into him, bloomed into a golden light, eating away at Samael's flesh and bones. It faintly reminded Kelera of the Beltane bonfire as she watched it consume him.

He did not cry out in terror or give any last threatening words as death came to claim him. When it was over, the flames subsided, leaving nothing but embers and ash lying on the lush, green grass. The ground around it was left untouched. Even the hot embers did not leave a mark behind as they died out.

Relief allowed Kelera to breathe fully for what felt like the first time since she encountered Samael's shadowy form at Cierine's reception. All the grief and pain Samael had caused was released like ashes blowing in the wind. Adrastus sighed heavily beside her and when she turned to him, she saw no regret for what they had done. He gazed down at her with love and devotion, running his hands through her hair.

"It is done. We are free." He leaned in and kissed her deeply.

As she returned the kiss, the Fae and mortals below erupted in celebration. They threw down their arms and embraced one another. Even the Unseelie Fae yelped and rejoiced in their new freedom. This was a victory for not just the Seelie who had triumphed in battle. All of Elfhame, Seelie and Unseelie, High and Lesser Fae, even the solitary who wandered Elfhame alone and the creatures who roamed the land could claim this day as theirs.

Kelera and Adrastus left the site of the great war and Samael's demise behind without a second glance. Their return to the Seelie palace was much anticipated and crowds of Fae stood gathered outside the gates, waiting for them. Their cheeks were flushed in the sudden warmth of spring that had returned when Kelera's magic had completed the prophecy.

The council, led by Bothwell, welcomed them with open arms and pride plastered on their faces. Even the Fae who had once stood with Herald bowed their heads in a show of respect. She didn't blame them for their loyalty and allegiance to the former King Consort, just as she wouldn't hold the Unseelie accountable for their decisions.

For so long, the Fae of Elfhame had been doing what they could to survive. The royal families had been playing a game against one another for centuries, leaving the rest of the realm to deal with the collateral damage. But there would be no more of that. Just as the land had been reborn, so had they. The slate had been wiped clean and Elfhame was free to be made into whatever they dreamed it to be.

For the Fae, that meant a life of peace and understanding. The ability to be who they wished without fear of repercussions. Not that it would be without strife. They would all have to work together to hold the peace. But with Adrastus there to guide them, Kelera had no doubts that it would all work out in the end. He'd been dreaming of this moment since he was a young boy.

For Kelera, it meant safety. A world that co-existed without expectation. No more would she be forced to pretend or exude an air of perfection. She had broken Samael's hold on the realm and, with that, the darkness that threatened to consume anyone within his reach was gone, too.

Gadreel sidled up to Adrastus and whispered something in his ear. Oliver smiled warmly at Kelera and winked at her. Adrastus thanked Gadreel and they each shot mischievous smiles in her direction.

Before Kelera could ask what that was about, Bothwell raised his hands and colorful light shot from them. They flashed in the air, creating bursts of beautiful sparks above them. The crowd cheered. The Unseelie, who had accompanied them back to the Seelie palace to see what would become of them and their world, gasped in awe.

Bothwell proclaimed, "All hail the Queen of Elfhame! Queen Kelera!"

Countless voices rang out in agreement, "Long live Queen Kelera!"

"Queen of Elfhame!"

"All hail the lost heir!"

"Heir of the Elfhame throne!"

Kelera's chest tightened, and she clutched Adrastus' hand firmly. Not Queen of Seelie. Queen of Elfhame. Just as the prophecy foretold. A ruler to unite all of Elfhame as one. It should have frightened her. That's what she thought the tightness was telling her to be afraid of. Afraid of letting them all down. Of failing. But as Adrastus raised her hand in the air in triumph, she realized the discomfort was coming from the endless possibilities. It was a nervous energy, brought on by the realization that the two of them had gotten what they wanted.

As the crowds dispersed—soldiers from both sides who needed to be healed, the creatures who had answered her call to be fed, and others to prepare for the celebration—Adrastus lingered with her.

Someone whistled to him from across the field, and Kelera turned to see Gadreel. Magic was rising from his palms in the shape of a beautiful arcing icicle. It glistened with purple light as it flowed through the crowd to her and Adrastus.

Adrastus gently squeezed the ice with his hand, shattering the sharp end. He closed his hand around something, and a mischievous smile splayed wide across his face as he turned to her. A few eyes darted their way as nosy courtiers and villagers were eager to watch their new rulers together. She ignored them, doing her best to give Adrastus her undivided attention. Something she would have to be sure to do for the good of their relationship as they ruled Elfhame together in the coming years.

A warm blush crept across the bridge of his nose as he opened his hand to reveal a silver ring. It was delicately carved like vines and held an array of precious stones. The smaller gems circling the larger one in the center were as black as Adrastus' shadows and twinkled in the sunlight. The one in the center was a deep emerald green like leaves in the Wildwood. It was the most beautiful piece of jewelry she'd ever seen and rivaled that of the crown on her head.

He shifted nervously as he held the ring out and slipped it onto her finger. "Gadreel is quite persuasive when he wants to be. He found a smith in the camp..." He shuffled his feet restlessly and chuckled softly. "I didn't get the chance to do this before. Like all things with you, I couldn't have predicted how these last few days would go and I admit I wasn't quite prepared to marry you in a battle encampment..."

"Dras, you know it doesn't matter to me how our wedding went. I would have married you in a hovel for all I cared."

Hair fell into his brow as he nodded, and she reached up to push it away. His eyes bore into hers as he spoke. "Still, you've stolen my heart, little thief, and for that, there is a price."

Kelera laughed and grasped his face between her hands, drawing his lips to hers. He smelled like blood and sweat, but he tasted sweet, like berries from the blackthorn trees.

She pulled away and whispered, "A life with you is a price I will gladly accept."

Epilogue
Three Years Later

The price had been a simple one. For the two of them to live out the rest of their days supporting and loving each other. It was one that she was truly happy to pay. They'd had three years of bliss. Rebuilding the realm and the relationships between the courts hadn't come without its challenges. But it had been made possible with the support of their friends.

Kelera ran her hands along the gray marbled walls as she walked. The palace Adrastus had constructed for them was a magnificent yet modest structure. The placement had been her idea. Putting a steady foundation in the heart of Elfhame. Right at the center of the four courts. If one were to go to the highest tower, they would look out onto the Spring, Summer, Winter, and Autumn lands. It was the perfect place for the Queen and King of Elfhame to reside.

She followed the deep blue rug lining the hallway until she came to the south terrace. The gardens were an ode to Elfhame itself. Housing flowers and plants from all the courts. Adrastus had put care into every detail of the palace, making it into the perfect home for the three of them.

Kelera smiled down at the marble fountain where her father was being chased by unruly children. It had been a dream come true when he had finally decided to move into the palace with them. Retirement looked good on him, even if it meant he now led children around the garden instead of leading knights into battle.

Dodger led the charge in the garden below with his adoptive daughter at his side. The girl Kelera had rescued from Samael's attack in the mortal realm had stolen Dodger's heart. And he, like her father once had, seemed to have found a balance between knighthood and fatherhood.

The smallest of the group drew Kelera's attention away from Dodger and the others. A girl of only two years old, who was beginning to look more and more like her father every day, tottered after them. The flowers braided in her raven hair had come undone and petals were left in her wake as she chased after the others.

Adrastus wrapped his arms around Kelera and nuzzled into her neck. "I thought I might find you out here. Are you hiding from Bothwell or Gadreel?"

Kelera laughed and rested the back of her head on his broad chest. "Both, I suppose."

Bothwell had just arrived from the Spring palace and was already laying documents in front of her for approval. They were miniscule things, agreements with the farmers to trade with the Autumn court, requests for more funding to build schools...Things she was happy to go over, but not today. Today was for celebrating.

Gadreel wandered through the garden, dodging the children and Sir Aldric's little game. The small girl with hair like the midnight sky waddled up to him and reached her little arms out. He frowned at her for a moment, before relenting.

She twisted his hair with her tiny fingers and said something that brought a smile to his worried face.

He looked up at the terrace, spotting Kelera and shouted, "I should have known the two of you would be up there shirking your responsibilities! Come and get this niece of mine and meet me at the altar. There are details to be sorted out before the ceremony!"

Kelera scoffed. "But look at how Mabine dotes on you! It is by no fault of mine that your niece misses her uncle. Perhaps if you left the Winter palace more..." She winked at him, knowing that he enjoyed the attention hers and Adrastus' daughter gave him.

"Very well!" He swung Mabine around to his back. "I shall just have to do everything myself." Then he jogged off with the child, who had begun giggling wildly.

Adrastus scoffed, "Did you know he really did paint the palace purple?" Kelera choked with laughter as he continued, "Oliver said the halls kept shifting whenever the servants tried to paint them and the carpet was such a mess by the end that it all had to be ripped out."

They both barked with laughter and when it finally died down, Kelera sighed. She turned to Adrastus and enjoying a moment of having his arms wrapped around her. "I suppose I should go down there and help him. Or else I'll never hear the end of it."

Cierine chimed in as she strode gracefully out to the terrace to join them. "Good luck. He's been high strung all morning." Her hair was piled wildly around her crown. Clearly, she'd had enough of the women at court trying to tidy her up.

"He just wants everything to be perfect." Kelera gave Adrastus a pointed look. If I recall, you, too, felt the same way about our wedding day." She stood on her tippy toes to kiss his stubbled cheek. "Perhaps you could go check on Oliver. Make sure he's not getting cold feet."

Adrastus chuckled. "Not likely. If living in the Winter palace for the last three years hasn't spooked him, I'm afraid nothing will."

He was right about that. Gadreel and Oliver had taken on the task of watching over the Winter and Autumn territories. With them righting the wrongs of the Winter palace's predecessors, the land and its people had flourished. Oliver didn't seem to mind that the hallways were constantly playing tricks on him and sending him to the wrong place at the wrong time. Instead, he had busied himself with brightening up the dark rooms and enchanting a garden to grow spring flowers all year long—a little piece of home for him.

The Winter Court wasn't the only one that was thriving. With Bothwell looking after the interests of the Spring and Summer territories, things had been going better than Kelera could have dreamed. The Wild Hunt had been joined by the Night Riders who had been freed from their curse. And they had all agreed to remain close at hand, ready to aid at any new signs of trouble. Even the stone and tree giants now roamed free amongst the Fae—a comfort to Kelera, both because of their freedom to live happily and that they would be there should she ever need them again. The crown didn't weigh quite so heavily, knowing she wasn't alone in any of this.

Even the relationship with the mortal court had been repaired—large in part to Cierine's leadership. She and Kelera had done their best to set things right for both parties. There was still plenty of work to be done, but it was a start.

Parting with Adrastus, she and Cierine wandered down to the altar, where a frazzled Gadreel was trying to create snowflakes to place on the hawthorn flowers. Mabine imitated his movements with her hands, and Kelera smiled as she knelt down beside her.

"Here, like this." She moved her hand gracefully over the flowers, calling on the ice of Adrastus' bound magic. Little snowflakes fell onto the petals, so cold that they did not melt in the afternoon heat.

Mabine's bright blue eyes widened, and Kelera's heart soared at the childlike wonder on her daughter's face. She was a baby born of mortal, Seelie, and Unseelie descent. When Mabine had been delivered after a long hard labor, and the healers had placed that tiny, perfect creation on Kelera's chest, she'd come to a realization. The Elders had actually been wrong about her. Kelera may have been the lost heir, but it would not be she who truly united the courts. Mabine—named for the mother Kelera hadn't had the pleasure of getting to know—was the true future of Elfhame. An heir that was tied by both realms and each Elfhame court by blood. One who would be raised to see all Fae as equals.

Kelera pulled Mabine onto her lap and squeezed her tight. Adrastus strolled down the path to join them and patted Gadreel on the shoulder. "Ready, brother?"

Gadreel clasped his jittery hands in front of him. "I've never been more ready for anything in all my life."

Adrastus took Mabine in his arms and held out a hand to help Kelera up. She swatted it away playfully and stood, dusting off her rose embroidered gown. Adrastus laughed, licking his finger and wiping away the dirt on her face.

He teased. "Your crown's crooked."

Kelera's hands flew to the crown on her head to find it intact. She rolled her eyes at him. "Very funny."

He bumped her with his shoulder. "Come on, little wife, we have a wedding to watch."

Kelera took her seat beside him as a band of horned Fae began to play. Gadreel stepped up to the altar, fidgeting uncontrollably, until Oliver appeared. He wore a dazzling suit of green, representing his ties to the Spring Court.

Her eyes drifted over the wedding guests. Mira and Diana waved merrily at her from their seats. Their skin was sun-kissed, and it appeared their time in the Summer Court had done wonders for their spirits. Kelera waved back and continued to gaze out at her people. Fae from all over Elfhame had come to see the sweethearts of the realm united in matrimony. But they did not take sides in their seating. Instead, mountain men from the Winter Court sat beside fishermen from the Summer Court. Spring and Autumn Fae welcomed one another and leaned in to share secrets. They were one. It was everything she and Adrastus had hoped for.

As Oliver walked down the aisle, a burst of flower petals rained down on him. He and Gadreel exchanged confused glances. But Kelera, spotting Mabine's little hands waving erratically in the air, laughed in understanding. Adrastus beamed with pride and ruffled her hair. Mabine clapped, appearing incredibly happy with herself.

Kelera's heart felt so full it could burst. Times like this were what made all their struggles worth it. True, they would run into trouble again. But it was these moments of happiness that they would tuck away in their hearts. Together, with her daughter and the man she loved, she would confidently face any threat that came their way. This, amidst a world of struggle and heartache, was total and utter perfection.

Acknowledgments

Wow! This has been such an amazing journey into the world of Faerie Folklore. This project all started as a seed and bloomed into something more beautiful than I could have imagined.

First I have to thank you, my readers, who have shown me so much love and support. I know that reading is a passion we all share and for you to take the time to open my books means the world to me.

As always, I have to thank my family for their support. Without them, I would never have had the courage to take this leap. To my husband, Zach, who is my rock and always tries to bring a smile to my face (especially when the work becomes overwhelming). And to my babies... I can never express how much joy you bring me. You two are the greatest story of all.

Next, I would like to thank the brilliant writers in my writer's group: Danielle, Emily F., Emily H., Kate, Samantha, and Jess, who never hold back. You have shaped me into a better writer and have given me a thicker skin. You've taught me so much about how to build on my strengths and how to improve on my weaknesses. And more than that, you have given me encouragement, love, and support. I truly do not know what I would do without you all.

Lastly, to my beta team: Ardena and Laura. I am so grateful to have been able to entrust the roughest version of this book to each of you. Without your fresh eyes and guidance, this story wouldn't be what it is today.

One thing I have realized since starting this journey is that it would be impossible without people around you who will love and support you. Through the ups and downs that have come with pouring my heart and soul into this story, every person mentioned here has kept me going.

My love to you all,
J.M. Wallace

ALSO BY J.M. WALLACE
A Legacy of Darkness
A Legacy of Nightmares
A Legacy of Destruction
Heir of Shadows and Ice
Heir of Embers and Ash

Novellas and More
The Princess of Sagon: A Smuggler's Tale (A Legacy of Darkness freebie in my newsletter!)
Born of Fire and Love (Claiming Elfhame-Read after Book 3)

About the Author

J.M. Wallace is a proud military wife. She has spent much of her adult life moving from place to place with her husband and their two children, making stories of their own. As a young girl, J.M. was fascinated with stories that she read and that she dreamed up on her own. Even when she was horseback riding, she was never in her own yard; instead, she was in an enchanted forest or riding into battle alongside brave knights. Today, she puts those stories to paper, to share with the world. She does this in the little pockets of her day between giving her kids snacks, naps, baths, and putting them to bed. *A Legacy of Darkness* was her debut novel.

www.jmwallaceauthor.com